## Acclaim for the authors of
### *Christmas Cinderellas*

#### SOPHIA JAMES

"Romantic, full of secrets and simmering passion this Regency romance is the perfect escape."

—Jane Hunt, author and blogger, on *The Cinderella Countess*

#### VIRGINIA HEATH

"If the front cover says Virginia Heath then you know you're in for a treat."

—*The Blossom Twins* on *Lillian and the Irresistible Duke*

#### CATHERINE TINLEY

"Catherine Tinley has a wonderful talent for writing Regency romances that sparkle with pathos, emotion and atmosphere."

—*Bookish Jottings* on *Rags-to-Riches Wife*

**Sophia James** lives in Chelsea Bay, on the North Shore of Auckland, New Zealand, with her husband, who is an artist. She has a degree in English and History from Auckland University and believes her love of writing was formed by reading Georgette Heyer on vacations at her grandmother's house. Sophia enjoys getting feedback at Facebook.com/sophiajamesauthor.

When **Virginia Heath** was a little girl, it took her ages to fall asleep, so she made up stories in her head to help pass the time while she was staring at the ceiling. As she got older, the stories became more complicated—sometimes taking weeks to get to their happy ending. One day she decided to embrace her insomnia and start writing them down. Virginia lives in Essex, UK, with her wonderful husband and two teenagers. It still takes her forever to fall asleep...

**Catherine Tinley** has loved reading and writing since childhood, and has a particular fondness for love, romance and happy endings. She lives in Ireland with her husband, children, dog and kitten, and can be reached at catherinetinley.com, as well as through Facebook and on Twitter, @catherinetinley.

# CHRISTMAS CINDERELLAS

---

Sophia James
Virginia Heath
Catherine Tinley

HARLEQUIN®
HISTORICAL™

Recycling programs for this product may not exist in your area.

ISBN-13: 978-1-335-50582-8

Christmas Cinderellas

Copyright © 2020 by Harlequin Books S.A.


Christmas with the Earl © 2020 by Sophia James

Invitation to the Duke's Ball © 2020 by Susan Merritt

A Midnight Mistletoe Kiss © 2020 by Catherine Tinley

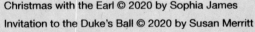

This edition published by arrangement with Harlequin Books S.A.

For questions and comments about the quality of this book, please contact us at CustomerService@Harlequin.com.

Harlequin Enterprises ULC
22 Adelaide St. West, 40th Floor
Toronto, Ontario M5H 4E3, Canada
www.Harlequin.com

**Printed in U.S.A.**

# CONTENTS

# CHRISTMAS WITH THE EARL

Sophia James

Dear Reader,

Christmas is one of my favourite times of the year, and for me it's all about family, friends, food and holidays. It's about relaxing in the sunshine here in New Zealand down at our little summer house, where we can swim, have barbecues, take long walks down beautiful beaches, and sit at night by candlelight under the stars and talk.

This year with all the fear and uncertainty around COVID-19, my husband and I have been isolating in our own little bubble away from family, so it will be even more important to reconnect and find again some sort of normality. I can't wait to sit at the long Christmas table with lots of dear ones around me.

I wish you all peace and joy at Christmas and hope you are surrounded by people you love in the places you love.

*Sophia James*

# Chapter One

*London, 8th December 1814*

A stranger dressed completely in black blocked her in the doorway, his height dimming the light of a crisp early December morning.

'Please let me pass, sir. I do not know you.'

Her tone was sharp, the shock of his closeness telling, but the man before her only smiled.

'If you could acknowledge me but for a moment, madam, I would be most grateful.'

Such entreaty held the sort of desperation that Ariana Dalrymple could not fail to hear and she observed him more closely. He had eyes the colour of wet autumn leaves and his face was one of a fighter. There was a scratch that went from one eye to his ear, and a bruise was swelling fast on his cheek.

'If someone dangerous is after you…'

'They are not.'

'Or if you have just had a fight…'

'Wrong again.'

A group of women were passing them now, and he tipped his head towards her as though to listen more carefully to what she was saying. The thick wool of his cloak effectively blocked all else out. His hat was pulled firmly down and his collar was up, and the small doorway in which they stood sheltered them from any recognition.

'Are you hiding from those women?'

She suddenly knew that he was, and he had the good

grace at least to appear remorseful. For a second Ariana saw in him something she liked a lot.

'Did she hit you?' Horror marked her words and he laughed outright.

'Hardly. I fell off a horse.'

'Where?' She looked around for a riderless steed, expecting one to charge through the throng on the crowded city street.

'Last night. At Stevenage.'

'The Duke of Horsham's estate?'

'Yes. You know him?'

'Vaguely. He seems a stern and sad man. Rumour has it there is an estranged son who has been a trial, so perhaps that is what ails him.'

She glanced at the group of fashionable women who had passed by half a minute ago and were now turning a corner, all chattering together like a clutch of noisy quail.

'I think you are safe, sir. Your huntswomen have gone. If you leave quickly and in that direction I imagine you would stay unnoticed.'

'Thank you, Miss…?'

'Mrs Ariana Dalrymple. But I am more usually called Aria.'

'Like a song in an opera?' There was a tone in his voice that was hesitant.

She nodded.

'I am North.'

'As in a direction?'

He began to laugh. 'No one has ever asked me that before. It's Northwell in truth—Christopher Anthony Stephen Northwell.'

Ariana swallowed back her horror. 'The Duke's recently returned and wayward son? The dissolute and unrepentant Earl of Norwich?'

'I am afraid so.'

She stopped herself from apologising as she sought to

remember the details. 'The stories about you are most specific, my lord. It seems you burnt the family mansion to the ground and left the country soon afterwards. Your father and mother only just escaped from being burnt to a crisp, if I recall it rightly.'

'Well, that was my mother's version of things.'

'There is another one?'

'Isn't there always?'

She swallowed. This conversation was one of the oddest she had ever partaken in. 'I am not certain. Perhaps you should tell me.'

'I'd rather not. My penance is over and done with and the Christmas season holds hope.'

'For reconciliation?'

'Personally I find that word overused.'

The smile hardened in his eyes and a new and far more dangerous lord stood where the charming womaniser had been before. Not an easy man at all. Her heart began to trip a little faster.

'Failing to take responsibility for one's faults is hardly something to fun about, my lord?'

'Hasty judgement is not a flattering trait either, Mrs Dalrymple.'

'So everyone is wrong and you are right? I had expected more of you.'

'Why?'

'Why what?'

'Why had you expected more of me?'

He had her there, and it was seldom people ever turned the tables on her logic.

'I'd hoped you might be kinder.' There—it was said, and the frills of good manners dispensed with. Because she had wished it so with all her heart.

Once he might have been kinder—once he might have taken her hand and kissed her fingers whilst apologising.

She was, after all, extraordinarily beautiful, this woman before him, with her dark hair and blue eyes and the sort of face that would never go unremarked upon.

But he was tired, and the afternoon was nearly spent, and all he wanted to do was to go home to the rented rooms in St James's and find a bottle of his very best brandy and drink the lot. A welcome oblivion as he sought solace.

It was becoming more difficult by the day, this façade of easy-going, casual happy-go-luckiness, and if he had erred in his judgement a moment ago, when she had mentioned reconciliation, then it was his own fault entirely. He didn't quite feel comfortable lying to her and it showed.

That admission had him stepping back. 'If there is any way that I can repay your good grace in humouring my small and recent difficulty I should be happy to hear of it.'

He watched her take a breath, saw conflict in her glance.

'Take me to the Shawler ball this Friday as your partner. I do not require more than one dance, a quarter of an hour at most of your time, and then you can be on your way. I shall not hold you to a moment longer.'

'You have a suitor you wish to…dangle? A lover who requires a push?'

'You have heard of me, then?'

'Who has not, Mrs Dalrymple? You are as infamous as I am.'

'There is no lover, my lord. I merely need to be received.'

'You were not invited, then?'

'I am afraid some hosts still cling to the old hopes of cloying submissive womanhood.'

'Those who marry well and never stray from the path of righteousness?'

'Not as far as I have, at least—and certainly not those who fail to apologise for doing so.'

'A questionable strategy in a town where manners are so strictly observed?'

'Well, sometimes even I am amazed at the things that I am supposed to have done.'

'The Hartley ball was one such *faux pas*, I suppose? I remember hearing of it years ago, just before I left England. The Simmons sisters accompanied you to the event and one of them lost her innocence.'

Blue eyes darkened at that, as if a sore spot had been rubbed.

'When others are hurt I generally feel some sense of remorse. But I am far wiser now, and much less inclined to extremes. Perhaps you are the same, my lord, after your extended jaunt in the Americas?'

'Perhaps. Who is it who looks out for you when you need help with your reputation? I know you to be a widow, and it is also said that you have lost both your parents.'

'Lady Sarah Hervey, Viscountess Ludlow, lives with me.'

North had heard of the woman and whistled, the sound piercing in the quiet of the day.

'A difficult protector—and one who has her own detractors.'

Again darkness surfaced, though this time it was tinged with a certain anger.

'Friday, then, at half past nine. At my townhouse on Portman Square. I will see you there.'

At that she turned, gesturing to her maid behind to follow, the stellar cut of her unusual cloak shimmering in the thin winter sun. A jaunty hat sat on the top of her head. A shapely bottom was outlined in the breeze and her dark hair lifted in the wind. The scent of some flower lingered where she had stood, and he tipped his head to try and identify it.

Lily of the valley. A beautiful but poisonous plant.

It suited her.


'Damn. Damn. *Damn*.'

She said this beneath her breath as she walked, each step punctuated by the word. She had known one day that she would meet a man who might make her heart beat faster, but why did it have to be this one?

She wondered just for a second whether she should turn around and cancel the plans that they had agreed on, but she needed to go to the Shawler ball in order to get inside the house. There seemed no other way to do it, and her aunt was depending on the outcome.

Christopher Anthony Stephen Northwell would not be pleased to be so duped if he found out the reason she'd asked him to partner her, but right at this moment she could not worry about that. She would need to create a new and flattering gown—one that would allow her the confidence she was far from feeling...one that might catch his eye and lead his thoughts away from her true pursuit.

Looking up, she swallowed. Once she had imagined that at twenty-five and a half years old she might be married to a man she loved and have children and a house and a life that was good and real and true.

And instead... She was alone and likely to remain so.

The rumours about her were mostly false. Who could have possibly slept with the number of men she was reported to have slept with? But she had been careless once or twice, soon after her husband had passed away, when she should not have been.

The Hartley ball with the Simmons sisters was one case in point. Susan and Dorothy Simmons had been far wilder than she had imagined them to be, and when the younger sister had crept off during the evening with a lover in tow Ariana had desperately tried to stop her and failed.

It had been a week later when Ariana had heard it mentioned that she was the one to blame, for her lack of care with their personages, and the gossip mill had begun to grind with startling vitriol. Pointing the finger of blame seemed to be what Society did, and she was enough of an outsider to make it easy.

Money had helped her remain in London—of course it

had—but she'd heard what was being said of her and felt isolated and different. 'The Merry Widow' was one name they called her, and nothing could have been further from the truth. 'The Fair Philanderer' was another.

She shook her head. Hard. There was a certain freedom in semi-ruination on top of inheriting a fortune, and right now it was her shelter.

The Christmas festivities and their accompanying joy were already in place. Just over two weeks until the twenty-fifth. Seventeen days of joviality and enforced excitement. She hated the season more and more each year, and wondered if such an innate melancholy would ever be shifted.

Her past had twisted her, she supposed, and her parents' wanting all the outward trappings of wealth had hidden a darker side that she still recoiled from.

Christopher Northwell reminded her of a pirate, with his dark brown eyes and night-black hair and the sort of face that was unforgettable. No wonder all those women were chasing him.

She tried to remember more about the scandal that had rocked the Horsham Dukedom.

His mother was a fragile woman, from memory—a woman who must have found being planted for years on an unfamiliar baronial estate while the first pile was being repaired difficult, to say the least. She had died just a few months ago from some illness, but Ariana had no recollection as to the malady. No wonder the Duke was sad and out of sorts, with his only child unrepentant and wild and his wife gone.

She frowned. There had been something in the expression of the Earl of Norwich that had not quite rung true, though, for in place of the guilt she might have expected there had been simply plain and unmitigated sorrow.

A shout from across the path brought Mrs Lucy Chambers to her side, all silky blonde curls and sky-blue eyes.

'I thought it was you, Ariana, but I could not be sure. Who was that man you were speaking with? He looked familiar.'

'The Earl of Norwich. It seems he is back in England.'

Lucy's mouth fell open. 'The Stevenage heir? My goodness—but is he not the most handsome man you have ever set your eyes upon?'

'Perhaps.' Ariana gave her reply with hesitation, because she did not wish to be thinking so as they walked on.

'His mother once told mine that her son was a saint, believe it or not. She said that it was love that made him burn the house down. Word was he tried to torch the stables as well, for Norwich loathes horses, by all accounts.'

'Well, he must hate them even more now. He said he had fallen off a steed at Stevenage yesterday.'

'Stevenage Manor has been completely rebuilt, you know, and it's said to be magnificent. The Duke is rather a recluse, however—especially since the death of his wife—and seldom graces any social occasion. My mother is adamant he needs more outings, for she swears a broken heart is relieved only when other people jolly one into life again.'

*Well, your mother is wrong*, Ariana thought, but smiled in the way she always did when the past forced memory into the present and claimed her. She had become so good at grouping her life into those things she wanted to remember and those things that she did not that surprise barely touched her now.

As if tired of the topic of conversation, Lucy had let her mind wander on to other things. 'I am going to the Shawler ball on Friday and I have decided to wear the new dark green satin gown which I have only just received from the workroom of Madame de Clerc.'

The talk of attire had Ariana's own mind wandering. Once she had loved clothes, and all the attending fuss. Now she only thought it a chore and a waste of money to be forever changing her gown for this event or that one. Besides, she'd sold her soul for a wardrobe when she was seventeen and had regretted it ever since.

Such ruminations brought sadness.

'I wish you would come to more of these society events, Aria. It would be lovely to have a friend in tow.'

Ariana took Lucy's hand. 'Tell me more of this dress you have purchased, because it sounds wonderful.'

As expected, such an opening brought a barrage of description and her friend's chattering was soothing, allowing Ariana to forget her strange and disquieting chance encounter with the enigmatic Earl of Norwich.


North visited White's as his next destination, and the first person he met was Alistair Botham, the Earl of Harding.

'I'd heard you were back, North, and was sorry to learn of your mother's passing. When did you arrive?'

'Last week. I took a ship from New York and it was a fair passage all the way across.'

'And your father?'

'Is the same as he always was.'

'So you're not at Stevenage, I take it? You're in Town.'

'St James's. I've rented a house on the square for the winter. After that I will return to America.'

'My youngest sister was right when she said she was sure she had seen you yesterday, surrounded by a group of fawning women, at the home of Lord and Lady Foxton. Any in particular take your fancy?'

'Nope. I was trying to escape.'

'Let's have a drink, North. I have the table over there, and Seth Douglas will be along soon. He married Pamela Charleston. You did know that, didn't you?'

North shook his head. 'Anna's sister?'

'It's been over five years since you left. Things change. I've heard you will be at the Shawler ball on Friday night, so you will see exactly how much. Marriage... Children...

Most of our friends have moved on. Who are you bringing with you as a partner for the ball, anyway?'

'Mrs Ariana Dalrymple.' He gave Alistair her name without thinking much of it.

'Hell, you are *not*. Andrew Shawler will kill you for it.'

'Why?'

'Because Mrs Dalrymple is unbending and ferocious in her attacks upon him.'

'Attacks about what?'

'His womanising and his lack of remorse in breaking hearts and thinking nothing of it.'

'Including hers?'

Alistair started laughing. '*She* certainly does not fall in love. Surely you should know at least that of her, North, for she was here in Society before you left for America.'

'I remember hearing her name, but it was more in connection with her looks. I never met her.'

'Well, Shawler will turn her away summarily, without a doubt, so I would save myself the embarrassment of such an insult and go alone, if I were you.'

'I can't. I have made a promise. That gaggle of women your sister mentioned at the Foxtons' was chasing me again today, and Mrs Dalrymple offered me shelter.'

Alistair was laughing so hard now that he could not speak. When he did it was in a breathless fashion.

'God, things were never boring when you were around, North, and I've missed that. What time are you planning on arriving at the Shawler townhouse, so that I can make certain I am there before you? Douglas will be there, too, so you will have friends to support you.'

'I won't need help.'

Further laughter made him frown.

North arrived back at his house in St James's Square late that night, with a feeling of empty tiredness in him that he could not shake. He'd been like this for a long while. Since his mother had died. Since fire had razed Stevenage to the ground on that late spring day, burning history, heritage and truth with it. The flames had leapt to the height of the oaks at the rear of the house, and the heat had been so fierce it had melted the steel in the forge and the anvil of the old smithy workshop in the barn beside it.

At least the horses had survived.

The scars on his arms tightened at the memory and he shook away his recall. He'd departed because he'd had to, and because lies had a way of scouring out love until nothing was left save bitterness and hostility.

The widow Dalrymple had a mouth that looked ripe for kissing and a twinkle in her deep blue eyes that he'd warmed to. She did not look run down by life or beholden to another. She was a woman making her way independently and without too much caution, and it was a breath of fresh air to find the truth in all its forms so baldly stated.

She dressed oddly. She looked one straight in the eye. She did not mince her words, and most certainly did not give one the feeling of neediness.

He wondered what she was doing now.

'That's finished.' Ariana put down the needle and held up the gown. Her stitches were careful things that gave no impression of a homemade fitting. 'What do you think?'

Aunt Sarah glanced up from the hat she was constructing with matching lace and long rust-coloured feathers.

'I have no idea why you do not simply go and get fitted for a new gown, Aria, instead of making these outlandish and colourful creations you insist upon wearing. You can well afford a thousand gowns, and Madame Berenger is always saying how she longs to style you in a proper fashion—one more suited to your circumstances and station in life.'

'It's the boredom of it all, Aunt Sarah. The tiring hours of fittings are a complete and utter waste of time, and in the end one has a garment which is no better than this. Besides, I enjoy putting odd hues together. Look at the colours here.'

She picked up the dress from her lap, turning the fabric in the light.

'Gold against leaf-green edged in red. Madame Berenger would put me in pink, or some ghastly pastel, and I should spend the night feeling like a flower, made wilted and sad by wearing such ordinariness.'

Sarah laughed and finished her substantial brandy. 'I have heard that Odette Northwell's son is well favoured...'

'You knew the Earl's mother?'

'Slightly. She was, of course, younger than me, but she was a girl of small opinion. She leaned on others to survive, which is not a flattering thing and is certainly an exhausting trait for whoever had to prop her up. Her husband is a domineering man, but I think she needed someone like that. The true pity is that their only son does not have more family about him.'

'No aunts or uncles?'

'There are two elderly grandparents on his mother's side, but apart from that nothing.'

'Friends, then? What of those?'

'Christopher Northwell ran with a wild set, and it came back to haunt him when the girl he was about to marry—a Miss Anna Charleston—fell into some river and drowned.'

'Was he there? The Earl?'

'He was. They had to pull him from the water to stop him searching when her body could not be located. Word has it that he contracted pneumonia as a result and nearly died.'

'He loved her?'

'With all his heart. I admired him for that—for, unlike his mother, he seemed to have strong beliefs and stuck to them. Until he burned down Stevenage. That was a step too far in anybody's book.'

'In the brief meeting I had with him he said that was his mother's version.'

'Interesting…'

'Why?'

'Because of the timing of his arrival back. Odette Northwell died four months ago, which is about the length of time it takes for a letter to be dispatched from London to New York and to take a subsequent return sea voyage, even given inclement weather.'

'You are saying he only came home because he knew his mother had died?'

'Families can be complex, Ariana. Of all the people in the world you should know that.'

'How did she die? Odette Northwell?'

'By suicide. She'd been threatening it for years, and finally managed it by throwing herself off the top of the newly finished Stevenage Manor.'

'Oh, my God! Is this common knowledge? I have not heard of this at all.'

'It isn't—although of course one does hear whispers. The doctor who attended her is a friend of mine and he asked me to keep it confidential, which I am sure you will, too. The story being put about in public is that it was a terrible accident and that the winds on the roof were unseasonably strong that day.'

'Do you think the son knows the true story?'

'Undoubtedly. His father is not the sort of man who would go to great lengths to make a lie more palatable. No…beautiful, fragile Odette Neilson Northwell never had a chance from the beginning, for extreme timidity runs alongside beauty in the Neilson bloodline. Her son, by all accounts, has inherited the looks of the Neilsons and the brains of the Northwells, for it is said he has made a fortune of his own in the Americas. All say he has been besieged mercilessly by interested females since arriving back and has had to swat them off like flies.'

\* \* \*

Ariana lay in bed that night and thought of her day. Christopher Northwell had smelt of wood-smoke and pine trees when he had pressed close in that doorway, his cloak enveloping her and his body feeling nothing like those of the simpering lords she was far more used to.

She wondered what he had been up to in the Americas, for she had heard little of his adventures—which, in itself, wasn't surprising, as she had barely arrived in Society when he had left it. He'd simply disappeared for the past five years, but he was now returned in all his full and former glory.

And bringing back a great deal of money, it seemed, for Lucy Chambers had regaled her with gossip about his sumptuous living arrangements in St James's and the freeness of his spending.

The puzzle deepened and Aria turned over, her face snuggling in to the pillow.

The women who had been chasing him had been undoubtedly fierce, determined, and very well dressed. She'd recognised a few of them, and knew they were females who usually had far more sense—girls from good families with strict upbringings. Women who usually behaved with far more decorum and modesty.

The frequency with which Christopher Northwell had been worming his way into her thoughts since their first meeting was worrying, and she slammed one hand down hard on the bed beside her.

Like a puff of smoke he disappeared, and she sat up and helped herself to a glass of the brandy she hid in the cupboard of her bedside table. Sometimes she just needed help to get through the darkness of the night, and this was one of those times.

Mama and Papa had not protected her—that was the trouble. They had thrown her into the lions' cage of the Dalrymple turbulence and expected her to survive. She had and they had not—though she wondered sometimes just who had received the better bargain.

Opening the drawer beside her, she found the pearl pendant that her aunt had given her a few years ago, and held it tightly.

'Help…' she whispered into the translucence, and then she said it louder, the echo of the word reverberating in all the frightened corners of her heart.

She needed purification, harmony and balance. She would never remarry—never again allow anyone such power over her. She was damaged beyond repair and it would not take much for anyone to see it should she allow them close.

The bells of St Clement Danes', one of the Island churches, began to ring: 'Oranges and Lemons'. The melody calmed her and she glanced at the clock on the mantel. Eleven already, and not a sign of sleep in sight.

Where was Christopher Anthony Stephen Northwell now? Tucked up in bed or drunk at one of his clubs. She knew he was a member at White's because Lucy had told her. She understood he was sad, too, because the sort of melancholy she had seen in his eyes was the kind that couldn't be hidden from one who knew it to the very bone herself—and, although she had liked his humour and his ease, she had been more intrigued by the darker things about him.

Would he come to escort her to the ball on Friday? Or would he find out more about her and decide to cancel? Personally, she would place her bets on the second option, but she hoped he'd be stronger.

*Please, God, let him have faith in me. Let him come.*

Anna Charleston had been beautiful. Ariana had heard the name down the years, and knew she was the tragic youngest daughter of Lord and Lady Duggan, but she had not known of the girl's relationship with the Earl of Norwich. He had been unlucky in love too, then, but not in the way she had been. Ariana imagined him searching the freezing waters of some river for his lost love and failing to find her, even as she thought of the sort of nightmares he must suffer as a result.

They were both alone.

They were both victims of circumstance.

Her eyes flicked to the banked fire on one side of the room. Orange flame had been transformed into ember, and the last warmth slipped into grey ash even as she watched.

Heartache was not fixed in time. It was only smoored like flame, until circumstance allowed it to escape and its heat rose again to eat into everything. Bitterness made deep runnels, and anger saw to it that nothing filled them up again.

The sum of her life rested precariously on the sharp edge of grief, loss and secrets.

She wished Christmas was over. She wished it was already January and a new year was upon them.

# Chapter Two

Aunt Sarah stood near the window and drew the curtain back. 'He's here.'

The words made Ariana's heart beat faster and she breathed in deeply to try and calm herself. She felt in her pocket for the small piece of paper folded there and was re-assured.

'Don't get caught, and once you have found the letters come home.'

Her aunt's instructions were explicit, but Ariana could hear the worry in her voice.

'Northwell is a friend of Andrew Shawler, by all accounts, so tell him nothing.'

She glanced at the clock. 'It will take a quarter of an hour to get inside the house, another quarter to find my bearings and the same to travel home again. I should be back before eleven.'

'If you are not I shall come looking for you.'

'No. If you do that I shall only worry, and I need all my wits about me. Promise you will not, Aunt Sarah.'

A terse nod was her only answer, before the butler knocked at the drawing room door and announced the Earl of Norwich.

He wore a black armband on the sleeve of his black jacket. For his mother, Ariana supposed, as his shaded brown eyes raked across hers. He carried a bouquet.

'For you,' he said, and stepped forward to place it in her hands.

The red of holly berries complemented the green of rosemary, with bay nestled amongst the pungent foliage of a young branch of fir.

'An American custom,' he explained, and for the first time she heard the slight burr of the colonies in his pronunciation. 'Soon it will be Christmas.'

'I am not a great believer in the season, Lord Northwell.'

'I am shocked, Mrs Dalrymple,' he returned, but the emotion playing in his eyes showed he was far from it.

Did Christopher Northwell know that she loathed Christmas? Had he been speaking to others and finding out what they thought of her? If that was the case it was a mystery why he was even here, and had not run for the hills with the haste most others were apt to do.

He turned to her aunt now and tipped his head. 'I am pleased to meet you, Lady Ludlow.'

Ariana was astonished as her aunt coloured and smiled back.

'I knew your mother once, many years back, and I was sorry to hear of her passing.'

'At least she is at peace now.'

He said this flatly, one of those stock answers people might articulate, but a certain hardness in the words belied the sentiment.

'How is your father managing?'

Her aunt asked this in the growing silence and a flicker of something akin to surprise filled his eyes.

'Badly.'

Aunt Sarah nodded. 'I always thought theirs was an unusual love story. Odette had found a rock to stick to and your father was pleased to provide her with the shelter.'

'I had not quite thought of it like that before.'

'Well, there are different ways to look at every story, I should imagine.'

Her aunt's words were slow and measured and Christopher Northwell smiled.

'I am completely in agreement with you on that, Lady Ludlow.'

Ariana could not remember her aunt being so wordy in the company of strangers. More usually she was tense and terse and could not wait to have them gone.

But the Earl had brought his notice back to Ariana now, his glance on her dress, his quiet humour apparent. Ariana wished she had not been quite so original with the cut and colour, but resisted the urge to worry.

'My carriage is outside, Mrs Dalrymple. Perhaps we should go?'

'Of course.'

Collecting her thick red coat and small jewelled bag, she said goodnight to her aunt and followed him out. He was so tall he had to stoop slightly at the lintel to pass through.

His conveyance was like one out of a fairy-tale. The polished gold of the chassis shone and the velvet cushions inside were numerous as she slipped in and sat down. She had never kept her own carriage, simply because the bother of stabling horses and hiring drivers had seemed like a great inconvenience, and she'd always been scared of the size and power in the animals.

'I feel a bit like Cinderella.' The words came as she leaned back into the comfort.

'Cinderella in a gown spun from many colours and a fairy godmother of indeterminate fierceness?' There was drollness in his query.

'My aunt has a reputation that is not always deserved.'

'Then I am glad for it.'

She felt for the note in her pocket, just to make sure she had not misplaced it. He sat next to her, his long legs stretched out. His clothing was understated but very fine. He was not a man who needed any artificial embellishment, nor one who wanted to show off.

'I would like to thank you for keeping your part of the bargain and for being here, Lord Norwich.'

'You thought I would not?'

'I am supposing that you do realise Lord Shawler and I have had our differences?'

He laughed at that, and she felt exuberant. He was not overcome by her, nor intimidated. He was only himself. And in the light thrown upon him from street lamps his smile was beautiful.

She thought of the bouquet that he had brought her, filled with the promise of Christmas. Fourteen days away. Gracious, how quickly Yuletide seemed to turn up, year after year. She wondered if he would still be enjoying her friendship by the time the day actually arrived, and decided he probably would not. There was tonight to get through, after all, and most men fled after a week in her company.

She smiled at that thought. Christopher Northwell didn't seem put out by her directness at all, nor by the fact that she was hardly a shrinking violet.

'A friend of mine—the Earl of Harding—tells me that you are a champion for the rights of women who have been wronged.'

'His Grace credits me with a large mission.' She said this with a dash of humour. 'The truth is that my aunt runs classes for women caught in difficulties. Sometimes I help her.'

'Just as you mean to help her tonight?'

'I beg your pardon?' Shock made her stiffen. Such perception was worrying.

'The Shawler ball. You need an invitation. Andrew Shawler is hardly a saint when it comes to his behaviour with women. I cannot see that you are going simply for the fun of it?'

'You think I would berate Shawler in front of everyone at a ball?'

'I don't know. Would you?'

He did not sound fussed either way, and such indifference was beguiling.

'What was it you did in the Americas, my lord?'

'I built towns where none existed and sold them.'

'An expensive undertaking, I should imagine?'

'And one that reaped large dividends.'

'An entrepreneur, then?'

'People need homes, Mrs Dalrymple. I provided them.'

'Why did you return to England, then, if things were going so very well?'

He did not flinch as he answered. 'My mother was ill. I thought I should come back.'

'But she died before you arrived?'

'I think she knew I was coming.'

That came with an honesty Ariana could barely believe.

'She didn't want to see you?'

'I didn't quite say that.' The smiling man had returned— the one who flicked off hardship and laughed at the world.

As the carriage slowed and pulled in behind a row of others the reality of what she was about to do made Ariana feel slightly sick. She knew her reputation preceded her, and that she would not be welcome. No, she was the widow Dalrymple—a woman with a past no one could quite understand, of whom the whispers were loud. A woman who did not fit into the rigid compartments that Society wished her to.

Three minutes later they were inside the entrance hall and her cloak was gone. The eyes of all those around were fixed upon her, and when Lord Northwell tucked her arm into his she was grateful beyond measure.

Andrew Shawler was receiving his guests. North saw him before the man glanced over at them, next in line. He was a jowly red-faced man, with too much weight upon him and an irritating countenance of superiority. Once they had run in the same pack of wild young men, but now he could barely see any similarity between them.

Perhaps he owed his mother more than he realised, because if he had not left England all those years before he

might have ended up exactly the same. Lost, bored and entitled, and wondering why life had passed him by.

Fury stamped Shawler's face as he caught sight of Ariana Dalrymple, but before he could say anything North leant
forward and whispered. 'There are things I know about you,
Shawler, that you might well wish I didn't. Be nice to the
lady.'

A look of uncertainty followed, and their host's cheeks
were infused with an even brighter red.

'Norwich.' The word was flat.

'Thank you for the invitation. I think you might already
know Mrs Dalrymple?'

'I do.'

Shawler made little attempt to conceal his dislike, but
with care North shepherded her past the man. Her hand was
cold against his own, her fingers clenched and solid.

'Don't worry. He won't make a fuss—though God knows
what you have done to make him hate you so much.'

'I hit him over the head with a statue last year, when he
seemed unable to understand the word no.'

'Hell.' The world stood still, all the gaiety around him
blurred by such a terrible truth. 'Did you knock him out?'

'Yes.'

'Good. Why the hell are you here, then? In this house at
a ball that you can hardly have wanted to come to?'

'For revenge.'

She said this quickly, the words clearly bursting forth in
her fright at Shawler's reaction. Unthinking.

'Your own?'

'No.'

Seth Douglas joined them before North could ask more,
his friend's arms coming around his body and lifting him up.

'My God. Alistair said you were back, but I did not believe him—five years is a damned long time without a word,
North!'

Anna Charleston's sister Pamela stood next to him, her

eyes taking in his face. He had not seen her since calling upon her family when he had finally been well enough to do so after Anna's death.

'My lord.' Her voice was so similar to her sister's he felt thrown back in time.

'Lady Douglas. I hear you and Seth are married? Congratulations.'

'And we have a little girl who is fifteen months old. Her name is Anna Joy.'

Layers of blame, guilt and fault shimmered, and North felt them keenly as the past reached through time to claim him.

Taking Ariana's hand, he brought her closer—because at least her truths were honestly stated, and right now it seemed it was just them against the whole world. Surprisingly she came with an easy grace, and he liked her warm soft curves, even in the ridiculously colourful dress that showed off far too much skin.

'We were sorry to hear about your mother's passing, North,' said Seth.

No one mentioned suicide, but he could see the ghost of it in their faces—see the horror and the question. He was glad his father had refused to follow protocol and had his mother buried in consecrated ground in the small family cemetery on the far side of the Stevenage chapel. In his book, an illness of the mind deserved nothing less than celestial and eternal peace.

For a moment North felt weightless and dislocated. The years he had been in the Americas had set him on a new path and he couldn't find the man he had once been. He had changed beyond recognition. The manners and deceits of the aristocracy held only unfamiliarity for him now, with their lack of truth and their careful treading around anything that was awkward.

Alistair Botham had joined them, and if there was one

thing about his friend that never failed it was his ability to put his foot in his mouth.

'I thought Andrew Shawler might have slugged you, North. I was hoping for more of a spectacle, or at least some insult that bore fruit and resulted in fisticuffs. Mrs Dalrymple. You are looking even more ravishing than you usually do.'

'Thank you.' Ariana gave her answer quietly, and in that particular direct way of hers.

'Shawler has the look of a bulldog that has lost its bone. Is that your doing, North? You always were good at raising his ire.'

'Nope. All his own doing, I think.'

'A lost soul, then.'

'And one as far from the promised land as is possible. God knows why we ever allowed him near us.'

'He has money,' Seth said, 'which makes it hard to take him down. You seem to have managed to find a chink in his armour, however, Mrs Dalrymple... I remember some scandal last year that involved a small statue used with force?'

'A faulty strategy that unfortunately has him baying for my blood.'

'Well, North is a great one to favour the underdog. At school he was always in trouble for it, so you are in good company.'

School. It seemed like such a long time ago. In America he had felt free from such memory and reborn into independence. A land of opportunity and equality... He wondered momentarily how long he might have to stay in England before returning.

Pamela Douglas had sidled across towards her, and Ariana could tell that she wanted to talk.

'I didn't realise you knew the Earl of Norwich, Mrs Dalrymple, but I think a friend like you will be good for him.'

A surprising turn of conversation. She frowned. 'You do?'

'You are said to be a woman who believes in justice. I hope that is true.'

'Because you feel he needs justice?'

'More than anyone else in this room, I think. There is only so much gossip one can hear before one starts to believe it.'

'Gossip about his mother?'

'No. I am speaking of my sister—Anna. He was going to marry her, but she drowned before he was able to and I think he has blamed himself ever since.'

'Something you don't think fair?'

'No one's happiness is the sole responsibility of another. Do you believe that, Mrs Dalrymple?'

'Implicitly.'

'Then I am glad of it.'

She could not quite understand what Lady Douglas was trying to tell her, but what she did know was that she liked the woman—liked her honesty and her lack of pretence.

Ariana glanced around the room to see where Andrew Shawler was, and saw that he was busy with a group of men she did not recognise. Christopher Northwell was busy too, his friends around him laughing at something he'd said.

Lady Douglas leaned closer and lifted her hand to shield her next words and prevent them from being overheard by others. 'Shawler is what the Chinese would call a paper tiger. He blusters and bridles about his businesses and his importance but there is nothing save his title and his fortune that prevents him from being forcibly ejected from Society. I think every woman in the room probably hates him, and well they should.'

This was a revelation to Ariana. 'You believe that women have the right to state strong opinions outside of the home?'

Lady Douglas laughed. 'I hear you are a champion of the feminine cause and I commend you for it. One day in the future equality for all will be a normal thing, and people will look back and wonder at the primitive times we now live in.'

'You surprise me. I have not heard these sentiments before from anyone save my aunt.'

The other laughed. 'There are many like me, Mrs Dalrymple. Hundreds and hundreds of us.'

Normal women. Women who held friends for ever and had large, loving families. Women who were in good marriages and believed in hope.

Ariana's past had always precluded her from being a part of these groups, and the lonely life she led with her aunt had seen to the rest. She was out of step, that was the problem, and it had begun all those years ago when her parents had betrayed her.

The room swam around her and she felt dizzy. She *never* thought of these things in company, and the horror of doing so here and now, in a salon full of prying eyes, was mortifying.

North was suddenly there, holding her up, making certain she was safe, whispering in a tone that was comforting and leading her out into an empty chamber off the main hallway.

When he had sat her down he took the space next to her on the large sofa. 'What happened?'

She could not answer him, even as she dug into her pocket for her handkerchief, extracting it to wipe her face and then wrench the fabric this way and that.

He leaned over and picked up something from the floor, and she saw that he held the map that her aunt had drawn. His brow puckered as he tried to make sense of it.

Resisting the urge to simply snatch it from him, she waited. Perhaps he would return it to her without realising what it was.

'It's a plan of this house.'

Her heart sank.

'This is why you wanted to come here, isn't it? To this ball? So badly? God, you spoke of revenge before. Are you a thief?'

She shook her head and took the piece of paper as he handed it back.

'Then why?'

'I told you that you only needed to give fifteen minutes of your time to me. I am sure it is past that, and I absolve you from any more.'

He sat there in silence for a moment, and she did too. Then he spoke.

'Vengeance has a dark side, Ariana.'

She was sure he was speaking of himself, so she waited.

'Bitterness drags you under until there is nothing left. You say you hit Shawler over the head and knocked him out. My advice to you would be to let that be enough and move on from it.'

He thought she was doing this for herself? Out of an ego-tistical vengeance? She wondered what would happen if she told him the truth.

She felt like simply giving it to him. She wanted to reach out and hold his hand—an anchor against the world, a safe harbour in stormy seas. She wondered what it must be like to have a man such as this on her side, aiding her, but of course she knew that was impossible.

With care, she folded the small map and stood. 'Thank you for helping me, my lord, but I think my night here is almost at an end, and it would be better for us to part now as friends.'

'Friends...'

He said this is a way that made her frown, for there was a tone in the word that sounded perplexed.

'Before you go, Mrs Dalrymple, could I ask a favour of you?'

'One?'

He nodded, and when she remained silent he continued.

'Would you consider accompanying me to Stevenage on a visit to see my father?'

Of all the things she'd thought he might say, this was the very last of them.

'Why?'

'He is a man whom people find difficult, but I think you might manage him. We are largely estranged, you see, and there are times when I would rather it were otherwise. Before I return to America I would like to make my peace with him.'

His honesty was startling. She wondered if he had ever told anyone else what he was telling her now, and thought it unlikely.

'When would this visit take place?'

'The day after tomorrow. We would stay at Stevenage for two nights and return the following day. Do you think your aunt might consider coming as chaperon?'

Ariana smiled. 'My aunt is as difficult as your father is purported to be, but if I asked her she would come.'

'And will you ask her?'

'Yes.'

He reached out and took her hand, and kissed the back of it in the way a gallant knight might have in one of the old tournaments, before the world had become modern. She felt the warmth of his mouth upon her skin and a shiver went through her.

'Now, Mrs Dalrymple,' he said, without looking at her. 'Before you leave I want you to tell me why you have a detailed map of the Shawler house upon your person.'

## Chapter Three

She felt her top teeth biting down on her bottom ones until they ached and then she stopped herself doing it.

'I have told you that my aunt teaches classes for women of limited means. She teaches her pupils things that might help them rise up in life and in employment. These are not Society women, so to speak, but the daughters of gentlemen who have fallen on hard times.'

'Of what do these lessons comprise?'

'Book discussions. Conversation. Music. The art of gardening. The expectation of manners. All the things that might help a woman find her place.'

She saw him smile and frowned.

'You think such an endeavour to be humorous?'

'No, I think it admirable. Do you help with these classes too?'

Now she saw why he smiled. He thought her far from the demure and decorous example of womanhood she was describing, and it was the truth.

'I do not. I am usually far too busy setting tongues wagging.'

'I don't believe you.'

That took her aback, though she did not pursue such a line of argument and went on with her own.

'Miss Josephine Leggett became a student last year, and my aunt had high hopes for her future—until Mr Shawler saw her on the street in Portman Square and decided he liked the look of her. She is delicate and dainty and blonde, you see, and inclined to be bashful, timid and coy. All the things that men find most attractive in a woman.'

'*Some* men,' he qualified, before he allowed her to continue.

'Unfortunately she sent him letters—unwise letters that held sentiments she should never have expressed so personally—and Mr Shawler has threatened to hold them against her unless she meets him...*privately*. My aunt found out, and we devised a plan to retrieve these unwise letters in the least visible way possible, thus putting a stop to any discourse between them and saving her reputation. Aunt Sarah was a friend of Shawler's grandmother, and drew the map from her memory of visiting the house years ago.'

'This map which shows the library upstairs as its end point?'

'That is where Josephine swears her correspondence will be. Lord Shawler described a red box to her once, as the place where he keeps his most valuable mail, and she noted the description. He mentioned the library at the same time.'

'You think this box will be just sitting there on a table for you to simply rifle through? Can you pick locks, Mrs Dalrymple? Would you be able to determine the complicated hiding places a man might use to secure important documents, should it come to that?'

He sounded angry, and she could understand his irritation. 'I cannot and would not, my lord, but the least I can do is to try to find them—and that I shall endeavour to accomplish.'

'And if Shawler catches you at your game?'

'Then Josephine shall be as ruined as I am, but I shan't go quietly.'

'How do you mean?'

'I shall shout out about his dreadful moral baseness to anyone who might listen—and his house is very full tonight.'

'And what if he hits you? What if he simply silences you in the first moment of discovery and bundles you up, to be taken somewhere so that you might never be found again?'

'This is England, sir. Lords of the realm do not kidnap ladies of means—they merely seduce them.'

'A man who attaches little importance to the word *no* is not one who will have a liking for semantics.'

She had to give him his due. Christopher Northwell had listened to all the things she had told him and he was a competent opponent.

'If I don't retrieve those letters Miss Leggett's future will be gone and my aunt's heart will be broken.'

She saw a muscle in his jaw grind along the line of his chin and his hands clench.

'Then I will do it for you.'

'I beg your pardon?'

'Give me the map and I'll find the letters.'

Her aunt had told her not to trust him, and yet she found herself handing over the map and stepping back.

'Let me come with you. I can help.'

North looked around, and she could tell he was thinking.

'If anything happens I will deny you are involved, Mrs Dalrymple. You have to agree to this. If I am caught you will simply leave and say nothing of this to anyone at all. I will say you followed me.'

'Why would you do this?'

'Because my reputation is something I have no concern for, whereas yours...'

'Is largely lost anyway.'

He smiled. 'Believe me, there is a lot further to fall than the position you now stand in—even in a dress that needs another yard of cloth in it to be decent.'

'You are a prude, my lord. This gown is hardly indecent.' But she said it kindly.

'And you are so impetuous I am wondering how you have managed to survive for so long in the most judgemental Society in all the world. God, its unfathomable—and damned worrying, too.'

Leaning forward, she kissed him—fully on the lips—and

found in his shock a lack of control that she had not expected.
He was beautiful and strong, and intimacy only underlined
such a fact. He was a good man, too.

'Tit for tat, Mrs Dalrymple. I shall owe you one.'

He drawled this as she stepped away.

'One what?'

'A kiss. In a far more private setting. A place where I
can kiss you back.'

For the first time in all her life Ariana blushed, hard and
true. She felt the burn of it cross her cheeks and move down
to the bare skin of her throat.

Checkmate. King to Queen. Captured. Startling.

Her world had shifted—because never before had she
been the one to make the first move, to want such intimacy
and to yearn for more on completion.

The frozen core of her was rearranging itself and melting,
and her surprise was so complete she merely stood there as
he moved to the door.

'Are you coming?'

His question released her from the trance and she followed him, the music in the salon disappearing into quietness, the rows of family portraits on the walls following
her with their eyes.

Finally they came to the library, and North shut the door
and turned to the desk.

'A red box, you say?'

She nodded, listening all the time for noises outside and
watching as he searched.

He used a short piece of wire that he brought out from
his jacket pocket to open the locks of all the drawers in the
desk. She wondered what sort of a man might carry such
a tool. Her own preparation for retrieving the letters was
woefully inadequate.

'There isn't any box here.'

He looked around and walked behind the desk, his hands
searching the solid wall with paintings hung upon it. He

found a hole behind the third portrait, revealing the front
of a dark steel door bolted before them.

'Can you open it?'

'I can—but Shawler will know it's been tampered with.
Once I have it open I won't be able to close it'

Within a few seconds he had the lock released and was
extracting the red box and pushing it towards her. The three
letters from Josephine were on the top of a pile of others,
and she placed them in her reticule. After she had done so
the Earl removed a card embossed with his name from his
top pocket and tossed it onto one corner of the desk.

'You will leave that there?'

'I have always found attack is more disconcerting than
defence.'

'Why would you do this? Take the blame?'

'Because Shawler is an immoral bastard who needs rein-
ing in, and because even as the reluctant heir to a dukedom my voice will be heard. Now we just have to get out of
here—because a scene tonight with all these people present
would be unfortunate.'

Ariana could barely believe he would do this—risk his
own name for the protection of an unknown and indiscreet
woman—and yet she found herself unable to refuse the offer.

She quietly moved behind him along the corridor and
onto the stairs. Just before the landing they heard footsteps,
and with nowhere to hide Christopher Northwell suddenly
pulled her into his arms and kissed her—hard, this time—
as if he meant it, and as if their life depended on the outcome. Which to a certain extent she supposed it did. It was
no quiet pretend kiss, but a full and sensual demand of her
body, with his tongue dispensing of any resistance.

A loud exclamation drew them apart and Andrew Shawler
stood there, looking furious.

'If we had wanted guests up here we would not have
placed a braided rope across the stairs, Norwich.'

North was not deterred.

'Which is precisely why I am in the only private space in the whole house.'

'You would risk further scandal, North, with a woman who is already tainted by it?'

The insult was specific, she knew. There was history between the two men—that much was obvious—but Ariana could not understand the underlying tension. A secret, she supposed, and one that bound them somehow. Both looked furious.

When the Earl turned to her and wished her goodnight she was astonished—and even more astonished when he bowed slightly and then disappeared with Shawler down the long corridor.

With little else to do, she returned to the main salon and found her cloak and hat, requesting a servant to call for a hackney to transport her home.

The events of the night had been surprising, and she could make no sense of any of them. Still, she had Josephine Leggett's unwise correspondence, and her aunt would be thrilled at the outcome.

She hoped with all her might that the Earl was not being set on by the obnoxious Shawler and his cronies right at this very moment—though in all honesty he looked like a man who could well deal with it.

North was glad when she left, and glad when he looked back and saw no sight of her. Once downstairs she would be safe, and he hoped like hell that she would have the good sense to call a conveyance and leave immediately.

He'd seen the small blade Shawler had in his pocket. The outline of steel against superfine was unmistakable. And he knew that, short of creating a scene that would draw attention, he had no recourse but to do exactly as Shawler wanted.

He had always known it would come to this, from the moment he had left for the Americas, with Anna's broken words at the river ringing in his ears.

Hell. That day drew back upon him—the coldness, the fear, the shock…

At the door that led into the library he pulled back. He needed to give Ariana Dalrymple time to leave, and he thought it wise to buy himself some time too.

'What's all this about, Shawler? I can see you are armed.' Better to confront him head-on and see where the conversation led. 'This is a ball, and as the host you are presumably needed downstairs.'

'The widow Dalrymple is no lady, North. You would do well to stay away from her.'

'Why?'

'Her baseness leads her to protect prostitutes and ladies of the night. She harasses every man who enjoys them.'

'Including you?'

'Her husband was ancient. She married him for his money.'

'Something many women in society would applaud her for.'

'After he died she sought comfort in the arms of others. She is a woman who is…immoral and bitter.'

North held up his hand. 'For old times' sake I will take your advice without rancour, but I don't want to hear any more. Do you understand?'

As they gained the library it took only a moment for Shawler to register the open door in the wall, the painting propped up beneath it, and the calling card upon the desk.

'Mrs Dalrymple was most adamant that three of the letters you kept in your red box were hers. She said something about blackmailing a vulnerable young woman who attends her aunt's school for ladies down on their luck, I think.' He paused as that sank in before continuing, 'If I were you, Shawler, I'd find another lock and then return downstairs without a fuss and count myself lucky that such ungentlemanly behaviour ends here.'

Shawler swore and leaned against the desk, his countenance ruddy and defeated. A deflated bully with sweat on his brow.

'You saw me that day at the river, didn't you? You saw me kiss Anna Charleston. She thought you didn't love her enough and she told you so.'

'Goodnight, Andrew. My advice to you would be to cut your losses and leave Miss Josephine Leggett alone.'

He turned then, and simply walked away. Away from this house and Andrew Shawler and from memories that made no sense but were engraved with pain. There was nothing left to say. Secrets did that—they burned into flesh and ate at certainty, and he did not wish them to do so for a moment longer.

Downstairs, Seth caught up with him and shoved a drink into his hand.

'You look as if you might need this. I saw Mrs Dalrymple leave.'

'Good.'

'You wanted her to go?'

'Can I ask you a question, Seth?'

'Of course.'

'How long did it take you to realise that Pamela Charleston should be your wife?'

'The first time she smiled at me I knew.'

North raised his glass. 'To wives,' he said, and swallowed the lot. 'And to truth.'

'You've changed in five years, North.'

'I have had to.'

'Your father is old. Don't leave it too late to make peace with him. He was heartbroken after your mother's passing.'

With care, North placed his empty crystal glass down on the silver tray of a passing servant.

'Age does not always bring wisdom.'

'I know that,' Seth said, shaking his head, 'but it can bring regrets.'

Leaving the Shawler house, North summoned his conveyance, which was waiting twenty or so yards down the street. When he threw himself in he was astonished to find Ariana Dalrymple there, shrouded in her dark woollen cloak, watching him.

'I sent my hackney on and crept in here while your driver was busy. I am good at being unseen.'

'A handy skill, that.'

'Not quite as handy as picking locks or drawing the enemy off his quarry. Not as honourable, either.'

'I've never been a saint, Mrs Dalrymple.'

'It isn't a saint that I need.'

'What is it you *do* need, Aria?'

'To say thank you. For your help. I would not have regained the letters without you.'

She stayed in her corner, sheathed in wool, giving him the distinct impression that she did not wish for him to touch her. Outside it was snowing. He noticed that with surprise, for it had not been snowing a moment ago, and it was a while since he had seen such weather.

'Was Miss Anna Charleston as kind and as beautiful as her sister?' asked Ariana.

'Yes.'

'Her death must have been quite a loss, then. To you.'

He stayed quiet.

'When my husband died I was nothing but thankful. At least your memories are happy ones. That is a comfort, I would expect.'

'Expectations are sometimes slippery things.' He couldn't believe he had said that.

'You searched for hours in a cold river, according to my aunt's recollections, and suffered with pneumonia afterwards. A high price to pay if it was not for true love.'

'Andrew Shawler was there at the river.'

More words that were not meant to be said. A new confession that he had never given anyone before.

'He kissed her, and she kissed him back. I saw them before she disappeared.'

'People make mistakes. People do things that they wish

they had not all the time. Yet one should not die for a dalliance.'

The hat Ariana wore had slipped, leaving one long feather at a jaunty angle across her hair, and the odd, mismatched cloak suited her colouring more and more as he looked at it.

Mrs Dalrymple was a woman of shadows, strength and depth, all topped with a beauty that was undeniably potent. She was unlike anyone else he had ever known. Original. Honest. Direct.

'Did Shawler know you had observed them?' she asked.

'Yes.'

'I see. But you never chastised him publicly?'

'The Charleston family did not need scandal on top of their grief.'

She smiled. 'And it takes so very little to set this Society agog.'

'A lot less than burning a house down, at least.'

'Or marrying a man forty years your senior.'

'Did you love him at all? The ancient Mr Dalrymple?'

Shaking her head, she looked out of the window. 'No, I did not. But my parents loved his fortune.'

'How old were you?'

'Seventeen. Just.'

'How long were you married?'

'Two years. Mr Dalrymple succumbed to the same congestion of the chest my parents had, and through the haze of it all the only hope I could see was freedom—which I have used to the best of my ability.'

'The series of lovers you are renowned for?'

'Two of them—and both disappointing.'

He laughed because he could not help it, this truth having been given with such directness. 'I can see why men of sense hold an admiration for you, Mrs Dalrymple. You are nothing at all like the simpering, clueless ladies they are used to.'

'Well, I try not to lie…'

'And you are not afraid of the truth?'

'Money allows one the choice of being frank, I suspect.'

'A weapon you use like a knife?'

'A rusty blade, given my age and situation. I have not welcomed anyone into my bed for years, despite what is said about me.'

'Is that a challenge?'

Unbelievably, she blushed again. Even in the dark he could see the rush of blood and the shake of her head.

'You have a gaggle of beauties falling at your feet—young women of kind and moral nature who would make comfortable life companions. And after your problems in the past...' She stopped momentarily. 'You seem like a man who might welcome peace.'

The conveyance had halted at the corner of Portman Square now, and the moon above them was full.

'Shawler won't bother you again,' he said.

He saw her glance at his hands.

'I didn't hit him.'

She smiled.

'I searched the river for Anna for so many hours because I felt guilty.'

'Of what?'

'Of a lack of love, I suppose. For her. She knew it, too. Her last words, shouted at me through the wind, said as much.'

'A fact that explains her unwise kiss with Shawler, perhaps? People can surprise you with their truth.'

'You surprise me, Ariana.'

He did not touch her as he said this, but something leapt between them. An understanding and a beginning.

He would have liked to draw her into his arms, but she looked distant and untouchable, caught in her own thoughts across the night, pledged to her freedom.

The lights were on at the Portman Square townhouse and two men had come out to greet them, opening the door before his own servants could and helping her out.

'Goodnight and thank you, my lord. It was a lovely evening and one I shall never forget.'

He saw her hand steal to her reticule, where he knew she had secreted the letters.

'Lovely?' he echoed, and thought of all the words she might have chosen, with this one the most unsatisfactory.

He watched her walk away, her cloak billowing in the breeze, her breath white on the cold of winter air. Upstairs a curtain flickered. Her aunt, he supposed. At least there was someone close to Ariana Dalrymple who would wait up to see her safe. That thought was comforting.

Ariana lay in bed and gazed at the bouquet that Christopher Northwell had given her at the beginning of the night. A winter bouquet.

The pungent smell of pine needles filled her bedroom. Strong and distinctive. Like the Earl himself. Untamed and unexpected. The bay held its own earthy tones, and the holly leaves shone waxed green under candlelight.

A Christmas composition, born in the cold and impervious to it. No small fragile flowers here, to wrinkle and curl in the frost. No, these specimens of greenery were sturdy, solid and resilient—as he had had to be, probably, banished to the Americas and away from all that was familiar.

She liked him. Which was unusual. More normally she found men annoying, cloying and difficult. But Christopher Northwell was none of those things. He had helped her retrieve the letters and protected her in a room full of people who had little reason to be kind.

Breathing in, she kept very still. Her heart was beating in the same fashion that it had before she'd kissed him—she could hear the quiet thump of it in the semi-darkness. But everything was different. For the first time in a long while she felt alive and excited, with all the possibilities she had thought long gone returned in one single night in the company of the enigmatic Earl of Norwich.

Her aunt had been waiting up for her when she'd returned, her thick dressing gown buttoned to the throat and her hair winding down her back in a long white braided plait. Ariana had felt her relief as she'd dispatched Josephine's letters into her waiting hands.

'How did you manage this, Aria?' Disbelief had been in her every word.

'With help. The Earl picked the lock on the door behind which they were hidden and left his own calling card on the desk.'

'Why?'

'I think he is a good man, Aunt Sarah, and there is also past business between Shawler and himself that demands recompense.'

'He told you this?'

'Yes.'

'A trustworthy man, then?'

'I think so. He has asked us both to Stevenage for a few days, the day after tomorrow. He wants to show us around.'

'Intriguing...'

'Why?'

'Because he is estranged from his father, by all accounts.'

'Well, perhaps he wishes for better relations between them and he needs us as a buffer? Will you come, Aunt Sarah?'

'Of course I will. I would not miss the chance to see the remodelled estate in all its glory for the world.'

Ariana smiled at the memory and reached out to the green waxed leaves of the holly, careful not to touch the wavy margins tipped with spines. No one had ever given her a bouquet before, and this one was so much more beautiful than the normal flimsy posies of indeterminate hue.

No one had ever kissed her as he had, either, but she shook that thought aside, because she could not understand where all this was leading.

She remembered the Honourable Mr Henry Dalrymple and shuddered. The few times he had come to her bed had been distasteful and frightening. The two lovers she had taken after he had died had been no better. Oh, granted, they had been younger, but the act of intimacy had held only horror for her and she had sent them on their way as quickly as she could, furious at herself for even imagining that such contact might help.

Four acts of lovemaking in all the years of her life. Two under the oppressive mantle of a distasteful marriage and the other two quick and forgettable things that had held no emotion whatsoever.

'The Wayward Widow' Mrs Dalrymple was a misnomer. But she had encouraged it because it meant men were wary of her, and she was not constantly swatting them off as she'd had to do when first she had come back to London from the north.

Turning over, she looked at the ceiling. The ornate sculptured rose that held the small chandelier made her smile. At least this house was hers, and she had money enough to live comfortably for the rest of her life. Marriage had given her that.

It had been a poor bargain, though—forced upon her by her mama and papa, who had seen her as the way out of their modest means and taken it. She had been unresisting and docile, because there had seemed no other alternative, and they had been clever in their bargaining.

Dresses. Houses. Furniture and carriages… She could barely remember the young, impressionable girl who had thought those things so important that she had sacrificed her future for them.

When her husband and her parents had died two days apart six years ago, in the coldest winter of living memory, she had not shed a tear. She had buried them with respect and decorum, and then she had sold up and departed—all the dresses and horses and furniture gone with the house, left behind. Accoutrements of a life that had been a lie.

She had taken nothing with her save her resolve never to be beholden to anyone again.

## Chapter Four

He saw her the next morning in the park as he walked—
a small figure alone except for the tall and well-built maid
trailing behind her.

'It is very early to be afoot, Mrs Dalrymple.'

'Oh, I've always preferred silence and emptiness, my
lord.'

Her formality this morning was difficult, for it left him
in a place that was hard to fathom, with the kiss between
them yesterday still causing heat inside him.

'You come here often at this time?'

'Most days. My aunt insists on a servant being dispatched
to accompany me, and I find resistance wearying, but the
girl follows at a distance so at least I can think.'

'You like being alone?'

'As much as you do, I should imagine.' She pointedly
gazed around. 'But then men can do many things that a
woman cannot.'

'And you think that unfair?'

'I do, my lord.'

Her prickliness hastened him on to another topic. 'Were
the letters we retrieved yesterday received well by your
aunt?'

'They were, indeed. She bade me thank you most sincerely for your help.'

'And she will accompany us to Stevenage tomorrow?'

'She will, if your invitation still stands?'

'It does.'

'Is your father...well?'

Her tone made him imagine the things she might have

heard of his family—dark things that he knew were whispered in the quieter quarters of the ton.

'Your aunt is somewhat correct in her assumption that my parents' marriage was a love story. My father, at least, put his whole heart into keeping my mother happy.'

'And was she? Happy, I mean?'

'Sometimes she was.'

He remembered her copious tears and desperate anxieties. He remembered her anger, too, but that he willed away.

'I hope the Duke will not mind guests at Stevenage?'

'It is my home too, Mrs Dalrymple, and he will not mind.'

'A home you shan't remain in, however? You said you mean to return to the American colonies.'

'My business is there, so I will go back after a winter here, when the shipping routes are safer.'

'You like it there, then?'

'I do. There is a freedom available that is rarely so in England. People take one another at face value, and the family they were born into or the school they attended has only small relevance.'

'It was a new beginning, then? A second chance?'

He smiled at the yearning in her query. 'Exactly.'

'And the change that you needed after the fire at Stevenage?'

'Are you always so inquisitive, Mrs Dalrymple?'

She shook her head and he saw her frown deepen.

'Never, as a rule, and I ask your pardon for my rudeness.'

He looked away and swallowed, trying to formulate an answer that would not be misconstrued.

'My mother found life difficult. I did not think she could weather any more scandal, so I left. I think my father was pleased that I had gone.'

'Because it stopped the questions?'

'And because he could protect her in the way he had since the day they were married.'

'And you? What of your protection?'

This time he did laugh, the release of it filling him with warmth. 'I did not need any.'

She nodded and moved back. And then, as she was wont to do, she changed the subject completely.

'I like the bouquet you gave me. This morning it is even more beautiful than yesterday, and its fragrance fills my bedchamber.'

'Reminding you of the Christmas spirit…the joy of the season?'

'I think you are jesting, my lord. I think you know that I have never relished all the joviality of Yuletide.'

He reached into his pocket and found what he was looking for. The small glass ornament felt fragile, hidden in its velvet bag, as he handed it across.

'Another gift?'

Ariana took the offering cautiously and, drawing the string of the bag loose, saw that it was a star of glass, its five points edged in gold and leaf-green and an unusual shade of red.

'I bought it last week in Regent Street, after you helped me. When I saw your gown, I realised the colours were particular to you…'

Ariana had to admit that as a truth. They *were* her colours…unusual, muted and different.

'What do I do with it?' The offering caught the light of the day as it sat on her palm.

'Hang it amongst pine needles. In America a small fir branch is cut and brought inside on Christmas Eve, to bring luck and happiness for the coming year.'

'A large promise for such a small thing?'

'Providence comes from unexpected sources, Aria.'

She did not miss his shortening of her name, nor the tone in which he gave it. Almost intimate.

'I was married on Christmas Eve.' The catch in her voice hurt, but she carried on. 'The memory is not a pleasant one.'

'Then make new memories.'

'Is that what you have done?'

'Yes.'

She could hear his certainty and was glad for it. 'You are making your way well in "the wilderness and the wasteland"?'

'Where is that from?' He sounded interested.

'The Book of Isaiah—though much rephrased. Before that scripture advises the reader to forget the former things and not to dwell on the past.'

'Did you know that a star is perceived to be a glow in the darkness?'

'Are you always so persuasive, Lord Norwich?'

Her fingers closed over the glass and she felt the prick of it on her skin.

'You will keep it, then?'

'I will—and I thank you.'

'Was your husband a good man, Ariana?'

'He was very old and very wealthy.'

'That was important to you?'

'I was young, and my parents were most adamant that my future would be more secure with such backing.'

She could not quite throw in the fact that it had been their own comfort they were more interested in.

'Stevenage burned down on the day of my birthday, yet I still celebrate that.'

Without meaning to, she laughed. He'd surprised her with his words, for there had been an implication there of the fire not being his own doing.

'Do you like horses, my lord?'

'I do.'

'I am pleased for it.'

'You change topic in your conversation a lot. Do you realise you do that?'

'I have heard it said that you burnt down the stables at Stevenage?'

'Ah, I see. You want to understand motive, then?'

'Or the lack of it, my lord.'

'The complications of family bear no logic, Ariana, and yours sounds about as complicated as my own.'

She liked talking to Christopher Northwell more than she had ever enjoyed talking to anyone. He was quick and interesting and solid.

*Solid?*

A strange word to use for a person, but it was what he *was*. The Earl of Norwich wasn't shallow or small-minded or petty. He was a man who could be depended on—a man who had backed her up in difficult circumstances and had not expected anything at all in return.

The kiss they had shared came to mind, and she wished he might simply lean forward and take her into his arms again, as he had yesterday. The small jolt of a thrill seared through her and she looked at him, hoping he would not recognise in her face what she felt all over her body. God, she had always been so frigid, so stand-offish, so reluctant to endure touch—and yet here she was, burning like a candle with sheer and utter want.

The star in her hand was warming…a small gift perfectly given. She would hang it above her bed tonight and watch to see how the moonlight altered each prism.

The glass star…the Christmas bouquet. Her chamber would be turning into an altar of worship for the season and she was welcoming it. Just as she was welcoming Christopher Northwell—although today he gave no impression of wanting anything more than just talk, and his stance was decidedly formal.

'My father may not at first be…easy company, but if you would allow him the time to adjust and get used to your ways I am sure he will relax.'

'My aunt once knew your mother, so perhaps that might help?'

'It might.'

He gave the words back as if he felt it would be the exact opposite, and such uncertainty resulted in a rare silence between them.

He was not telling her everything—she was sure of it. He was afraid for his father. Her amazement grew. Was there something wrong with the Duke of Horsham? Some character trait that his son did not wish for the world to know?

She had heard gossip in Society which stressed that the Duke and his only offspring did not get along. She had heard it said too that Christopher Northwell was wild and undisciplined. And yet she had never seen one glimpse of that side of him. If anything he seemed always in control, and he was indisputably logical.

Nothing quite added up.

'It has not been many months since your mother passed away, so perhaps he needs longer to come to terms with his changed circumstances. At least you are back now—and blood, for all its complexities, runs thicker than water.'

'Was that the way in your family?'

She glanced towards the lake in the distance. 'No. I used to wonder if perhaps I had been adopted as a baby, or found under a bush, or simply swapped with another child who might have grown up…happier. But I looked quite a lot like my mother, so such a wish was groundless from the start, but…'

'But you still hoped?'

'From this distance, and with hindsight, I think I should have been stronger. It is one thing to try to fit in, but another entirely to lose yourself altogether.'

'You seem to have made up for such an early lack, Ariana. If I could pick one word from the air that would describe you best I might choose the word "strong".'

Such a compliment both astounded and delighted her out there in the misty cold clear December morning, with the bare branches of the oaks and the elm above them, out there in the quiet hour before the city truly awoke and all the noise began.

A cocoon of calm...

She wished they were alone, and that her appointed and curious maid was not standing twenty yards away, watching them and waiting. Already she could see other silhouettes further afield, and she knew that their allotted time of privacy was over. Christopher Northwell knew it too, for he straightened and tipped his head.

'Until tomorrow, Mrs Dalrymple.'

Then he was gone.

She did not ask a servant to bring in a tree branch that might suffice as an anchor for her ornament. Instead she found red cotton and strung it from one bedpost to the other, dangling the star in the middle between them, above her pillows, so that she could reach up and touch it if she pleased.

A place of honour and purpose.

A point of light in her darkness.

She had not told the Earl all of it. When he had asked her if Henry Dalrymple had been a good man she had fobbed him off with other facts. She had not told him of the actions which lingered here in the dark all around her. Unforgettable and shameful things.

When Henry Dalrymple had coughed his last she had simply sat in the plain oak chair beside the bed, overcome by a sense of relief.

She remembered there had been Christmas candles in the bedroom when she had first been brought to him by her father. She remembered how her new husband had lifted away her nightgown and pinched one of her breasts hard with his old, thin fingers.

'A bonny girl and well worth the coin. You may leave her to me now, for I will look after her.'

Her father had not hesitated, even with the red whorls of her new groom's hurt blooming on her breast. He had left her there with the promise of payment and had expected her to behave.

Her mother had not asked anything the next day either, her watchful eyes tracking her progress down the stairs when she came for breakfast, with Henry Dalrymple at her heels and close.

And when her parents had left the following day her mother had departed with a warning. 'Do not anger him, Ariana. Do nothing to raise his ire and you will be safe.'

She had not seen them again until two years later, when they had arrived late one autumn with further pleas of financial hardship in their eyes. A week later they had all been dead. Her husband and her father and her mother. And the snows from the north had fallen down on their graves, leaving the newly dug black soil scattered with white in the Dalrymple cemetery.

The star shifted in the wind—a quiet, small movement that caught the candle flame, burning by the bedside, threading the glass with colour.

A comfort. A solace. A tiny prism of faith and belief.

Had Christopher Northwell known it would be so? Had he given it as a guiding light? She could almost believe that he might have, for the smell of the winter bouquet complemented the brittle glass somehow, creating a sensory wholeness.

Tears ran down her cheeks, warm against her skin, trickling onto the pillow, dampening the linen. She had not cried for years. Not when her parents had died. Not when her husband had hurt her. Not even when she had found her small dog Topper, frozen solid in the courtyard, having been locked outside for the night under the orders of the man she had married.

Yet here in her room, in the warmth and the quiet, she did weep—because for the first time in a long while hope had wormed its way up into her world, steadfast and unwavering.

She swallowed and held her hand over her mouth willing away any sound. She must not expect more. She could not allow herself the feelings that she felt crouched there, the possibilities that would never come to pass...

# Chapter Five

Stevenage Manor was bigger than she had imagined it. Much bigger.

The country seat of the Horsham Dukedom spread across a great deal of the flat top of the hillock upon which it sat, towering over the landscape, its windows glinting in the midday sun.

The Earl's carriage had transported them south, with the same comfortable interior she had enjoyed after the Shawler ball swallowing her aunt and herself up as they sped across the countryside. The Earl had accompanied them on his own steed—a magnificent huge grey stallion that she had caught sight of now and again out of the window.

It was a crisp blue day and the sight of Christopher Northwell's figure on top of his horse had been riveting. Her glance had kept straying to find him, and even her aunt had commented on how well he looked upon a horse.

She remembered seeing similar rolling countryside out of the window on her trip down to London six years prior. She had never left the city since, and the views and the trees in this part of the south of England were far more beautiful than any she recalled in the north.

She felt nervous. Nervous about meeting the Duke. Nervous about the Earl's expectations and her own limitations. Nervous about not being enough.

She had chosen the least outrageous clothes in her wardrobe to wear, and while they could probably not be called muted they were at least of quiet hues. The Duke of Horsham was, after all, an older man, and she had no wish to offend him.

'The fire has allowed a phoenix to rise in the place of weariness.' Her aunt's words were said with breathless wonder as she observed Stevenage. 'No wonder Odette loved the place so much.'

'The Earl, however, has indicated that he will not be staying in England any longer than he needs to. He has work back in America that he enjoys. He builds houses on the east coast, and there are many people there needing shelter.'

'Well, I hope we can be of help in the repair of relations between father and son, at least.'

'Thank you for coming, Aunt Sarah.'

'Wouldn't have missed this for the world, my love.'

The front door opened as the carriage drew up on the stones of the circular driveway and a succession of servants spilled out of the portal, all dressed in similar clothing of white shirts and navy trousers or skirts. The women wore caps on their heads and the men neckties at their throats. The Earl had dismounted now. A man was taking his horse and he came across to stand beside the carriage, his face flushed from the ride and a look of freedom in his eyes.

'Welcome to Stevenage Manor.'

'It is a very lovely house,' said Ariana.

'I think the fire improved it.' There was humour in his face and his smile flashed as he stepped forward to help her aunt from the carriage first and then herself.

Ariana thought that in all her life she had never seen a more beautiful man, so solid and comfortable in his skin.

'My father is waiting inside, no doubt. Nothing pleases him more than awkwardness.' His hand cupped her elbow.

'A daunting thought, for my reputation will surely provide him with enough of that.'

'And this is why I so enjoy your company, Mrs Dalrymple. You are unnervingly direct.'

'As opposed to cunningly duplicitous?'

Laughing again, he let her go. 'My father requires firm

management. Without it he is wont to get his own way. I have faith that you will manage him with aplomb.'

Once inside the house, Christopher Northwell led them into a small room to one side of the main hall.

Sitting by the fire with a blanket over his lap was an old man bathed in the sunshine that dappled across him through the windows. He was thin and bent, but his glance was sharp.

'Papa, I would like to introduce you to Mrs Ariana Dalrymple and her aunt, Lady Sarah Hervey, Viscountess Ludlow.'

After a quick sweeping glance over them both, his father's eyes came back to Ariana, their colour almost exactly the same hue as his son's, though much more wary.

'I have heard of you, Mrs Dalrymple, but I had not imagined you to be so young.'

This was said with a decided stiffness.

'I am going to be twenty-six on my next birthday, Your Grace, and I have enough years to know that what is said of one is often embellished and overstated.'

This brought a frown to his forehead. 'You are telling me that the rumours abounding about you are false?'

'Embroidered, I think. I consider myself a person who has made mistakes and learnt from them.'

He lifted a glass from the table beside him and held it up to her. 'Join me in a drink and we shall toast the power of truth. North, pour us all a brandy. It will at least warm you after the long ride.'

Her aunt was smiling as she fell into a graceful curtsy. 'Thank you for the kind invitation to Stevenage, Your Grace.'

The Duke tipped his head in answer. 'I take it that Mrs Dalrymple is your niece, Lady Ludlow?'

'She is, Your Grace. We are related through her father, who was my nephew two times removed.'

'A distant relation?'

'But a close connection.'

Turning, the old man continued. 'My son tells me you are a widow, Mrs Dalrymple?'

'I am, Your Grace. My husband died six years ago.'

'Then I am sorry for it. My own wife——' He stopped and caught his breath and did not continue further.

Ariana remained quiet as the Earl stepped into the silence with glasses of brandy and words.

'Lady Ludlow and Mrs Dalrymple champion the rights of women in need—vulnerable women who might otherwise be lost to proper Society altogether.'

'An endeavour to be admired…'

There was hesitation in the Duke's words, and Ariana thought there was also sadness. It seemed, by all accounts, that his wife, the Earl's mother, had been a vulnerable woman, so perhaps it was of her that he was thinking.

As the Duke asked her aunt a further question Ariana caught the Earl watching her.

'It is good to have you here.' His words were quietly said.

'Your family's house is very beautiful, inside and out, my lord.'

He smiled, but made no effort to answer, a man caught in a setting he must be well used to. It magnified all the differences that lay between them.

Why had he asked her here?

She almost voiced the thought, but stopped herself, reasoning that with her aunt and his father in the room he would hardly be verbose.

'I hope your trip down in the carriage was comfortable?' he asked.

'It was, thank you.'

They were words that meant nothing, empty fillers in the awkwardness between them, and Ariana was pleased when a maid knocked and entered the room with a tray of tea and biscuits.

With nothing else to do, she sat and watched the girl pour, seeing small plumes of steam disappearing into the air as she did so. The Earl of Norwich did not partake in the refreshments, though his father and her aunt did, and Ariana was grateful to have the cup and saucer in her hands, and the warmth of tea to finish what the glass of brandy had started.

She noticed that although father and son were in the same room they did not communicate at all. Rather they avoided any contact completely, with the presence of her aunt and herself in effect creating a buffer.

This was why the Earl had wanted them here.

That thought was followed quickly by another one.

She was a convenient guest—one with an aunt who could act readily and easily as chaperon.

The hopes she had journeyed down with today withered somewhat, her expectations suddenly seeming childish and silly.

Sipping at her tea, she wished she was anywhere but there.

Aunt Sarah addressed her then, and the quiet puzzlement in her eyes was concerning.

'The Duke has asked if he can show me his wife's paintings. Odette was most proficient as an artist and I asked after them.'

The Earl was quick to step in. 'Then I shall take the opportunity to show Mrs Dalrymple the garden behind the house. Is that something you might be interested to see?'

Ariana nodded, pleased that she would be able to get out of this room and away from her aunt's notice.

Within a few moments they were in the open air, the crisp blueness of the day making her turn her face to the sky and simply breathe.

'My mother was a woman who enjoyed beauty. This garden was her idea and it was she who directed the planting.'

The scene before her was one of winter, with brown vines pruned around canes and the soil plied with compost. But the bones of the garden were there for all to see, and Ariana could imagine the greening abundance come spring, the layers and the levels, the crawling lower plants and the taller shrubs behind them.

Like a canvas.

She suddenly had a better idea of this mother who was no longer here, and her vulnerability and her need disappeared into more interesting character traits. Odette Northwell had been stamped with the startling beauty of her Neilson roots, and also with an obvious ability to make a house even as grand as this one a true home.

'You loved your mother?' she asked.

'I did.'

'Was the garden damaged in the fire? It looks well established.'

'Not really. The main damage was to the front façade of Stevenage and to the stables.'

'The horses...?'

'Were saved.'

It was strange, talking about the event like this, distanced from the fact that all gossip pointed the finger at the Earl as the arsonist. She wanted him to tell her that the grim act of burning his family home almost to the ground had been someone else's, not his.

But he didn't.

He merely pushed back one sleeve and picked the dead head off a spiky flower.

As he did so Ariana saw a raised and shiny scar that widened across his wrist then moved up to his forearm and disappeared under the cloth of his jacket.

Burns.

She knew exactly the appearance of such because her mother had been afflicted with a similar scar, received from flaming fat, on the skin above her elbow. It had never faded into oblivion. A constant mark that could not be removed.

If he saw her notice he gave no sign of it as he snapped off a twig bedecked with bright red shiny berries. Holly.

He presented it to her with a smile. 'Some say holly protects the home from malevolent faeries—gives it shelter against evil intentions, if you like.'

'And you think Stevenage needs that?'

'I think it needs some Christmas decoration to ward off sadness, at least.'

'Did your mother mark the season?'

Ariana imagined a woman of an artistic bent must have enjoyed seeing the symbolism of Yule displayed inside the stately salons of the mansion before her.

'I think my father enjoyed it more,' he returned, and broke off more stems of shiny green and red.

She frowned, for it was getting closer to Christmas Day and she had not seen a single sign of that inside the house as they had walked through—which was surprising, given the Earl's presents to her.

He had quite a handful of greenery now, however, and when he noticed that she was looking at it he smiled. 'Celebration makes something out of nothing. A redemption, if you like, against all that has been taken away.'

'And rebuilt?'

'That too.'

'But the stories of the fire…' She could not quite continue.

'Stories are only that. Supposition. Conjecture. They swirl for a time, as fodder for gossip, and then they fade and other speculation fills in what was there before.'

'A hard truth for the one who takes the blame if it was not theirs in the first place.'

He laughed then, loud and long, and when he had finished he took her hand in his and raised it to his lips, bestowing a small warm kiss on the skin above.

'You have shouldered your own burdens by the sound of things, Aria, and yet you have not betrayed those you love. I have never heard your family history whispered of in anything but general tones. Not once.'

'It is shame that stops me from speaking, but I think in your case it is honour.'

He didn't answer her right away, but looked at the hills behind them, rising misty in the cold. Finally, he spoke. 'I was an only child, and I loved both my mother and my father, even with all their faults. They were brittle people, and set in their ways, whereas I could change easily and did.'

'Your voyage to America?'

He nodded. 'And the coming back.'

What was it he confessed? Ariana could not quite make sense of his reasoning and she frowned.

'It isn't long until Christmas Eve, Ariana, and without decoration Yule will pass unnoticed and unobserved at Stevenage. Will you come with me to the woods to find suitable branches to bring into the house?'

'I thought you said this should not happen until the night before Christmas? Something to do with luck?'

'Sometimes you have to make your own good fortune and to hell with superstition.'

His smile was beguiling and his eyes were filled with the sort of humour that she had never been a party to. Not as a child, nor as a young bride. Not as a widow in Society either, with a reputation that slashed at any hope of a normal life.

His hand came out, its long fingers asking her to join him, and when a redwing swooped down from a branch above them she took it as a sign. A travelling bird, here for the moment. Like her.

Reaching out, she felt his warmth come around her gloveless hand. 'How will we cut them?'

'With force. I'll hang on the end of some of the lower branches and they will give way.'

He was leading her off to a small copse a hundred yards away from the house. The snow was deeper here, but the wind was held off by the bulk of the trees. It was a silent, beautiful place, smelling of pine.

'This one is good.'

Letting go of her hand, he swung on the branch. As it cracked he smiled, and then the whole thing fell.

The next branch was more difficult and he asked for her help, signalling her to move to one side of him and then counting. When he reached three she pulled with all her might and the fir branch snapped suddenly, sending them both tumbling on top of each other down into the snow.

Just them, in the greenery, with the rubbery fir underneath them and the pine sap strong and fresh.

He didn't wait but drew her close, beneath him. The world darkened with his shadow until his lips came down across her own, asking for things she had no notion of, wanting, desperate and warm.

She let his ardour comfort her, felt the slick pressure of his tongue inside her mouth as her head went back. Opening. To him. Writhing under a promise that she had never understood until now. Wanting to be closer, wishing for the things she had only ever imagined in the dark shadows of her bed.

He moved so that he was at a different angle now, no longer gentle, and his aching need was exemplified in the way his hands grasped her hair and bundled it into a knot. Then he was at her neck, demanding, his hands moving lower, his thumb tweaking across one nipple.

No longer tender. Passion ruled him. And the hot need of it dragged her in as he whispered things that she could make no sense of.

His mouth was wide across her own, demanding more and more and more. And she gave it wordlessly, undeniably, moving her own fingers against his nape and in his hair, feeling the darkness of it tangled in her fingers.

'I want you, Aria.'

His words were hot breath against her cheeks, no guessing in them. She could feel the hardness of his body along her own, virile, young and impatient. An ardent suitor, an experienced lover, a man who was not afraid, nor bound by manners, expectation or even propriety.

He would take her here in the snow if she allowed it. Already she could feel her nipple under the fabric of her dress, rising where he touched her, and she parted her legs as if to welcome him in.

He did not offer love or lies. He only offered himself. Fully and without constraint.

When she breathed out she heard the shake of surrender in it.

But so did he.

He cursed even as she watched him, his eyes refocussing and flattening.

Hell. He was like a beast. He would have had her here in the snow, a hundred yards from Stevenage, in full daylight, with the winter against her skin already causing redness, the ache of cold all around them.

He took in breath and held it, claiming calm, finding sense. The Christmas fir pricked at them and her hair fell in long wet strands.

Even to consider it. A woman who had told him her history of an unwanted husband and two nothing lovers. What was he thinking? Was he going to rip up her skirts and enter her, spilling his seed into the wet warmth of her centre and then…?

She deserved more. Much more. She deserved the delight of the season and the care of his ardour. And yet even now he was hard pressed to rise and end it.

His hand cupped her chin and he raised one finger along the line of her cheek. 'You are the most beautiful woman I have ever laid eyes upon, Ariana Dalrymple, and I promise you right here and now that you will know the truth of what I say soon.'

'The…the truth?'

'I want you. I want every piece of you. Your soul, your heart and your body. I want to see you in the moonlight, unclothed and ready, arching up for my touch, melting under my caress. I want to enter you and know that you want me too. Until the very end. Until we are so far into each other

that there is no beginning. Melded. Spent. Only one heart-
beat of infinity.'

He saw how she shivered at his words, at the promises
and the stated intention.

'I would always keep you safe, sweetheart.'

He added the endearment because he could see she
needed it—and because he needed it, too.

'I haven't been...' Her words were whispered.

'I know.'

With care, he stood and helped her up and the world came
back. Stevenage, the day, the fallen branches, people waiting. Like a drawing done in ink and clambering into colour
right before his eyes.

Ariana was straightening her hair, pulling at it with cold
fingers, fastening it back with the pins that had loosened.

He lifted the branches onto his shoulders. He wanted to
say more but the moment was gone. Reality was settling
back, his father and her aunt were waiting, and a servant
was hurrying towards them with an offer of help to carry
the fir boughs.

There was no quiet time here—no way of taking her off
into oblivion.

He tried to smile, and she did too, but all he could think
about was the looming night-time and the possibility
of more.

# Chapter Six

The Christmas boughs were set along the mantel and the fragrant candles placed in the spaces between the branches were lit. There were oranges there too, and small red paper flowers that had been brought in by a maid. It looked festive, and unusual, and Ariana felt her happiness at the sight bubble up.

A proper Christmas. A family Yule.

Her parents had never bothered with the tradition, and Henry Dalrymple had scorned her for even mentioning the thought.

But Christopher Northwell's enthusiasm was catching and touching. People who loved Christmas loved life, she decided, for they had not given up on joy, had not settled into the nothingness of disappointment.

She admired his resilience, and his tenacity, and elected to make more of an effort with her own. Their tryst in the snow was still warming her blood and sending shards of delight through her, adding to the heat that was rising in her with each passing moment.

He wanted her. He had said as much. And she wanted him back with a longing that was surprising.

She wished she had met him six years ago, when first she had returned to London—before the two ill-chosen and disastrous lovers, before her reputation had suffered as a consequence.

But perhaps there was such a thing as a second chance, and Christmas with all its promise and exaltation seemed particularly suitable.

Looking at the decorated green boughs, she smiled. And

Christopher Northwell caught her eyes, his brows raised in question.

'Merry Christmas, Ariana, and may the joy of the season stay with you all year long.'

'Perhaps you are persuading me to think more of the tradition than I used to.'

'Then I am glad for it. In America I once stayed with a family who celebrated Christmas by draping the walls of their cabin with evergreen garlands. The decorations were all natural. Little pine cones, nuts and bright bittersweet berries that took the place of holly. They also had many activities, such as kissing under the mistletoe, storytelling and charades. Dinner would be of the best quality possible, including mincemeat pie and plum pudding made with fruits that grew close by in the forest.'

Ariana could imagine it—a far-off Christmas in the woods of a new land, full of all the games, decorations, food and fun that she had never known. She wished all of a sudden that there might be mistletoe hung above them here—a way of getting closer again, sharing laughter.

She was so tired of trying to survive on her own, picking at the small bits of the life she had been left with, keeping her head down, trying to be brave.

Christopher Northwell was showing her a life that could be lived if she took a chance and simply reached for it—left the past behind and moved forward without looking back.

As her aunt and the Duke returned from their viewing Ariana knew that there were as many undercurrents in the Northwell family as there had ever been in her own: a very public scandal with the burning of Stevenage, and the more private battle of suicide disguised as an accident.

The Duke looked as though he had barely weathered these things. He looked as broken as she was, and Ariana felt a kinship with him.

'You have only been in London for six years or so, I hear, Mrs Dalrymple? Do you enjoy the city?'

North's father asked this as he reached for a glass of brandy. Ariana noticed that his hand shook quite badly.

'I always thought I did, but coming here to the country and seeing the beauty and the peace...' She stopped, suddenly unsure as to what she intended with her answer.

'My wife loved it here, too...'

There was a hesitation after that, a quick glance towards his son and a decided withdrawal. The Duke had not directly addressed his son once in all the time she had been in his company, but now Christopher Northwell tempered his father's words with his own.

'Loved it enough to die for it.'

Unexpected words. Jagged and furious.

The brandy spilt as the Duke slammed it down on the small table beside him. 'Loved it enough to understand that it needed an heir, too.'

With a short click of his heels the Earl departed the room.

'This family obviously has its troubles.' Her aunt said this to Ariana as they readied themselves for dinner. 'Odette Northwell made painting after painting of the fire in her studio, until there were too many to count, stacked as they were one on top of another. Her son's face stares out of the flames in nearly every one of them, contorted and disbelieving.'

'What are you saying, Aunt Sarah?'

'I think she had gone mad. I think when she finally threw herself off the top of the Stevenage ramparts a few months after returning here she welcomed death because she had lost her son. And I think the Duke blames the Earl for her madness and her dislocation. They don't speak, Ariana, have you noticed that?'

'Or when they do it's with anger. It is why the Earl invited us, I imagine. He wants to try to mend bridges.'

'Well, it's not working. If anything, having us here seems to have aggravated things further. The Duke told me Odette wrote to her son every week when he was in America, and yet she never received one answer.'

A new mystery. The Earl had not struck her as a harsh man, or a resentful one. Why would he not reply to the mother whom he said he had loved? Why would he arrive home only after her death?

'Were there other paintings that held a different subject matter?'

'A few. One of a dog, and another of a cottage in sight of Stevenage, with its silhouette looming in one corner. They were both propped on easels, which is why they were so prominent. The Duke asked me if I thought they would fetch a good price in London. It made me wonder about the fact that although he has considerable assets he may need ready cash.'

'His son is said to have come home with more than a fortune…'

'Perhaps he does not wish to share it?'

'Christopher Northwell was adamant that he wanted to make peace with his father.'

'But he has not. Every word that passes between them is toned in fury. If there is no significant improvement on the morrow then I think we should leave, Ariana.'

'Leave?'

The word went round and round in her head. Leave the hope of another kiss? Leave the Earl in the heartbreak of his discordant family? Leave him to weather the storm without anchor, without anyone on his side?

Because she was, she realised suddenly, on his side— cheering him on, willing him to find at Stevenage some sort of a home that would not send him rushing back to the Americas.

'You look pale, my dear. I hope you are not coming down with a cough.'

Turning at the words, Ariana caught herself in the mirror and barely knew the woman who stood in its reflection. Her eyes glittered and her lips looked swollen. She had chosen a gown tonight that covered almost all her skin, for hidden in the high folds of her collar were the marks of ardour…quiet, unseen things reddening with each passing hour.

This was a new, less broken version of her old self. And she smiled because in the transformation she felt only strength.

Dinner that evening was as difficult as the afternoon had been, with both men circling as though they wanted to rip the other's head off.

Her aunt, in her own inimitable way, carried a great deal of the conversation and Ariana was glad of it—because she herself could never have managed it with such aplomb. Her heart ached for father and son, and the green boughs on the mantel, alight with candles, seemed to mock the cold uncertainty in the room and its lack of joy.

Finally she took her chance to speak quietly with Christopher Northwell as her aunt and the Duke talked of people known to them once in Society many years before.

'For a man who is advocating a truce, you are making a poor show of it.'

He didn't answer.

'It's Christmas, after all. A time of family and good will.'

This time he looked at her directly. 'I thought you did not believe in the season?'

'With candles and baubles threaded through pungent green fir only a few feet away from the table it is hard not to.'

'An unwilling convert?'

'I just want you to be happy.'

There—she had said it. Blurted it out with no finesse and little thought.

'Why?'

'Because I like you.'

He straightened and put down his fork. 'Do you like me

enough to want to kiss me again?' The beginnings of a smile pulled at his lips.

'Yes.'

'Enough to join me in the library for a drink when the others go to their beds?'

She nodded, her heart beating so hard she thought he must see it in her chest under the thin velvet of her gown.

Her aunt seldom stayed up late, and she imagined the Duke would take to his bed early as well—though a sudden sound had her looking round to see that the older man was bent over and choking.

Her aunt was on her feet, but the Earl was quicker, wrapping his arms around his father's chest and squeezing with force.

Nothing happened. The Duke's face was set in surprise and fear, his mouth opening without sound as he pulled at his collar.

North tried again, this time making it a double movement so that the first squeeze came directly after the second. A piece of roast beef shot out from the Duke's mouth and he began to breathe again—hoarse, desperate tugs of air at first, relaxing into more normal ones.

Tears ran down his cheeks, and as his hand slipped into his son's the similarity between them was apparent. 'Th-thank you, Christopher. If you had not been here...'

He couldn't continue, the shock of his narrow escape making him shake.

'You are all right now—although you might have a few bruises from my ministrations come the morning.'

'I can live with those.'

The Duke had brushed the tears away and looked more himself. The distance was back, the isolation returned, though there was something in the air that was different. A sense of resolution, Ariana thought, on the part of the Duke. But she had no idea as to what that might mean.

He excused himself then, and a servant came forward

to shepherd him off. The Earl stood there watching, with a look on her face that broke her heart.

'It is lucky you knew a method to make certain he could breathe again,' she said.

'He's a tough old thing. It would take more than a piece of beef to kill him.'

'Though perhaps your mother's death broke his heart?'

'It was broken long before that, Ariana.'

Picking up his drink, he finished it in one swallow—just as her aunt stated her intention of going up to her room and resting.

'All this excitement has exhausted me.' Aunt Sarah's voice sounded small.

Then there was just the two of them, and the servants fussing around, cleaning up the shattered glass that had fallen from the table and putting away the food and plates.

When both her aunt and his father were gone North held out his hand and turned to her. 'Come—the library will be warmer and it is a much nicer room.'

She took his fingers and wondered at the coldness in them.

The library was a beautiful space, small and well furnished, and the leather chairs near the blazing fire were welcoming. All over the walls were pictures of sunny landscapes and gardens, and an earlier version of Stevenage Manor, with no flames in sight.

'Your mother did these?'

'She did.'

'What was she like?'

'Fragile. Uncertain. Loving. Needy.'

'Everyone is a mix.'

'Are you?'

The question was a serious one, so Ariana took some time to answer.

'I think I am a hidden person and have been for a long while.'

'Secrets do that to one, I suppose. Veiling what has happened for fear of what might occur next is too important.'

'Like the glass star you gave me…full of prisms that show parts of it from different angles but never the whole.'

'There's protection in that, I suppose. No one is ever all good.'

'But neither are they all bad.'

His smile reassured her.

'I like talking to you, Ariana. I like being with you. More than any other person I have known.'

'Thank you.'

He smiled again. 'Come with me to America. Come and see a different land.'

She shook her head. 'I don't know what you are asking…'

'Do you not?'

He leaned across and took both her hands in his. He was about to speak when a servant came rushing in to find him.

'It's the Duke, my lord. He has insisted on sitting up on the roof and I cannot get him to come in again.'

North was on his feet immediately, and she followed, up one flight of stairs and down a corridor. The window of the Duke's bedchamber was wide open. Small drifts of snowflakes were coming in to the room, and two manservants hovered by the lintel.

'If you will wait outside, Mrs Dalrymple and I will deal with this.'

The servants did as he asked and then it was only them and the old Duke, perched a few feet away on the roof, his feet bolstered by the raised stones that ringed the lower end of the guttering.

In one easy movement the Earl vaulted the window ledge and joined his father, sitting next to him but not touching him at all.

North wanted to grab him and hold on tight. He wanted to cradle him and rock him and make him understand that his mother had never meant any of it. But he wasn't sure if his words would incense his father or calm him.

'I won't jump, Christopher. I just want to sit here for a while and remember.'

'Remember Mama?'

'Remember our family a long time ago, when things were good.'

'She was sick, Papa. She didn't understand what she was doing. She loved Stevenage, I think, but her demons were stronger.'

His father laid his head in his hands and breathed out. 'And I let her get away with it. I let her ruin you.'

'It was not your choice.'

'Wasn't it? You were crucified for our secrets. You bore the brunt of your mother's madness with the scars on your arms and your isolation...'

He didn't seem to be able to carry on.

'I've survived—prospered, even. America is good for me and to me. Without it I'd have been like Andrew Shawler, directionless and lost. The burning of Stevenage did not break me, Papa, and what happened next was my choice.'

'No.' His father's fisted hand slammed down. 'It was my shame. The shame of wanting your mother to survive above all else. And that was wrong because I failed you.'

'You protected her, just as I did. We both did that because we could do nothing else and she needed help. It's Christmas, Father, the season of goodwill and new beginnings. Let's make one now—tonight, this Christmas. I think Mama would be pleased in her place above if we should agree to bury bad feelings and concentrate on what is left between us, now and in the future.'

He watched his father nod.

'She would have been pleased to meet Mrs Dalrymple, too, Christopher, I am sure of it. She is the only woman I have ever seen you truly happy with. And she is strong. Like you are. Together you will be invincible.'

North felt his words as a warmth. 'Come inside now, Papa. It's cold out here.'

He put his hand out and his father grasped his fingers tightly, almost as if he might never let go.

Ariana was waiting at the window, her eyes worried.

'It's fine. Father just wanted to remember my mother at Christmas.' He said this as they climbed back inside.

'I understand,' she returned, and her smile lit up the room around them, making him wonder just how much of the conversation on the roof she might have heard.

But it didn't matter. Soon there would be no secrets whatsoever between them.

In the library again, after seeing his father into the hands of his servants, North looked tentative—a man who was thinking of words to say and searching for the right ones.

Ariana had not been able to hear much of his conversation with his father from her place in the room, but had heard the mention of his mother more than a few times. She sat and waited, her fingers clenched.

'I am not quite as people imagine me, Aria. The rumours—' He stopped, as though taking stock. 'My mother was different. I am sure you must have heard. Everybody said so.'

He waited until she agreed.

'The thing is she was also...mad is the wrong word, I think. Perhaps delusional is a better one.'

'Delusional about what?'

'About things that were trying to get into Stevenage Manor to hurt us. Hurt Papa and me. She thought there were demons and she wanted to stop them. By fire. She thought it was the only way.'

Everything suddenly dropped into place.

'It was her and not you.'

His eyes looked desperate, and the pulse in his throat was thumping.

'You took the blame for your mother?'

'I did. Because she could not have weathered it and nei-ther could my father.'

'You tried to put the fire out?'

'I got the horses out of the stables, but after that... Fire has a sound to it, and a smell, and when the flames reached higher than the rooftops I knew I was defeated.'

She imagined him there, beating back flame as well as fury and horror and sadness. She imagined him afterwards too, crucified and alone, burnt and banished, the son of bro-ken people in a circumstance that was unthinkable.

'I love you, North.'

The words came simply, quiet and true, one after the other, bare and honest, with no hidden meaning and noth-ing held back.

'I am not a saint.'

'You have told me that before, and I say again that I do not require you to be one.'

'But I am a man who will love you in the way that you deserve, with care and passion and devotion. For ever.'

She began to cry, because it was all she had ever wanted. *He* was all she had ever wanted.

'Will you marry me, Ariana, as soon as we are able?' He lifted the gold ring off his middle finger and held it out to her as a token of all he promised. The diamond in the gold winked in the light. 'I don't want a big wedding but I want a quick one, here at Stevenage, as soon as I can acquire a special licence.'

'Yes!' Throwing her arms around his neck, she felt her-self being lifted and held close. 'I've loved you from the first moment of meeting you, North.'

He breathed out—as if he had been holding everything in for far too long, as if Odette had finally been freed from the place inside him. Trust and love was a formidable thing...a force that could not be chipped away by doubt.

Then his lips came down across her own, and the same

joy and elation that she'd known every time he had kissed her returned. But this time there was also the knowledge of love, and it was a powerful force.

He shoved the lock into place as he passed the door. One of his legs disengaged the pile of cushions on the large leather sofa, and his fingers were at the small pearl buttons along her back, causing the gold wool of her gown to fold back. Next he slipped off the sleeves of her silk petticoat and untied her corset with skill. Her breasts came loose and into his hands, waiting there to receive them, their full flesh goose-bumped with nerves.

Would he like what he was seeing? She was twenty-five, after all, and no longer young…

'You are so beautiful…more beautiful than any woman I have ever seen or dreamed about.'

His voice was hoarse, emotion threaded through the words, and then his mouth came down upon one nipple, softly at first, and then with more ardour. Passion rolled through her and she felt the years of sadness washed away by love.

'I love you so much, North, that it hurts.'

She clenched at his hair, saw the darkness of it contrasted against the white of her skin. His fingers were kneading her other breast, so that sensation made her stiffen, searching for more, wanting what she could feel coming, rushing towards her.

Then it was there, breaking over her in hot waves of airlessness, a feeling rising from within and covering her as she stretched out for it, willing it to last.

His hand was before her, one finger brushing the tears from her eyes, another tracing the line of her cheek. Telling her without speaking that she was cherished and that he would always keep her safe.

She felt as if she was floating into him…as if reality had been suspended and the whole world lived just in them and just in here.

'I want more.'

He laughed.

'I want you to show me how you do this…how you make me feel beautiful.'

The air around them became quieter, all humour fleeing. 'I might not be able to stop, Ariana, if—'

She raised a finger to his lips. 'I don't want you to.'

'You are sure?'

'More sure than of anything else in my life.'

His fingers loosened more of the buttons down her back and she felt the fabric pool around her feet. Left in her corset, stockings, garters and shift, she watched him. What would come next.

Unexpectedly he swore, a ripe and heartfelt curse, and her hands crossed her chest in self-protection.

But he shook his head. 'Even Aphrodite would not hold a candle to you, my love, and she was said to be matchless.'

His fingers came to her waist and he pushed all the clothes away, leaving her bare and vulnerable.

'No, the goddess of pleasure and passion would pale against your beauty, the sheen of your skin, the curve of your breasts, the softness here and here…'

He stroked her stomach, and then her thighs, before finding the warmth between her legs. All the time watching to see if she might refuse him. He hoped she could not feel how his heart beat in his chest, could not see how he was struck by desire and also thankfulness. But she did not waver. Rather her legs opened and allowed him in, her eyes closing and her head falling back.

Trust.

She gave it without words, but it was there.

He wished he could lay her down in a bed of rose petals as dewy as her skin, but already his manhood was hard. Undoing the buttons on his fall front, he allowed it space.

The Aubusson carpet underfoot would have to do, and the fire would warm her.

Outside, December rain hit at the windows—an oncoming storm making itself felt.

Just them. He had never before lived in the moment like this, but the past and the future were lost in the now as he lifted her against him, her clothes left behind, only beribboned garters and sheer stockings left.

He felt indomitable in a way he never had before, with the truth of who he had been, all his secrets uncovered into light. Well, not all of them, he thought quietly. His scars from the fire lay hidden still beneath the linen of his shirt.

Laying her down, he followed, pulling her to him so that their bodies touched, the heat of her propelling him on as he sought her centre. Poised on the edge of softness, he waited, tipping her face to his own and letting her understand his need.

'I love you.'

He said it as a promise, whispered so that she could hear the echo of feeling in his blood and his bones. Then he was within her tightness, seeking entry, slick and hot. Deep and deeper. His hands under her hips tilted her, so that still he penetrated, fully embedded now, inseparable.

'North...?'

She breathed the question and his lips came down, taking the word inside him, his answer silent.

He moved. There was no latitude or freedom from such a surge. He wanted Ariana Dalrymple fully as his—wanted to feel her sex cling around his own, asking for more, needing relief as much as he did.

Her fingernails dug into his back beneath the shirt, small pinpricks of pain that drove him on, his breath ragged with need.

'Come with me, sweetheart, to the very edge of life.'

He felt her release even as his own started.

\* \* \*

She was lost in sensation, floating in a world she had never known, taken by North to a place that was wondrous and astounding. All the pieces inside her were letting go of each other, until there was only a thread remaining in a tide of heat and promise and feeling.

Even breathing was difficult as her body stiffened, the far-off response coming closer and taking over her entire body, waves of it streaking inside her like magic. He held her still as she collapsed down on to the carpet, soft beneath her, and she held his hand across her stomach, finding the echoes and pressing.

The resonance continued, and when she opened her eyes she found his upon her, watching and knowing. There were no words for what had just happened, what was still happening, the wetness between them and the heat. She could only stare and find in the depths of his gaze a pledge that was for ever.

It was astonishing and shocking. For so many years she had thought lying with a man meant hurt and shame and suffering. Yet here, now, it was beautiful and fine.

She felt tears pool in her eyes.

'Are you hurt, Aria?'

His words were given in concern.

She shook her head. 'No, I am healed—and that is something I never thought I could be.'

'By love?'

She reached her arms around his neck and drew him in, glad to feel his lips against her face and then on her mouth.

This kiss was different again—softer, more gentle, with a cherishing carefulness that was so very wanted.

He hardened inside her and she smiled, the very thought of it all happening again bringing a pleasure that was wondrous. 'Love me, North.'

'I do.'

* * *

She woke to birdsong in a room she had not seen before—
a large chamber with a substantial fire burning and shelves
of books on each wall. The bed was enormous, with four or-
nately carved wooden posts around it and dark green velvet
drapes caught back by tassels of braided gold.

North lay beside her, still in his unbuttoned white linen
shirt, though his trousers had long gone. He was asleep, his
face gentler in slumber than it was when awake.

As if aware of her regard, he opened his eyes.

'Good morning.' His voice was rough with sleep and
there was a dancing lightness in his gaze. 'Did you rest
well, my love?'

She felt the blood rise quietly in her cheeks. 'You know
that I did not.'

'You were wonderful, Ariana. Wonderful and uninhib-
ited.'

His hand dived beneath the crisp sheets and the covering
of a feather quilt and she felt it trail across her stomach, then
lower. With care, she opened to him, and he came again to
the secret place that was waiting. She felt him push in further, stretching her, one finger and then another, the swollen flesh gathering around him.

'I want you.'

She smiled, and closed her hand around his sex as she
guided him home.

Much later she awoke again to hear rain. Heavy rain that
darkened the morning light. The clock in the corner showed
it to be the hour of eight. Still early enough to escape detection. Still early enough for a little more time.

His shirt was gone now, pulled off in the heat of their passion, and the scars on his arms were easily seen even in the
gloom. Fire had ravaged him, leaving the skin rippled and
misshapen, and his absolute beauty everywhere else made
it even more shocking.

Knowing he was awake, she reached out to touch, feeling the pain he must have known with a jolt and understanding his bravery.

'The fire spread to the stables,' he said as she traced one long indentation. 'I saved the horses.'

'Who tended you…after…?' She could barely speak.

'Alistair Botham. He took me to Wales, to his seat there, and nursed me better. When I could walk, I left for America.'

'You did not see your mother again?'

She knew he had when shards of pain crossed into his eyes.

'My parents came to the Harding seat. They came to make sure my mother's name remained…untainted. She could not have borne the slurs otherwise, or the threat of being sent to a place that might contain her madness. I agreed. My father took me aside and made sure that I realised she would not be long for this world. He told me that afterwards I could come home again.'

'Still a betrayal?'

'I don't think he saw it like that, then. I think he viewed it as a duty.'

'But not his?'

'My mother wouldn't have survived a day without him.'

'So they sacrificed you instead?'

'My mother left me a note before she threw herself off the roof. I found it here in my room, tucked into my writing desk, when I returned. She wrote it in one of her moments of lucidity and told me that she was sorry but she could no longer live at Stevenage, with all its memories. She also said that love was not always an easy thing and she thanked me.'

Ariana's hand rested on North's and she pressed down. 'Yet sometimes it can be an easy thing, can't it? It is here, with us.'

'Strength banishes the difficult, I think. That is what I loved about you when we first met, Ariana?'

'In that doorway on Regent Street?'

'You didn't apologise for who you were perceived to be, and it was so very liberating to be with a woman who was unrepentant even in the face of gossip.'

'Imagine what they might say of us now—here in your bed, dishevelled after a whole night of lovemaking.'

'I think every man I have ever known would be jealous of me—but I also think we should be married quickly to avert more rumour.'

'When?'

'As soon as I can procure a licence.'

She began to laugh. 'You don't do things slowly, my lord, or in halves.'

'Indeed, I don't, my beauteous will-be wife,' he said, and his mouth came over hers to seal the bargain.

# *Epilogue*

*Stevenage Manor, Christmas 1815*

Ariana walked around the room, putting the final touches to the candles, ribbons and glittery red paper amongst the green of pungent fir. She'd had a tree brought in from the woods and decorated that, too, with small china ornaments of various shapes and sizes that trailed from its boughs. Mistletoe hung above the door as well, the white waxy berries alluding to all that might happen beneath.

In the corner, away from the cold of the windows, sat a small cradle, its occupant fast asleep and warm. She checked him every few moments, just to gaze in on his face and make sure that he was breathing.

Such a thought made her smile. Their precious bundle of a small son was unusually quiet. More often he was crying to be fed and held and loved, and North and she were more than willing to comply.

Footsteps outside had her turning. Her husband stood there, a bouquet of holly in his hand.

'Christmas has come to Stevenage Manor early this year,' he said, looking around.

'You have made me believe in the season again, my darling, so how can I fail to render the house joyous? Besides, we have a son to tutor in the art of Yuletide celebration, and there is nothing better than starting him young.'

He laughed, placing the holly on the table as he wrapped her in his arms.

She could feel the cold of outside on his clothes and his skin and she shivered. 'Where have you been?'

'In the stables, helping with the birth of a new foal.'

'That's very late.'

'Or extremely early. I thought we might train him for Alexander to use.'

'He's only three months old, North.' Her hands covered his, giving him some heat. 'I think we can wait a while.'

'But he's bonny and strong. Like his mother.' Tugging her over to the cradle, he gazed down at their tiny dark-haired child. 'I still can't believe we have him...that he is our flesh and blood.'

She watched him tidy the sheet and make certain the woollen blanket was well across him. A protective father. A good man.

'The Duke has spent the morning in here, telling me stories of your childhood. He is most insistent that Alex looks just like you did at that age.'

'Papa is happier, isn't he? I think having us here suits him—and you are the crowning jewel of his family, Aria. You know he loves you like a true daughter—especially since you refused to leave Stevenage.'

'Well, returning to America didn't seem like an option any more, with Alexander coming.'

'And the house reaches out somehow to claim you, too, doesn't it? Reeling you in with its history and its solidness? Is your aunt coming to stay for Christmas?'

'She is. And your father was pleased to hear it, for he enjoys her company.'

'Alistair Botham is arriving with all his family as well. Seems he is feeling lonely over there in Wales. And Seth Douglas has asked me if they can join us, too, if there is room.'

'A long table of good friends and family,' she replied. 'What could be better than that?'

'A night alone with you,' he returned without pause, and kissed her soundly. 'You are curvier now than you were on the night we first made love, Ariana, and I like it.'

'The night Alexander was conceived...'

'And I pray to God we will have other children as easily. Lots of them, I hope. But a girl next time, with your eyes and smile, would be agreeable.'

A cry from the cradle had them both bending, and she lifted her son in her arms and rocked him quietly.

'Your papa is just instructing me on your brothers and sisters, sweetheart. How do you feel about that?'

When he closed his eyes again and fell back into slumber they both laughed.

'We have some time now, if you are willing?' North whispered.

'When am I not?' she whispered back.

'Ariana, I love you more than I have ever loved anyone before—a thousand times more. If I had not jumped into that doorway on Regent Street—'

She interrupted him. 'We would have found each other anyway. I swear it. We were meant to be together, and all that had come before for both of us was only leading up to this.'

She put Alexander down and tucked him in. She would ask the nanny to come and sit with him while she took North upstairs, but first...

Leading her husband over to the lintel of the door, she bade him look up.

'Mistletoe?' The smile on his face was knowing.

'You told me it is a custom that began in Greece in marriage ceremonies, because of its association with fertility, and I know the Georgians continued it in the games they enjoyed at Christmas.'

'You are an expert now? A reformed lover of the season? A woman with an abundance of Christmas knowledge?'

'Only because of you, my North,' she answered, and leaned in to kiss him.

\* \* \* \* \*

# INVITATION TO THE DUKE'S BALL

Virginia Heath

For Grandpa Reg, who loved Christmas and always put his tree up in October.

Dear Reader,

For me, Christmas is all about the giving. Sure, it's nice to receive gifts, but nothing tops the heady feeling that comes from witnessing the sheer delight on a loved one's face as they unwrap something that touches them. It is never about the money—it's always about the thought. Because it is the thought that always makes things extra special.

I spend months contemplating, planning and sourcing things to make sure I get it just right and, if I say so myself, my track record for inducing awe and wonder among my nearest and dearest is pretty spectacular. But I have to say it isn't one-sided. My husband and kids are all about the thought, too, so I get to unwrap some fabulous gifts myself on Christmas morning. The best gift of all, though, is always the unguarded and heartfelt reactions of my family. I hope you have a merry and thoughtful Christmas, too.

*Virginia Heath* xx

# Chapter One

*December 1818*

Eliza Harkstead was, without a shadow of a doubt, the blandest person in the room.

In a sea of jewel-coloured silks and sumptuous warm velvets she was an insipid, uninspiring and monotonous festival of brown. From the unruly and nondescript dark curls pinned ruthlessly to the top of her head to the tips of her practical tan boots she was as drab as a dust sheet in a gloomy old attic. And, visually at least, as dull as dishwater that had been used to wash a sink full of chocolate pots.

Instantly forgettable and practically invisible.

So brown, in fact, that she blended perfectly with the panelling.

To test that theory, Eliza was sorely tempted to splay herself against the Duke of Manningtree's ancient woodwork in the forlorn hope that she might miraculously disappear from his depressingly cheerful Yuletide festivities completely before they had really started.

Two hours in and already she knew it was doomed to be a depressingly long three days. At this punishingly slow rate it would feel more like three weeks by the time the wretched masquerade ball crawled around on the day before Christmas Eve.

Eliza loathed balls at the best of times—largely because she was always on such a tight budget that she felt miserably underdressed. But at a masquerade, where everyone went ridiculously over the top, even in her very best coral frock she was doomed to be uninspiringly underwhelming. Although at least it wasn't brown.

She stared down at her mud-coloured skirt and sighed. Her own stupid fault, she supposed. When she had been told this was an informal 'getting to know you' afternoon tea, which would be followed by an invigorating tour of the grounds, she had believed it. But, while she was sensibly dressed for the anticipated walk, everyone else had obviously come here to shine.

Dukes did that to people.

All the gentlemen wanted to become his friend and all the ladies—all the many, many, *many* hordes of single ladies, gathered here in their droves—wanted to become his wife. Her silly cousin Honoria included.

And while they waited for the Duke to return from his 'urgent business elsewhere', those same ladies swarmed around his tall, dark and handsome brother. She had met the dashing and effervescent Lord Julius Symington before—not that he would remember her, of course. He was quite the catch in his own right, with his own estate and fortune bequeathed to him by his eminent father, so if the ladies failed to snare themselves the Duke on this visit at least they still had the spare.

The poor man would have to beat them off with a stick if they became any more boisterous. Already those eager girls were practically climbing over one another to inch a little closer to his person.

All rather pathetic, in Eliza's humble opinion, but mind-numbingly predictable. For surely every single female of good breeding wanted a husband of even better breeding in order to feel complete. That she didn't made her the exception, she knew.

'Do you think he will be more handsome than his brother?' Honoria was not only openly staring at the viscount, she was doing so longingly. Fluttering her eyelashes and simpering over her fan for all she was worth. 'Because it is hard to imagine anyone being more handsome than Lord Julius.'

Her poor cousin had only been out a year, and at just eighteen, in Eliza's unsought opinion, was much too young to be making doe eyes at a man a decade older. She was still a child—albeit one encased in a petite but fully developed woman's body—and was still to develop an ounce of common sense.

'Stop gaping, Honoria. It's undignified.'

'I want him to be aware of my partiality...just in case the Duke decides to cast his net elsewhere.'

'Men don't want to be handed a woman's affection on a plate. They prefer the thrill of the chase. Look at Lord Julius's face.' Currently surrounded by seven equally simpering and fluttering young ladies, he appeared ready to bolt at any moment. 'He is not enjoying any of this attention.'

'Do you think I should go over there too?'

It was like talking to a brick wall.

'Absolutely not! Stay here. Stop staring at him like a starving dog at a butcher's window and try to be a bit mysterious.' If she was any more obvious, poor Honoria might as well be carrying a placard. 'Better still, turn your back to him and focus your attention on this magnificent art collection. It's lauded as being one of the best in England.'

She steered her immature cousin in the direction of the fireplace, where a very stern-faced ancestor of the Duke posed resplendent in Tudor garb, captured for posterity in vibrant oils.

'Look—that's a Holbein.'

'I always thought Holbein was a place in town. I am sure Mama has taken me shopping there a time or two.'

Eliza almost groaned aloud. 'That is Holborn, dearest. This is a *Holbein*... E. I. N. He was a sixteenth-century painter who—'

'Honoria!' The dulcet tones of Aunt Penelope came out of nowhere. 'What are you doing over here when Lord Julius is over there?' She grabbed her daughter's arm and pierced Eliza with irritated glare. 'Shouldn't you be attending to Lady Trumble?'

Eliza bit her lip at the insulting jibe. 'Great-Aunt Violet is having a whale of a time with her friends.'

Aunt Penelope might want to deny that Eliza was actually part of the family as well as her great-aunt's companion at all costs, but if it didn't bother Great-Aunt Violet, and it certainly didn't bother Eliza, she was not going to deny being a blood relation purely so the social climbing Penelope could save face.

'As you can plainly see, she doesn't currently require my assistance in any way.'

Not that she ever did in reality. Great-Aunt Violet was as sharp as a chisel and as wily as a fox. She needed a companion about as much as Honoria needed to simper over Lord Julius.

'Then at least go and sit over there.' Penelope gestured to the empty line of chairs at the very back of the room. 'Out of the way. You are not an invited guest, Eliza.'

Something her aunt had been at great pains to remind her all the way here.

'You are here in a servant's capacity. And, as such, you really shouldn't be socialising.' She cast a critical eye over Eliza's brown walking dress and rolled her eyes. 'Especially not in a frock as dull and plain as that one.'

With her daughter clamped to her side, Aunt Penelope marched off in the direction of the Symington spare, sliced a path amongst her silly daughter's rivals and practically thrust the child at him while they both simpered for all they were worth.

It was painful to watch.

Then, to make Eliza's living hell complete, another group of young ladies, thus far excluded from the space to simper, set up shop before her and began an overly boisterous game of charades in the vain hope that they might draw the gentleman's eye. Each considered and narcissistic mime was accompanied by much squealing and artful breathy laughter which grated on each and every one of Eliza's sensible nerves.

It all begged the question—if they were this desperate to court Lord Julius, what nonsense would they resort to for his brother the illustrious Duke?

Longingly, she stared towards the open door to her left. With the Duke's arrival depressingly imminent, would anyone notice if she slipped away?

A quick glance to the right confirmed that her indomitable Great-Aunt Violet was in her element and thoroughly enjoying holding court amongst the gaggle of older matrons ensconced in the corner. As she was the only person in the room likely to miss her, or even talk to her for that matter, and Aunt Penelope would be delighted to see the back of her, Eliza decided to seize the opportunity and escape, secure in the heady knowledge there would be a book in what was bound to be the well-stocked library with her name on it. Because there was always a book with her name on it, and she would much rather lose herself in its fascinating pages than sit here slowly dying inside from the interminable boredom of the most tiresome of all house parties.

A friendly footman pointed her in the correct direction, and after a full five minutes of walking the length of a gallery aptly named the Long Gallery, she finally found Jerusalem. The biggest, tallest, most book-stuffed library she had ever seen.

The dark oak shelves spanned between shiny marble floor to the towering domed ceiling, covering every inch of wall. Enormous arched windows flooded the space with light, while a fireplace which must be a good eight feet wide by eight feet tall crackled brightly with enough comforting warmth to effectively banish the brisk December chill outside, irrespective of the sheer size of the space.

Overwhelmed and overawed, she spun in a slow circle

and inhaled the wonderful aroma of print-covered old pages. Perhaps this dreadful week wouldn't be quite so bad after all now that she had found this oasis?

There really was nothing like the comforting smell of books. Books that would expand her mind or whisk her away to exciting places and great adventures she secretly yearned for but was too sensible to chase. There was enough here to keep her thirsty mind sated for twenty years or more, and in the absence of any chance of a decent conversation, which the outspoken and inquisitive aspects of her character adored above all else, it hinted at salvation.

Spoilt for choice, she ran her fingertips over a row of leather spines in the closest bookcase until she found an old friend—*The Ingenious Gentleman Don Quixote of La Mancha* was one of her father's favourites, and he had read it to her and her mother, from cover to cover when they had been snowed in at an inn one Christmas. Seeing as she was stuck here now, albeit without all the snow and the lively company, it seemed a rather fitting choice.

With the book in her hand, she went in search of a chair to sit in, but bizarrely found none. What sort of person had such a magnificent library and didn't put a single seat in it?

The sort that didn't read, that was who.

What a criminal waste of all this knowledge and escapism.

Her already low estimation of the elusive but doubtless pompous and self-absorbed Duke of Manningtree went down several notches. Even his enormous windows failed to have windowsills big enough for her to rest her bottom on.

In desperation, she wandered to the furthest end of the library, only to discover it continued via a narrow book-lined passageway tucked into the corner and hidden from plain view. Intrigued and determined, she followed it, turned the corner of some more bookshelves—and stopped dead.

His head bent over a huge desk in this small anteroom, a tawny-haired man in spectacles was scratching copious notes into a huge ledger with economic haste. At her gasp, he looked up, clearly surprised by her intrusion, bright blue eyes blinking back at her through the lenses of his glasses.

So very handsome it quite took her breath away.

Like her, he was plainly dressed. He wore an austere dark coat over an equally plain dark waistcoat. The comforting uniform of those born to serve.

'I am sorry to have bothered you, but I was looking for a chair...'

And the only visible seat seemed to be the cosy-looking leather chesterfield on the opposite side of this small and secret reading nook.

'And finally I have found one. Do you mind if I sit here for a little bit and read?'

She waved *Don Quixote* for good measure. He didn't smile. Which was a shame, because he had a very pleasant face. An excellent pair of shoulders too, if the fit of his un-fussy black coat was any indication.

'I promise I shan't disturb your work.'

Apparently he needed to give her simple request some thought, which he did with an exceedingly put-upon expression, before he huffed out a sigh. 'If you *must*.'

He might well be good-looking but his manners could do with some improvement she decided, and she seriously considered telling him so before stomping off to find some-where else to while away the afternoon. But as this distant and silent library was the farthest she could get from the house party without leaving the house, and because she was much too stubborn to be bullied out of this magnificent li-brary by a man with undoubtedly the same lowly rank as she, Eliza dug her heels in.

It was one thing being put in her place by Aunt Penelope—after years of consistent censure whenever they collided she expected nothing less from her—but it was quite another thing entirely from a complete stranger with an inflated sense of his own importance.

'Oh, I *must*, sir. As I fear my very sanity depends upon it.'

She wouldn't allow his lack of manners to spoil her bliss-ful and very likely short-lived stretch of freedom. Her sen-sible papa would urge her to use diplomacy to get what she wanted, rather than the pithy observations which came to her naturally, so she forced herself to smile, acknowledg-ing that she might be feeling tetchy more because of Aunt Penelope than because of this clerk.

'You have my word I shall be as quiet as a mouse.'

Despite her obvious olive branch, he failed to smile in return. Instead, looking bemused and a tad irritated at her intrusion, he went back to scratching whatever it was he was scratching so intently with his quill while she settled into the sofa, opened her book and tried her damnedest to forget he was there.

Which, for some reason, and despite her stubbornness, proved to be completely impossible. Perhaps because she could sense he was staring at her and, for some inexplicable yet overwhelming reason, she really wanted to stare back.

# Chapter Two

Marcus tried to ignore her while he waited for the inevitable nonsense to begin. As much as he tried to shield himself from the voracious husband-hunters at what could only be described as his mother's annual Yuletide menagerie, there was always at least one dangerously intrepid young lady who took matters into her own hands and calculatedly sought him out, recklessly unchaperoned.

To say it was an irritation, when everybody else, including his mother, thought him to be with his solicitor on urgent business until two, was an understatement. A quick glance at his pocket watch conveniently placed next to his ledger on the desk, showed he had a scant ten minutes of freedom left, and he really needed each and every one of them if he was to get the weekly estate accounts finished today.

Clearly he should have hidden in his dressing room instead of the library. But because he loved the library, and it was usually the last place any of those determined young ladies ventured, and because he'd had all the chairs removed as a precaution, an unwelcome unaccompanied female visitor here so early in the proceedings was a surprise. Especially as there was so much going on in the drawing room on this, the first interminable afternoon of three interminable days.

Yet she had gone duke-hunting on the off-chance anyway.

Any second now those exceedingly pretty eyes would lift from the pages of the book she was pretending to read and she would either gaze up at him through those ridiculously long, dark lashes shyly or she would do it boldly.

They both knew that *she* knew he was the Duke of Manningtree.

He might have deftly avoided the cloyingly predictable balls in the *ton* for the past year, but he had been dragged to hundreds of the damn things before that so he had to accept that his face was instantly recognisable. But alas, Marcus the man wasn't anywhere as attractive or interesting as his Dukedom, and he sincerely doubted any of those women ever really *saw* him anyway. Which was why he had withdrawn from blasted society in the first place.

He was so bored with the game.

Supremely aware of the vixen on the chesterfield, he waited for her to make her move, supremely confident he already knew them all. Any second now, she would try to engage him in conversation. Flirt a little. Perhaps even push the boundaries of propriety to their very limits in the hope he might be daft enough to take the bait.

She wouldn't be the first to try and ruin herself in order to marry him and, depressingly, she probably wouldn't be the last. Dukes seemed to bring out the worst in some women. And thanks to his meddling mother's unsubtle attempts at matchmaking—here in the sanctity of his own damn house—they had plenty of opportunities.

He flicked his suspicious gaze to the intruder. She didn't look like his mother's usual type of minion. Mama always sent him diminutive effervescent blondes with irritatingly tinkling laughs, even though blondes had always appealed to his brother Julius more than to him.

Not that his mother knew that.

Marcus had always been very careful about letting her know his taste ran towards brunettes in case she sent him irritatingly tinkling brunettes instead.

He blamed his eyes for his love of dark hair. Marcus had never been able to discern colours properly. What others called red or green looked much the same to him. He recognised yellow—vaguely—but it was so muted and insipid to his eyes it tended to blend into the background. But dark colours popped and dazzled against his odd canvas.

Surreptitiously, he watched her very fine pair of dark, almond-shaped eyes follow the words on the page in front of her and conceded perhaps she *was* reading while she awaited the right moment. But when one minute ticked by, and then five, the waiting started to drive him mad and much to his chagrin, she began to intrigue him.

'It is rude to stare.' She didn't even bother to lift those fine eyes from the book as she told him off. 'And most disconcerting.'

'My apologies.'

Why was he apologising? This was his house. His library. She was pretending to read *his* damn book!

'Are you not enjoying the entertainments?' His mother always put together a punishingly packed schedule at Christmas. Everybody, bar him, always raved about it.

Her head lifted. Two beguiling dark brows edged together in consternation at the interruption before she realised what they were doing and ruthlessly ironed them flat in order to appear polite. It was an entirely different tactic from what he was used to and, all credit to her, it had captured his interest.

'I was promised a walk...'

She seemed put out, but resigned. Wistful, even. Those lovely eyes wandered briefly to the window to gaze out before she dragged them back.

'But, alas, charades won out and instead of spending a pleasant couple of hours wandering these beautiful grounds and gazing at the superior scenery, I was on the verge of being saddled with the sight of two dozen silly girls ferociously outshining one another in the vain hope they might be the lucky one to catch the eye of the Duke.'

She rolled her eyes as she said the word 'Duke', as if it were offensive, then grinned as if dukes in general were all a big joke.

'Or his *dashingly* handsome and *charming* brother. So I did the sensible thing and escaped.'

'Because you didn't find Lord Julius dashingly handsome nor charming? I hear he is quite the catch.'

'I am sure he is considered quite the catch in certain circles—but, alas, they are not the circles I move in, so I really could not care less about impressing either him or his *illustrious* elder brother. I hate these sort of society parties—all enforced and false gaiety, when really most people are simply determined to outdo everybody else.'

He lay down his quill, both misguidedly fascinated by and pragmatically cynical about her unique and original approach. She was either a very good actress indeed or, unbelievably, she really was blissfully oblivious of his identity.

'And which circles do you move in, Miss…?'

Because he was certain they had never crossed paths before. He would have remembered. This minx had the sort of face and body any hot-blooded man would remember long after they had parted company.

'Harkstead. Miss Eliza Harkstead.'

She smiled then, and it transformed her face from exceptionally pretty to breathtakingly beautiful, although not in the fashionable way. She was too dark. Her features too bold. Her intelligent eyes too animated and amused. The thick, rebellious tendrils of hair framing her face curled in their own way, rather than being curtailed by the conventional ringlets favoured by the masses nowadays. He could tell already those rebellious curls mirrored her personality.

Miss Harkstead was different. Alluringly different.

'I am companion to Lady Violet Trumble.'

He instantly recalled Lady Trumble. She was a regular and raucous fixture in society and a frequent guest at his mother's parties—but she had never come with this fascinating creature in tow.

'Have you been her companion long, Miss Harkstead?'

'Four months…give or take a week here and there. Although as you can see, I am not a particularly good one.'

'Why do you say that?'

Using her index finger as a bookmark, she waved his father's favourite, overused and well-loved copy of *Don Quixote* at him.

'Because the purpose of a companion is to be *present*. Not to gleefully abandon her employer at the first available opportunity to pursue her lifelong love affair with books. Give me a book over a tedious house party or duke any day.' She grinned as she said this. 'Although, in my defence, I did check to see that Lady Trumble was occupied before I initiated my break for freedom—and, to be frank, she has no real need of a companion.'

'Then why does she have one?'

'I am still not altogether sure.' She discarded the book and leaned forward, dropping her voice conspiratorially. 'Other than the fact we are family and she feels sorry for me. Although I am not supposed to mention that here, so kindly keep it to yourself.'

'Lady Trumble disowns you in public?' How appalling.

'No—Great-Aunt Violet doesn't give two figs about my background. But my aunt Penelope does and as the original invitation came to her, and because we all travelled in her carriage, she made me promise not to report the connection.'

Now she really had him intrigued. 'Why on earth would she do that?'

'Because I hail from the shunned and scandalously impoverished side of the family. Although I am not supposed to mention that either so kindly keep that to yourself, too.'

He nodded solemnly, though he was vastly amused by the way she tossed about refreshing honesty like confetti. 'Shunned *and* scandalously impoverished? How did that come about?'

'My aristocratic mother fell head over heels for a lowly bookkeeper and rashly eloped with him within a week of meeting him. To Gretna Green, actually. It made all the newspapers—or so I am told—and caused quite the scandal in its day. My aunt Penelope—my mother's dreadful snooty sister—has never got over it.'

'Because your mother recklessly married a fortune-hunter?'

'Not in the slightest.' She seemed unoffended, as if the very suggestion was absurd. 'Whilst I *will* admit the elopement was uncharacteristically reckless for him, Papa is a man of substance who cares little for material things. He also loves my mother to distraction and she him. They claim it was love at first sight—although I am not sure I believe all that nonsense—and when they were denied permission to marry they were forced to take matters into their own hands. Which did not go down well with my mother's side of the family for obvious reasons. Her father wanted her to marry someone with a lofty title, not a lowly bookkeeper.'

She shrugged, unperturbed at the circumstances of her birth, and he admired her for that.

'But thank goodness they did, else I wouldn't be here. And by "here" I mean here on this planet, rather than here at this tedious house party.'

'We shall blame Lady Trumble for that travesty. Curse her kind heart for feeling sorry for you.'

She leant forward, those bewitching dark eyes dancing, and he found himself doing the same and enjoying it.

'Between you and me, I suspect the real reason my great-aunt Violet insists on having me as her companion is purely because it irritates my aunt Penelope so very much.'

'You don't say...?'

'Oh, I do.' Amusement made her eyes sparkle in the most attractive way. 'Having such a lowly mongrel as a niece is a frightful embarrassment to Aunt Penelope, and one which might prevent her *vigorous* social climbing.'

If she was trying to seduce him, confessing her lowly connections while simultaneously insulting his hospitality seemed an odd way of going about it. Although it was working. Against all his better judgement, Marcus was already thoroughly seduced.

'Not that I am allowed to call her Aunt Penelope while I am here of course. *Here* I have to call her Lady Broadstairs, in case anyone learns of my shameful parentage and it somehow taints *her*. And, of course, she is of the firm opinion that my mere existence under his *illustrious* roof might put off the Duke...'

'From what?'

'From marrying my cousin Honoria, of course.'

She laughed at that. And it didn't tinkle in the slightest. It was brash and loud and gloriously abandoned.

'Aunt Penelope has quite set her mind to it, regardless of the fact poor Honoria is as dim as she is beautiful.'

'Do you think Honoria stands a chance with...um... His Grace?'

'You might know the answer to that better than I, sir.' She flapped one elegant hand towards his ledger. 'You work for him after all.'

'I do...'

Was it wrong to lie when she was speaking so freely and would undoubtedly clam up the moment she realised who he was? Or, worse, begin to fawn and defer to him when he adored it that she didn't.

'As a bookkeeper, Mr...?'

'Bookkeeping is one of my many duties here at Manningtree.'

'More an estate manager, then?'

'Yes...' He experienced another pang of guilt. 'Sort of...'

'And what is he like?'

'Well...' How to describe himself without sounding like a braggart? 'He's a decent sort...by and large.'

She laughed as if she didn't believe him. 'A very diplomatic answer, sir. I am heartily impressed by it. You are a much better employee than I could ever aspire to be, Mr...?'

'Why do you say that?' He was not ready to tell her

who he was, but he was curious to know what people really thought about him when they weren't being crushingly well-behaved and polite. 'Do you doubt he is capable of being fundamentally decent?'

'Well…he *is* a duke.'

There it was again. That dismissive, heartily unimpressed roll of her eyes.

'I am not entirely sure we can blame him for that any more than we can blame you for being scandalously impoverished, Miss Harkstead, can we? He was born to be one after all.'

'Indeed. But like all men of his ilk, I suspect he is probably imbued with arrogance and perhaps prone to be a little pompous, as all dukes inevitably are.'

'I take it you speak from a wealth of experience with the breed?'

'Not with any dukes, specifically, but I have collided with more than a few earls and viscounts—not that I expect any of them to remember colliding with *me*. I am far too lowly for them to notice. Which is exactly the problem with titled men. They cannot help it. It is in the blood. And what isn't is learned in the crib. Fed to them by their similarly entitled ancestors along with their milk until they believe they are better than everyone else.'

'If you don't mind me saying, that's a rather sweeping generalisation to make about the Duke of Manningtree specifically, based on no evidence whatsoever. Especially when you have already admitted you haven't yet met him.'

Although technically she had and was unlikely to be very happy about it once she found out.

'Or any other duke, for that matter.'

'You are quite correct. I haven't met him. Yet already I have the evidence to corroborate my suspicions. Even in his absence the eminent Duke of Manningtree lords it over everyone else and probably does not even realise he is doing it.'

'He does?'

This was news to him. He had never consciously lorded it over anyone in his entire life. He had neither the time nor the inclination and he abhorred all those that did.

'In what way?'

'For a start, there are close to fifty people in the drawing room eagerly awaiting him. They have been there two hours already and as far as I know, he hasn't said hello to a single one of them. What is that if it isn't *lording*?'

The way she said it made him feel a tad guilty for purposely avoiding them all.

'Surely you have to concede your employer would never get away with such poor manners if he *wasn't* a duke?'

'I suppose that is a bit rude, now you come to mention it… Although, as I understand it, he is frightfully busy…'

His eyes drifted to his pocket watch again, his heart plummeting when it told him his time here was almost up. He'd promised his mother faithfully he would be there at three.

More binding and unbreakable still, he had made a solemn pledge to his brother he would relieve him from all the fawning of the determined husband-hunters at precisely three o'clock, too. Julius had done his allotted two hours of torture and now it was Marcus's turn. It was the only way the pair of them could tolerate all the nonsense. Worse still, he'd now have to work by candlelight till the small hours to get the accounts done.

A very long, dull day of ducal duty stretched before him.

'Too busy to say a quick how do you do? When they are all here expressly for him?'

'*He* did not invite them. They are his mother's guests. I am fairly certain *he* has little interest in any of them—your beautiful cousin Honoria included.'

Seeing as she was being brutally honest, he would be too.

'Between you and me, the Duke knows this whole tedious affair is his mother's ruse to thrust a bride upon him and he is merely rebelling by disappearing. It can be hard work, being a duke.'

She tilted her head and studied him thoughtfully for a moment. 'You like him, don't you?'

'He is an easy fellow to like.' Marcus shrugged, feeling oddly keen to defend himself from her indiscriminate and wildly incorrect assumptions. 'I have never found him to be the least bit arrogant or pompous. If anything, he is decent and rather self-effacing, truth be told. Forward-thinking and egalitarian, actually. A model employer and a generous landlord. In fact, he prides himself on being so. He recognises the individual worth of all the many people who toil so diligently for the Manningtree estate because the place wouldn't work without them.'

A sound piece of advice his beloved father *had* drilled into him from the crib.

'The Duke judges the measure of a man—or a woman, for that matter—by the strength of their character and by their deeds rather than their titles. In fact, he is not the least bit obsessed with his rank.'

If he was, then his trusty and efficient bookkeeper would be here now, balancing the accounts, rather than enjoying a well-earned Christmas holiday with his family hundreds of miles away in Northumberland, and Marcus wouldn't have to be working until goodness knew how late to balance the books in his stead. But, because he had been taught diligence by his father, and because he believed in fair play to the roots of his soul, the accounts needed to be settled so that the many suppliers to the estate were not out of pocket and the weekly wages still had to be paid. His loyal army of people depended on him.

She blinked, then scoffed in disbelief. 'He might *think* himself an egalitarian—and perhaps he is as far as his staff are concerned—but he certainly doesn't practice what he preaches with those *not* in his employ. From the second we arrived we all knew exactly where we fitted in the pecking order.'

'I doubt there is actually a pecking order—'

He found himself staring at the suddenly raised palm of her hand and realised he hadn't been so ruthlessly cut off mid-flow by anyone—not even his mother or brother—since he had succeeded his father. Dukes were not interrupted.

'Clearly you have not been apprised of the dining arrangements, then, for I can assure you they are all the proof any of us needs to *thoroughly* know our place.'

Of *course* he hadn't been apprised of the dining arrangements! Any more than he had been apprised of *any* of the blasted arrangements. His mother had presided over all the arranging like Wellington at Waterloo, cloaked in Machiavellian secrecy, and now only deigned to tell him and his brother what was happening on the day, in case they fled screaming from the proceedings or, more likely, created a pressing engagement elsewhere well in advance.

'I am not sure I follow, Miss Harkstead. Surely the Duke feeds all his guests equally?'

He'd seen the bills. Was still wading through them all. They were feasting on the best beef and salmon tonight, a veritable glut of it, and certainly not on humble pie.

'He might feed us all the same food—but the way it is to be served is most definitely different. Those of us who are not deemed worthy enough to dine with the Duke have been relegated to take separate repasts in the Oriental Room every mealtime, where I am told one of his uncles is to host.'

That brought Marcus up short. And left a bad taste in his mouth. It also explained why his ever-present Uncle Horace was *never* present at dinner during one of his mother's never-ending duke-snaring house parties.

Why had he never noticed that before? Or paid enough attention to ask why? He should have known that. Was heartily ashamed of himself that he didn't. Had thought himself forward-thinking and egalitarian.

'Oh…'

'*Oh*, indeed.'

Miss Harkstead made no secret of the fact she thought it

an outrage. Disgust at his apparently shoddy treatment of his less titled guests was written all over her lovely face.

'But apparently we might catch a glimpse of his eminent personage and his dashing brother afterwards, when the two parties briefly merge before the gentlemen disappear for their port.'

She huffed out a heartily unimpressed long sigh.

'Lucky us…to be so favoured by his majestic presence. Although I am sure the many poor young ladies pitifully vying for his attention will be grateful for those few crumbs and will doubtless make the most of it as they all stampede to catch His Grace's superior eye.'

'But not you, Miss Harkstead?' Why did that depress him?

'Not me.' She made a point of shuddering at the suggestion. 'It takes more than a hereditary dukedom and a ludicrously absurd fortune to earn my respect. But it should be entertaining to watch. More entertaining than the silly charades at least.'

'Unless you happen to be the poor Duke.'

Out of the corner of his eye he saw Gibson his butler appear in the passageway, come to remind him that his time was up, and winced—because it was. In more ways than one.

As much as he would love to be play the ordinary bookkeeper indefinitely—especially around the refreshing Miss Harkstead, who clearly held bookkeepers like her father in far greater esteem than dukes—as a depressingly sensible pragmatist he realised he was what he was and it was ultimately pointless to pretend otherwise, considering the circumstances.

He could barely hide from the party for two hours undiscovered. Three days would take a blasted miracle and a level of duplicity the upright, upstanding and annoyingly noble aspects of his character were incapable of perpetuating.

His butler coughed politely. 'It is precisely two o'clock, Your Grace.'

her talk without thinking first. She had been uncharacteristically reckless and still couldn't fathom why.

Of course, this afternoon, she had thought she was conversing with an equal. A fellow servant of sorts. From the grey middle ground. Too educated to be from the working masses, too poor to belong to the merchant class, yet too common to be welcomed into the lesser gentry.

'Absolutely not! I would hate you to miss out.'

'I shall hardly be missing out…' Her great-aunt was now rifling through her meagre trunk, so she had to make do with pleading to her back. 'You know I dislike these sorts of functions and would appreciate the opportunity to have some time to myself.'

'You took three hours this afternoon, missy—don't think I didn't notice. I even went hunting for you so I could introduce you to the Duke, and you were nowhere to be found.'

That was because she had been curled up in a mortified ball in her room, awaiting an ominous knock at the door which would herald her unceremonious marching orders. The last thing she wanted now was to be formally introduced to him by her well-meaning and overly romantic great-aunt. That would be beyond excruciating.

'Although I cannot say I blame you for escaping this afternoon's melee,' her great-aunt continued. 'As soon as the poor Duke arrived it rapidly descended into noisy carnage. The drawing room was so full of excited, high-pitched giggling I could barely think straight, let alone hear. Let's hope all those silly girls are over the initial shock of meeting a duke and will behave with a tad more restraint this evening.'

*And pigs might sprout wings and fly.*

With a triumphant tug, Great-Aunt Violet held aloft Eliza's well-loved coral silk. 'This is perfect. So much better than that sludge-coloured monstrosity you are wearing.'

'It's deep plum.'

It was hardly sludge-coloured and, like her practical brown dress, the soft wool had been an absolute bargain.

Thanks to her mother's talents with a needle, the cut was quite modern too.

'And it's hardly a monstrosity. Only last week you said it was very becoming.'

'For taking tea at the vicarage, perhaps—but not for a formal dinner in the home of a duke! How on earth is he going to notice you wearing that, Eliza? Put this on.' Her best dress was thrust at her. 'It's much more appropriate for tonight.'

She set her shoulders and lifted her chin defiantly— because, frankly, stubborn pride was all she had left after her enormous *faux pas* with their illustrious host. 'Firstly, I do not want him to notice me.' The absolute truth. 'And neither does anyone else.' More truth.

Aunt Penelope in particular would have an apoplexy if she thought for one second her disgraceful niece was attempting to compete against her dim-witted daughter.

'And secondly, if I wear that gown tonight I'll have nothing for the masquerade.' Although that might well be a blessing, all things considered. 'This dress is perfectly appropriate for *a companion* to wear, and as I am dining in a separate room from all the important people anyway...' thank goodness for the Duke's aristocratic 'lording' '... I doubt anyone will care what I am wearing.'

'I care.'

'You're not dining in the same room as me either, so it hardly matters.'

'Even so...just once I wish you would let your hair down, Eliza.'

Because that had gone so well earlier in the library, when she had been tempted to flirt with a bookkeeper.

'You are a very attractive young woman, staying in one of the largest and most beautiful houses in England, attending one of the most sought-after house parties in the kingdom, and your host is a handsome duke with an equally handsome brother... And it's Christmas, Eliza.'

'What does that have to do with anything?'

'If you cannot have an adventure at Christmas, when can you? Two handsome and eligible bachelors, a masked ball, hopefully some snow…and let's not forget all the mistletoe. The Duchess has been wonderfully liberal with the mistletoe this year. It would be a positive tragedy if you didn't get waylaid under some.'

'Oh, for goodness' sake!'

'Your mother ran away with your father at Christmas time,' said her great-aunt. 'She said one impromptu kiss under a stray piece of mistletoe was all it took.'

'But you are forgetting one tiny but significant detail, Great-Aunt—I am not my mother. If I am like either of my parents, I am more like my sensible and level-headed father.'

'Who also ran away after an impromptu kiss with your mother under the same piece of mistletoe! Which *he* stole, I believe—just in case you've forgotten that significant detail, my dear. It takes two people to create a deliciously romantic scandal like your parents did, so why shouldn't I have high hopes for you?'

Her meddling aunt held up the gown once more.

'Just this once, Eliza, don't be stubborn. Be spontaneous. Wear the coral silk! Loiter under the mistletoe! I promise I'll find you something else for the masquerade.'

'Absolutely not!'

This was all going from the sublime to the ridiculous. As if the handsome Duke would want to loiter under the mistletoe with *her* after everything she had said to him.

'I happen to like this dress—and, even if I didn't, it is too late to change now.'

Before her equally stubborn great-aunt could argue further, Eliza marched to the door. Loiter under the mistletoe indeed! That would make her as silly and as desperate as all the other girls here, chasing the two Symington men.

'Dinner is in ten minutes. We should go. It is poor form to be late—especially when one's host is a duke.'

Displaying a woeful lack of diligence, Eliza abandoned

her charge just shy of the door to the formal dining room and
darted to the necessary sanctuary of the Oriental Room on
the other side of the hallway as if her life depended upon it.

It certainly lived up to its name. Every stick of furniture,
every piece of art and sculpture, and even the sumptuous
silk of the curtains positively screamed that it hailed from
the Orient. Even the two intimidating, intricately decorated
suits of armour flanking the red-lacquered double doors
were Samurai. But it was a lovely room, made lovelier by
the sea of unimposing aged spinsters, companions and un-
important ladies and gentlemen who were in the process of
taking their seats.

Being a bit shaky on his legs, Sir Horace, the Duke's
uncle, was already seated at the centre of the long table.
Eliza politely greeted him, then scanned the place cards at
the empty chairs for her name amongst those of the other
twenty or so lesser mortals who had also been banished here.
Typically, she was deemed to be of such woeful insignificance she was right at the end, furthest away from the door.
Which meant she would be the last served too.

A slight which was probably the illustrious Duke's doing,
and frankly she couldn't blame him in the slightest. She had
unwittingly and unabashedly called him arrogant, pompous and rude.

Her toes curled each time she considered some of the
more shocking and irresponsible things she had said when
she had thought him a bookkeeper. All done to show off a
little because she had assumed—no, *felt* they were cut from
the same cloth. And also, she was ashamed to acknowledge,
because his handsome face and the intelligent eyes behind
those scholarly spectacles had appealed a little too much.

Clearly the Harkstead apple hadn't fallen far from the
tree. Just like her mother, she had been waylaid by a bookkeeper and uncharacteristically thrown caution to the wind.
She would happily laugh at the irony if the situation wasn't
so unbearably awful.

The next three days were thoroughly doomed to feel like three weeks.

With a resigned sigh she took in the table as Sir Horace called for quiet and began to make a welcoming speech. Almost all the chairs had been filled now, except the one next to Eliza and the one directly opposite. While everyone else had someone to talk to, it seemed she was to be left in the lurch.

As the rest of the guests listened to their host with rapt attention she surreptitiously glanced at the name on the place card beside her and nearly groaned aloud. Lady Audley was a nice old dear, but as deaf as a post. So much so, all she ever did was smile. If the guest seated opposite was in the same league as Lady Audley, then this dinner was going to be worse than purgatory.

She was about to reach across the tablecloth and peek at the card when she felt a slight draught on her neck and instinctively turned towards it—only to see that purgatory was a forlorn hope now that hell beckoned from behind a secret near invisible door in the panelling.

Because the gentleman who quietly and, at least as far as the other guests were concerned, stealthily slipped into the chair across from hers was none other than her worst nightmare—the dratted Duke himself.

He pressed a finger to his lips to silence her—which was probably just as well because she was sorely tempted to scream—then mouthed *Good evening* as he unfolded his napkin and placed it across his lap.

Completely thrown by his presence, Eliza attempted to listen to Sir Horace, who was now blathering on about the importance of friends and family at Christmas time, but after a painful minute had ticked by she couldn't hold her words in any longer.

'What are you doing here?' The question was part stunned whisper, part outraged hiss. Because surely he was only here to make her suffer?

'I'm practising what I preach and being egalitarian.' He

smiled at the footman, who was topping up the glasses for the toast, and the footman broke rank to smile back—as if he smiled at the Duke all the time. 'Seeing as I apparently have two dinner tables for this god-awful house party, I thought it only right and proper that I visit both of them.'

'But you are supposed to be in the other room!'

'Says who?'

He wasn't wearing his spectacles tonight, so those unshielded bright blue eyes, which co-ordinated perfectly with his cobalt silk waistcoat, positively shimmered with mischief.

'Because the last time I checked, Miss Harkstead, I was in charge here, and so long as my mother is kept completely out of the equation, what I say goes.'

'But surely your other guests will miss you?'

The desperation in her voice, even in such hushed tones, was unmistakable, and that annoyed her. She might well want him gone, but her pride would not allow her to alert him to the fact that his unexpected intrusion, so soon after her horrendous and cringe-worthy blunder, had thoroughly flustered her.

Now, thanks to Great-Aunt Violet's outrageous suggestion that she loiter under the mistletoe, she could feel herself blush.

Fighting for composure, she tried to use reason. 'Your important guests will see your absence as a slight. Surely you do not want to insult them? It is the first night of the house party after all.'

'Interesting...' He pretended to mull this over. 'Only earlier you criticised me for neglecting the guests seated in here, and now it is the people across the hall which most concern you. Unless you simply want to be rid of me because you are hideously embarrassed to be facing me so soon after you accused me of being inherently arrogant and pompous...and rude.'

There was no denying it, so Eliza fell on her sword. 'I am very sorry about all that.'

That tawny head tilted as he stared her dead in the eye. 'Why?'

'Because it was unfair of me to pass judgement and indiscreet of me to gossip about you behind your back.'

Which was a ridiculous thing to say when she had gossiped about him clean to his face—something he had actively encouraged, as she recalled.

'Although in my defence, Your Grace, you did provoke me with all those leading questions you kept asking...and you *did* lie about who you were.'

'I never once claimed to be someone else. Did I give you a name, Miss Harkstead?'

'No, Your Grace. You did not. On purpose.'

She might well be insignificant in his eyes, but her outraged pride would not allow her to kowtow. Not when she was in this tiny instance in the right.

'You also referred to yourself in the third person on at least two occasions that I can think of during our short conversation, specifically to entrap me into believing you really were the lowly bookkeeper I had assumed you were.' A not inconsequential detail she was justifiably still annoyed about. 'And you were having fun at my expense when I repeatedly enquired as to your name.'

Defiantly, she tilted her chin, daring him to deny that.

'In my defence...' He paused, and for the first time appeared contrite before he sighed. 'I have no defence, Miss Harkstead. Other than the fact that I was enjoying our conversation and knew full well you wouldn't have been quite so indiscreet if I had made you aware of my real identity. Besides, you were also having fun at *my* expense, so I believe we are equal.'

As if they could ever be equal!

It was on the tip of her tongue to tell him so when the toast finally came to a rousing end and they all had to clink glasses before a battalion of liveried servants swarmed the table wielding soup.

This proved to be the time when a few of the other guests at their end of the table noticed the Duke was there, and used the efficiently brisk and silent communication of the nudge to alert the rest of the diners to his illustrious presence.

Like toppling dominoes, Eliza was able to judge the impressive speed of those enlightening nudges by the way each person in receipt of one suddenly sat straighter as their eyes immediately swivelled his way.

And hers.

Instead of quietly blending into the panelling, as she had hoped, she was being made a spectacle.

By him.

It was a cruel and cunning method of revenge.

With the deaf Lady Audley still absent, she had nobody else to talk to—or in Lady Audley's case talk *at*—so Eliza had to resort to swishing her spoon in her soup to cover her discomfort rather than look at him blatantly enjoying his.

'If you don't mind me saying, you seem irritated by my egalitarian gesture Miss Harkstead.'

And now he was baiting her.

Papa always cautioned that she count to ten before responding to an incendiary comment, and she made a valiant attempt at heeding his sage advice—before outrage overwhelmed her shortly after the count of three.

'Probably because I *am* irritated, Your Grace!'

If she was going to be tossed out on her ear, she might as well go with her trademark honesty. Skulking off with her tail between her legs had never been her style. Being a shrinking violet felt wrong too, when Eliza usually exited all confrontation in a blaze of glory as a matter of principle.

'Whilst I will admit my earlier comments were, for want of better words, ill-considered, narrow-minded and grossly misplaced, I think it mean of you to have made it your business to come here tonight simply to make me suffer. Because believe me, I have suffered enough all afternoon, reliving every painful flippant comment in my mind and nervously awaiting your censure—or your mother's, or my pretentious aunt Penelope's. It is no fun at all waiting for the axe to fall, I can assure you. And, as justified as my punishment undoubtedly is, gloating is unbecoming. Frankly, considering your rank, you should be above seeking such petty satisfaction. If you want to chastise me for my insolence, and my complete lack of thought and decorum, the decent thing to do is to send me packing with the minimum of fuss. Not prolong the torture simply to prove a point.'

He made no secret of the fact he found her anger amusing, even pausing with his spoon midway between his bowl and his upturned lips as he listened to her subtle, whispered yet impassioned rant in its entirety.

'I promise you—I am not gloating.'

'You look as if you are gloating.' For some bizarre reason she couldn't seem to stop herself speaking her mind now that the hounds had been unleashed—even though that same mind was simultaneously screaming at her to shut up. 'You are openly laughing at me.'

'I am smiling, Miss Harkstead. Because—although for the life of me I cannot think why—I rather enjoy talking to you.'

That took the wind out of her sails. 'You do?'

She felt her eyebrows knit together in confusion and was sorely tempted to give in to the urge to gape at him dumbfounded, but didn't.

'I do...'

In fairness, he appeared as bewildered as she by this bizarre turn of events.

'I find your forthrightness and honesty strangely... refreshing.'

He took a thoughtful sip of his wine while they studied one another, like two territorial tom cats sizing each other up as they decided whether or not to fight.

He broke the peculiarly loaded stare first, with a befuddled shrug. 'You are the first person in a very long time who has actually spoken to *me* rather than the Dukedom—outside of my immediate family, of course. And I have to confess... I liked it.'

'You *liked* being insulted?'

'You weren't really insulting me. You were passing comment based on your particular experiences. I wasn't the least bit offended by it at all.' He frowned again and sighed, then shook his head. 'Not strictly true. Being accused of "lording it" over people stung, I cannot deny. But after I had had a cold, hard look at myself I realised my absence at the gathering earlier *could* be construed as lording. As, too, could the differentiated seating arrangements for dinner and breakfast. I don't usually trouble myself regarding mealtimes and menus and such—but, thanks to your insights, I have decided some alterations to this gathering are necessary. Therefore, starting tomorrow morning the allocations will be more *ad hoc* and everyone will be mixed up. Including the hosts. It bothers me immensely to think I have unintentionally used rank to put people in their place and that will cease henceforth, Miss Harkstead.'

Eliza did gape then. Because she couldn't have been more shocked if he'd suddenly jumped on the table and danced a Highland jig.

He toasted her stunned expression with his glass. 'I can see that this Duke has surprised you, Miss Harkstead.'

'You have, Your Grace. I am...' *decidedly off-kilter and ever so slightly impressed* '...all astonishment.'

'Then my next request should startle you more. I have a proposition.'

Instantly her pleasant surprise turned to disappointment. She'd had quite a few propositions from titled men in the last few years. All of them quite improper.

'You do?'

Her disgust must have shown either on her face or in

her tone because he laughed out loud. 'Do not panic, Miss Harkstead—what I am about to propose is neither illegal nor immoral. Although your complete lack of faith is both hilarious as well as insulting. I can only imagine all the previous dukes you encountered before me were beasts. Which of them gave you such a high opinion of the breed?'

As she did not know nor have any experience of dukes personally, and as his question had caught her on the hop, the truth leaked out before she could stop it. 'It's not so much dukes, *per se*, as titled gentlemen who consider themselves in such high regard they assume any untitled woman is fair game, and should be grateful for their unsolicited and unseemly attentions.'

He seemed genuinely appalled. 'That's dreadful! And such men have made overtures towards you?'

'On more than one occasion, Your Grace—which makes me predisposed to be suspicious of sudden propositions.'

'Then allow me to put your mind at rest about mine. What I am proposing is perhaps a tad revolutionary, but I am a progressive by nature so I hope you will find it in your heart to indulge me.'

Experience meant she wasn't entirely placated. 'Go on...'

He leaned closer, sending a delicious waft of spicy cologne her way, and lowered his deep voice to a silky whisper which, much to her chagrin, caused excited goosebumps to bloom on the sensitive skin of her neck and back.

'It cannot have escaped your notice, Miss Harkstead, that I—or rather my title—bring out the worst in some people... young ladies in particular.'

'You are referring to all the eyelash-fluttering and simpering?'

'All the fawning and deferring, yes.'

He looked delightfully awkward as he dropped his voice another octave to prevent those closest from eavesdropping. Something they had been doing with varying degrees of unsubtlety since their conversation had begun. Hardly a surprise, really. Dukes and companions usually did not mix, let alone have intensely private discussions which excluded the rest of the table.

'I loathe it. To such an extent I was rather hoping we could make a pact, Miss Harkstead, whereby I give you my word that I shall not behave in the least bit duke-like if you faithfully promise not to fawn or defer to me under any circumstances and remain at all times the forthright, pithy and entertaining person you quite obviously are.'

He found her pithy forthrightness *entertaining*? Such a novelty when so few did.

'I cannot tell you what a relief it would be to me to have at least one guest under my roof with whom I can have a decent and honest conversation. Like you, I hate this sort of society party. If my mother hadn't thrust it upon me, I confess I would have moved heaven and earth to be anywhere else.'

# Chapter Four

Marcus awoke feeling surprisingly enthusiastic about the long day ahead, entirely because he knew Miss Harkstead would be in it.

They had talked non-stop throughout last night's dinner, about absolutely everything and nothing, and they had laughed constantly. So much so, it had been with great regret that he'd left her when his mother had dragged him away to take port with the other gentlemen in attendance, as expected. Something about her made him feel lighter and less burdened with responsibility.

He had been left in such good spirits that in an unguarded moment of weakness he had happily agreed to accompany the whole party on an excursion to the village for shopping, which he loathed, followed by wassailing, which he also loathed.

Why anybody thought it enjoyable to knock on some poor, unsuspecting neighbour's door and inflict upon them tipsy, unrehearsed, out of time and tuneless singing was beyond him.

It was an irritation when, as lord of the manor, it was inflicted upon him, and nothing short of abject humiliation when he was forced to take part in it. To make matters worse, as the Duke he was also expected to participate at the front and centre of the rag-tag choir, rather than hide at the back as he preferred. Hiding at the back, according to his mother, was apparently a slight upon the villagers, so not only must he be at the front, he also had to muster up the strength to appear enthusiastic as well.

No mean feat when all one's muscles and sinews were contracting in cringing protest.

Regardless, he had still agreed to it, and he rather looked forward to hearing Miss Harkstead's pithy but insightful observations of the inevitable debacle as they wandered from door to unsuspecting door, demanding figgy pudding for their woefully inadequate efforts.

'Well, you've certainly put the cat amongst the pigeons.'

Never one to stand on ceremony, his brother Julius wandered into his bedchamber without knocking.

'Certain people are outraged by the breakfast arrangements—our dear mother included—for how can anyone possibly know precisely where the two most eligible bachelors in Essex are without a seating plan set in stone and cast in iron?'

'Allowing everyone to choose their own seat, and indeed their own dining room, merely struck me as a nicer, less formal way to begin the day. This is the season of goodwill, after all—what better way to spread goodwill than to dispense with the stuffy and unnecessary restrictions of rank?'

His brother eyed him dubiously while Marcus finished shaving. 'And you came up with this radical idea all by yourself, did you?' He stared at him as if he had suddenly sprouted two heads. 'It has absolutely nothing to do with the chestnut-haired vixen you were glued to all evening?'

It had everything to do with her. Not that he would admit it to his brother. Of all the people he knew best, Julius was the one who would tease him mercilessly for his sudden interest in a woman. Especially a woman at one of their mother's hideous duke-snaring, husband-hunting house parties.

'I was hardly glued to her. I conversed with Miss Harkstead over dinner, that's all.'

'After you suddenly decided on a whim *not* to take your allotted seat as host in the main dining room and unashamedly abdicating all those responsibilities—which then forced *me* to shoulder the burden of the unpleasant task.'

'I am aware I owe you for that.'

'Good. Because I flatly refuse to traipse around the village today with all those young ladies. It's my turn to hide from mother's rampaging army during daylight hours, and I intend to claim every single one of them from breakfast to dinner. Especially after you left me to the vultures alone again last night.'

Marcus owed his brother for that too. Instead of joining them all in the drawing room, as he had been supposed to, he had dallied in the Oriental Room with Miss Harkstead until the last possible moment.

'Is there someone in particular you are avoiding, big brother? Because I have to say Mama has invited a tenacious bunch this time. Several of the young ladies are significantly bolder than usual—which, after the last party, I didn't think possible—and a couple of the mothers are, frankly, for want of a better word, terrifying.' He shuddered while pulling a face. 'I've never encountered house guests like it.'

'They do seem a bit more forceful this year. Or are we simply more jaded?'

'It's hard not to be jaded about it when their ulterior motive is so obvious.'

There was no arguing with that. A hopeless romantic at heart, their mother was convinced neither of her sons could be happy unless they were wed.

'If I had my way, like you, I'd avoid them all. But it's Christmas…' The third without their father.

'Indeed it is. If only our dear mother wasn't an expert in laying on the guilt.'

She claimed to find Christmas the hardest time of all, because she had met their father at a yuletide house party, fallen head over heels in love with him at first sight, realised he was 'the one' after their first rashly stolen kiss and married him within the month.

To celebrate their whirlwind romance, the devoted couple always held a festive house party here at Manningtree, to mark the occasion, and in honour of her dead husband their mother had insisted they continue with the tradition.

And then she used it ruthlessly to fill the house with unwelcome guests, banishing her grief by completely occupying herself with fervent matchmaking instead. All because she was a hopeless romantic who believed in fate, fairy tales and Christmas miracles, and fervently hoped history would repeat itself for her sons.

Marcus and Julius simultaneously shrugged miserably, accepting there was nothing to be done about it except continue to be the good sons they were, while divvying up the workload as most eligible bachelor in the room for the sake of their own sanity.

'Have you collided with Lady Broadstairs yet?'

His brother's tone was cautionary as he mentioned Eliza's pretentious aunt. She had cornered him briefly last night, when he had finally graced the drawing room with his presence, before Gibson had practically frog-marched him into the billiard room, where he'd been late to take port with the gentlemen.

'She's the worst of the bunch, so avoid her like the plague. Absolutely shameless! While you were missing in action I was thrust opposite her at dinner and forced to listen to an hour-long liturgy on the many attributes of her silly daughter, whose blasted name escapes me.'

'Honoria.'

'You've met her, then?' Julius pulled a face.

'Not yet. But she was mentioned in my conversation with Miss Harkstead. They are cousins.'

'Are they? Then I hope for both your sake your Miss Harkstead is nothing like the other branch of the family. That would have made your dinner very tedious. But if they are related, why wasn't she seated with them?'

'Because she is companion to Lady Trumble—also from the scandalously impoverished side of the family—and Lady

Broadstairs likes to pretend there is no blood connection between them.'

'Ah…' His brother rested his behind on the dressing table and, arms crossed, watched Marcus splash on some cologne. 'That explains it, then.'

'Explains what?'

'Your newly democratic approach to mealtimes. It's nice to see you finally taking my advice about seizing the day, big brother.'

Julius winked. He was all about 'seizing the day', like their mother, whereas Marcus was predictably calm and measured, as their father had been.

'If everyone sits where they want, you get to sit with *her*. She must be very nice indeed for you to abandon your usual tendency towards tortured staidness and painful good manners. You've become very dull since you became the Duke. Too sensible. Or at least you were till you found a distraction. Perhaps Mama is right after all? Perhaps there *is* a magical spark when you find the right one which encourages you to throw caution to the wind? It would certainly explain your uncharacteristic behaviour…'

'Idiot.' Marcus rolled his eyes, deciding not to dignify such fanciful nonsense with more of a response, and hoped to divert him by gesturing to the bed. 'On a sensible note— which of those two waistcoats goes best with that coat?'

As everyone in the family knew he couldn't discern colours, it was a run-of-the-mill question.

'They are both typically plain and boring, as you are so tediously prone to be nowadays, so go with either. Whichever you choose, you will look like a dreary accountant or a dull solicitor. Old beyond your years.'

Not at all the effect he had been aiming for. 'Which would you wear?'

His brother stared at him thoughtfully. 'That depends…'

'On what?'

'On what my motive was. If, for example, I was trying

to appear impressively ducal but devoid of all humour I would choose this insipid green one.' He pointed to the left waistcoat, which looked as brown as the right one to Marcus's odd eyes, and frowned. 'It screams staid and suitably boring. But if I wanted to be sensibly ducal still, but with a vague nod to the cheerfulness of the season, I would choose the mustard.' He pointed to the other, looking thoroughly disgusted with the valet's choices.

Julius suddenly strode to the wardrobe and flung it open, his fingertips skimming the neat line of waistcoats quickly until he found one which appeared to Marcus as brown as the other two and held it aloft, grinning.

'But if I forgot, for one blessed and reckless moment, my mountains of ducal work and responsibilities, and had my mind set on impressing Lady Trumble's devilishly attractive but scandalously impoverished companion, I would choose *this*.'

He presented the garment like a French sommelier, delivering the rarest and finest of wines.

'Being burgundy, rather than red, it subtly speaks of confidence, with just a hint of flirty mischief, while still exuding the necessary gravitas one expects of a duke in the midst of his *vigorous* prime.'

The word *vigorous* was accompanied by a salacious wiggle of his incorrigible brother's eyebrows.

'I am not trying to impress Miss Harkstead.'

A flagrant lie, when he had practically jumped out of bed in his eagerness to linger over his toilette after contemplating her all night and wondering what it would be like to kiss her.

'And I certainly don't have the time for flirting.'

Not that he had ever been any good at it anyway. More was the pity—because she was exactly the sort of woman he would be inclined to flirt with, if he'd possessed Julius's enviable talent for flirting.

Marcus could hold his own in a conversation, could even be amusing and witty, but if he tried to flirt he came over as awkward and ultimately made a hash of it. Ergo: flirting and flirty waistcoats were probably best avoided.

'If you say it is a cheerful nod to the season, I shall wear the mustard.'

Even though he was suddenly desperate to wear the burgundy, especially if it imbued him with the powers of flirty mischief. And she *had* made him feel *vigorous*. Very vigorous indeed and decidedly off-kilter. The sort of off-kilter which made him yearn to be rash and frivolous for a change, rather than staidly sensible and depressingly dependable. The sort of vigorous which tempted him to seize the day, and say to hell with his mountain of ducal responsibilities, flagrantly flouting all calm and measured reason.

Before he could grab the lacklustre *brown* mustard, Julius whipped it away and tossed the identical-looking *brown* burgundy at him instead.

'For the love of God, live dangerously! Besides, you always look jaundiced in mustard. I cannot, in all good conscience, allow you to spend the entire day looking as if you have a liver complaint.'

Then he sauntered to the door with the offending garment still crumpled in his fist, in case Marcus had a mind to argue, when in truth he was relieved to be forced into the vigorous and flirty garment instead.

'Out of interest, which room will you be breakfasting in today?'

Whichever one the bewitching Miss Harkstead ventured into.

'I haven't decided yet. Probably the one with the fewest husband-hunters within it.'

'Then be assured I shall see you there.'

Twenty minutes later, and feeling very dashing in burgundy, despite being unable to see it, Marcus took the servants' stairs down so he could peep through the concealed entrances in the panelling, in the hope of locating Miss Harkstead before everyone else located him.

Bizarrely, aside from Uncle Horace and a few of the older gentlemen, the bigger formal dining room was deserted. Before he could do a similar reconnaissance of the Oriental Room, Gibson appeared out of nowhere, effectively blocking the route.

'If you are looking for all the ladies, Your Grace, then you should probably know that, despite your dear mother's best efforts at chivvying them, almost all of them are using every excuse they can muster to loiter, crushed in the hallway, until you or Lord Julius make a decision regarding where to eat this morning.'

Marcus knew the bland delivery was his butler's preferred way of telling him off.

'Then we expect a veritable stampede.'

'Ah…'

'You should also know that Cook is fuming, because her perfectly coddled eggs are cooling on the sideboard and she is resolute she will not be making more when she has slaved for hours since dawn making the things.'

The butler stared at him unblinking as the unmistakable cacophony of excited feminine noise from the hallway beyond the dining room finally permeated the door he was hiding behind.

'However, if Your Grace is not looking for *all* of the ladies, but seeking somebody in particular, the ladies not in the hall are Lady Trumble and her companion Miss Harkstead, who are currently the only two people enjoying perfectly coddled eggs in the Oriental Room.'

'The only two?' How gloriously typical of Miss Harkstead not to be impressed enough by his title to wait around for him. 'Then that sounds like the perfect room for me to quietly break my own fast, Gibson. You know how I enjoy a bit of peace at breakfast time.'

'As you wish, Your Grace.' His wily retainer did not appear the least bit fooled.

'To that end, I wonder if you could…um…'

'Unsubtly hint to the baying hordes so eagerly awaiting you at the foot of the stairs that you will imminently be heading to the *formal* dining room, Your Grace?'

'That would be splendid, Gibson.'

'Very good, Your Grace.' Gibson bowed. 'I shall quickly don some protective armour and tell them. I shall also ensure there is a physician standing by in case anybody is trampled during the charge.' Then he smiled. 'I hope she is worth it, Your Grace.'

His butler had been gone less than a minute when the swarm of young ladies, followed by their ambitious mamas, flooded into the formal dining room, all scanning the place settings for the optimum position. Marcus watched them, baffled, through a crack in the door as the most intrepid flung themselves into the chairs nearest the head of the table and breathed a sigh of relief he wouldn't have to suffer them as he stealthily retreated along the warren of corridors which led to the Oriental Room.

Exactly as Gibson had said, the object of his fascination was indeed sitting prettily sipping tea. Looking positively ravishing in brown. Or green. Or hopefully flirty red.

Completely unsure of what he was going to say, but mindful he probably had less than five minutes alone with her before the unsuccessful overflow of guests gave up trying to secure a seat in the other room and were forced to venture here instead, he smoothed down his waistcoat, checked the knot in his cravat, neatened his cuffs, took a calming deep breath and then opened the door.

'Good morning, ladies. Would you mind if I join you?'

# Chapter Five

At the unexpected sound of his deep voice behind her, Eliza almost choked on her tea. She managed to avoid choking only by sloshing half the contents of her teacup into the saucer, and then half of that onto the pristine white tablecloth. She winced at the sight of the spreading brown stain blooming on the starched linen and he winced back.

'G-good morning, Your Grace.'

She had positioned herself in order to see both the main door and the secret door he had emerged from yesterday, on the off-chance he might turn up and because, being proudly sensible by nature, she wanted to appear thoroughly nonchalant if he did. So to say she was more than a little stunned to learn there was yet another concealed entrance, through which the wretch had slipped at the precise moment she had been daydreaming about him was an understatement.

'You startled me, Your Grace.'

'And you almost gave *me* an apoplexy!' Great-Aunt Violet clutched at her heart as she scowled at him, before her irrepressible good humour returned. 'Although I can hardly say I blame you. It is absolute chaos out there.'

She gestured to the chair opposite them, and for some inexplicable reason Eliza's pulse quickened as he sat in it.

'And by all accounts, Your Grace, chaos entirely of your making.' Great-Aunt Violet slanted them both an odd look before she picked up her cup and stared at the Duke over it. 'I am curious, young man…what on earth possessed you to change things?'

'Well, I…er…'

Before he could form an answer a wide-eyed and breathless Aunt Penelope bustled in, dragging Honoria. 'There you are, Eliza *dearest*!' The beaming smile she bestowed upon her niece did not touch her eyes. 'We've been looking everywhere for you!'

As her aunt never called her 'dearest', nor beamed at her—or even smiled, for that matter—it did not take a genius to work out her scheming aunt was here solely for the Duke.

She had been spitting feathers last night when she had discovered, third-hand, that Eliza and the elusive Duke had dined together. In fact, she had been so annoyed her niece hadn't immediately come to fetch both her and her cousin to join them, Eliza hadn't dared inform her aunt Penelope that dinner had been their second encounter yesterday.

She hadn't quite found the opportunity or the words to confess that to Great-Aunt Violet yet, either, preferring to claim it had been a chance meeting at dinner, rather than one brought about entirely by the handsome Duke's design after she had so shockingly called him arrogant, rude and pompous.

But she knew her great-aunt would read much more into his actions than mere happenstance. She would convince herself he was interested in more than Eliza's forthrightness and undeferential conversation, and then everything about this house party would become unbearable. Romantic people like her great-aunt were incapable of being sensible if they sniffed even the vaguest whiff of the chance to matchmake. No matter how far-fetched that chance was.

Aunt Penelope practically threw Honoria into the seat next to Eliza, before settling down beside her and pinning the Duke with her stare. 'I did not have the opportunity to introduce you to my daughter last night, Your Grace.' She framed her daughter's face with her outstretched arms like a painting. 'Although I daresay you must have already noticed her. My Honoria is widely regarded as an incomparable.'

*Only in her aunt's mind.*

'And she has only been out for one Season.'

'I am delighted to make your acquaintance, Lady Honoria.' The Duke politely inclined his head before his gaze wandered briefly back to Eliza's, amused. 'Your cousin has told me a lot about you. You too, Lady Broadstairs. She holds you both in *great* esteem.'

Would it be wrong to kick a duke under the table? Before she could consider it properly, her foot shot out and clipped him on the shin. Her insolence was rewarded by a very naughty smile, which suited him immensely.

'In fact, you are to be commended in your generosity, Lady Broadstairs—not many would be so sympathetic towards such a *scandalously impoverished* relation as to welcome them so completely into the bosom of her own family. I applaud your egalitarianism.'

Oblivious to the irony, Aunt Penelope took his words as a gushing compliment. 'We do what we can for poor Eliza, and we are grateful to you too, Your Grace, for condescending to speak to her last night. It was most benevolent of you.'

He nodded solemnly, clearly enjoying himself. 'Yes, it was, wasn't it?'

Before Eliza could kick him again, Great-Aunt Violet nudged her with her knee.

'And here he is again... Being egalitarian once more by honouring *us* with his presence rather than breakfasting with the masses. What an *unexpected* privilege.'

'Thank goodness!' Never one to squander an opportunity, Aunt Penelope gave a smile that was all teeth. 'For this gives us a chance to get to know one another properly, away from all those other silly girls.' She dismissed them with one flick of her wrist. 'I know my Honoria has a million questions for you, Your Grace. Don't you, Honoria?'

There was a pregnant pause, during which Eliza could only imagine her supercilious aunt pinched her poor daughter's thigh hard under the table, because Honoria suddenly sprang forward, eyelashes fluttering for all she was worth, her expression decidedly panicked.

'I do indeed…'

But then the poor thing floundered, until her mother stepped into the fray to save her. 'You wanted to ask him about his favourite…?'

'Colour!'

Honoria was clearly relieved to have remembered one of the many questions her mother had relentlessly drilled into her during the carriage ride on the way to Manningtree, attempting to school her in the subtle art of charming small talk and the not so subtle art of flattering an eligible gentleman.

'I wanted to enquire as to your favourite colour, Your Grace.'

Judging from the brittle smile now pasted on her face, her mother was mortified at the choice, which made Eliza want to hug the poor girl close and tell her she had done well in trying. Honoria was only eighteen, and desperately wanted to please everyone. Most especially her mother.

'Well…um… I suppose my favourite colour is…'

'That is entirely and singularly the most pointless question to ask my brother, ladies.'

The Symington spare suddenly filled the door frame, making a point of standing still to take in every face around the table, before finally resting his eyes on Eliza. He grinned.

'He's not one for the frivolousness of colours—but if you were to ask me the same question, I'd say it depended entirely on my mood and the situation. Today I have a penchant for lilac.'

Which just so happened to be the exact shade of the sensible woollen walking dress Eliza had donned for the planned trip to the village.

Two dark eyes nowhere near as disarming as his brother's fathomless blue ones twinkled. Then continued to study her as he sat down in one of the vacant chairs beside his sibling.

'Aren't you going to introduce me to your lovely new

*friend* Marcus? Seeing as she is the only person at this table I have not yet had the pleasure of meeting?'

'Miss Eliza Harkstead—my brother.' The Duke's tone was unusually clipped. Either he was annoyed by his brother's mere presence, and his shameless flirting, or he was annoyed at his insinuation that she and he were friends. 'Lord Julius Symington.'

Eliza politely shook his hand, and then waited for two footmen to pour hot beverages. While everyone else took more tea, she and the Duke took chocolate. She tried not to read more into that pathetic coincidence than was wise, but did so anyway. What *was* it about this Duke which made her suspect they were kindred spirits?

As she pondered this, she felt Lord Julius staring at her, and in turn realised she had been staring at his brother. To cover it, she smiled and returned her attention to the latest arrival. 'Actually, we have met before, my lord.'

The darker sibling looked surprised by this. 'We can't have… I'd have remembered.' Then Lord Julius grinned wolfishly, earning him another censorious glare from his brother. 'You make quite the impression Miss Harkstead.'

'I couldn't have made that much of an impression as it was only last month, my lord. We briefly collided by the refreshment table at the Renshaw ball. I was fetching Lady Trumble some lemonade.' Which was an entirely inconsequential detail which nobody would have any interest in. 'And you were—'

'Oh, stop, Eliza! Can you not see you are embarrassing the man?'

In true Aunt Penelope fashion, she couldn't hide her true colours for long and, in view of her obvious annoyance that her niece was currently receiving more attention than her daughter, she took great pleasure in publicly knocking her down a peg or two.

'Why would he notice a decrepit old lady's drab companion in a ballroom full of the highest in society?'

Then she turned to the Duke and his brother, apparently all concern and totally oblivious to Great-Aunt Violet's shock at the insult.

'Bless her, but dearest Eliza does tend to fade into the background. Sadly, she inherited her father's drab colouring.' She managed to say this as if the mere mention of Eliza's papa was distasteful. 'He is a bookkeeper, don't you know?'

There was true malice in her eyes when she leant forward, her next words an octave above a whisper to ensure everyone heard them.

'But of course you *must* know. When my foolish sister ran away with him to Gretna Green it caused quite the scandal. It even made it into *The Times*.'

A fact Eliza's parents had always worn like a badge of honour. A declaration of the real strength of their love. She had always admired them for that and occasionally, when she wasn't being cynical, she wished she might one day find someone who would be happy to brave a scandal alongside her.

'My poor sister was thoroughly ruined, of course, and has not dared to show her face in society since. But, being of liberal mind and charitable nature...' she grabbed Eliza's hand and squeezed it hard '... I have opened my arms to her daughter and pray she is not completely tainted by her mother's rash actions all those years ago.'

Whatever effect Aunt Penelope had hoped her poisoned dart would have, it wasn't the heavy veil of awkwardness which immediately cloaked the table like smog. To their credit, both the Duke and his significantly less handsome brother seemed appalled by her aunt's bad manners. Great-Aunt Violet was silently shooting daggers at her, still not over being called decrepit, and for once even Honoria wasn't oblivious to the tension because she looked every inch like a startled rabbit.

It was the Duke who finally broke the silence. 'Are your

parents still nauseatingly pleased with their rash decision, Miss Harkstead?'

Those bright blue eyes were kind, yet behind them she saw the challenge, daring her not to give a fig.

'They are, Your Grace. Neither has regretted it for a second. They treated the story in *The Times* as their wedding announcement rather than a scandal.'

Great-Aunt Violet joined the rescuing cavalry charge too. 'Eliza's mother and father enjoy one of life's rarest gifts, Your Grace—a genuinely happy marriage. They are as nauseatingly besotted still as they were the first moment they met.'

'Then it all happened for the best.' He toasted her with his chocolate cup. 'My parents were lucky enough to share much the same feelings. They met, fell instantly in love, and married just three short weeks later.'

'At Christmas time,' added Lord Julius with a surreptitious wink in her direction. 'I believe that caused quite the scandal in its day too. Back then, dukes were not supposed to marry into the merchant classes.'

'Our maternal grandfather was an importer of goods from the Orient, Miss Harkstead.' The Duke gestured around the room with a smile. 'And *his* father was a midshipman on a merchant frigate.' His next smile seemed only for her. 'So, you see, I am not a particularly *illustrious* duke after all—all things considered.'

A blessedly quiet Aunt Penelope had been put securely back into her box, and along with the growing trickle of clearly confused guests hovering outside the door, wondering where they were supposed to go, the Duchess arrived and forged a determined path through them all, like Moses parting the Red Sea.

She shut the door behind her before she glared and said, '*There* you are!'

Both Symington males winced, looking like two naughty schoolboys caught doing something wrong, then plastered on twin smiles before answering in unison. 'Good morning, Mama.'

'I will grant you it *is* morning, but I can assure it is not a good one! You've created pandemonium, Marcus! And we shall be having words about it! Many, *many* words! Just as soon as this lawless debacle of a breakfast is over.'

Obviously furious, she sat down next to her eldest son.

'Cook is beside herself. She slaved for hours over the coddled eggs.'

Then she leaned across the Duke to address his brother.

'And do not think for one second you will escape my censure, Julius! It has not gone unnoticed that you chose to skulk off just now rather than assist me with our confused guests!'

Instead of appearing chagrined, Lord Julius grinned and gestured to Eliza. 'Have you met *Miss Harkstead*, Mother?'

The change in their mother was instantaneous and dramatic. 'So *you* are Miss Harkstead…' All trace of fury now gone, she stared curiously at her across the table. 'I am delighted to make your acquaintance, Miss Harkstead.' An odd look passed between the Duchess and her younger son. 'I have been looking forward to meeting you, though I must confess you are not at all what I imagined…'

Before Eliza could respond to such an unexpected comment, the Duke stood decisively. 'Shall we all eat?' He seemed uncomfortable. Suddenly eager to be gone. 'Cook will have my guts for garters if I allow her famous coddled eggs to go cold.'

'I'll wager they are already cold!' The Duchess skewered him with a terrifying glare before she also rose. 'And that is assuming you have some of your guts left intact after I have finished with them, my dear. And believe me—that is yet to be decided.'

Then she glided to the sideboard first.

# Chapter Six

All Marcus had wanted was five minutes at breakfast to get to know Miss Harkstead better. When that had failed miserably, thanks to everyone else, he had hoped he might be able to grab some time for a quiet chat during the interminable shopping trip to the village, but he had been thwarted at every turn by every other young lady present, all of whom were now determined to do whatever it took to outshine her, or to scupper his attempts even to exchange a few mere pleasantries with her without a vast audience.

A similarly frustrating evening of the dreaded wassailing loomed before him, and already he was at his wits' end. The herd of duke-snaring husband-hunters now circled him on the driveaway and there was still no sign of the object of his fascination.

But her aunt Penelope was there. Front and centre with her daughter in tow, practically glued to his side and doing her utmost to convince him that her child was the woman of his dreams.

'Oh, you really must hear her sing, Your Grace. My Honoria has the voice of a nightingale. Many people have commented upon it. Perhaps tonight, if we place her next to you during the carolling, you will hear her. She has such a talent for—'

'Sorry to interrupt. Urgent estate business...'

Julius grabbed his arm and pulled him away, striding from the suffocating crowd at speed towards the stables.

'Thank you! I owe you. Again.'

'You most certainly do.'

His relief at being saved was temporary. 'That doesn't mean I am not still peeved at you for this morning.'

'I cannot think what for,' Julius said.

How to put it without sounding pathetic and jealous? 'For having so much fun at my expense over breakfast and for flirting outrageously with all the ladies throughout it. The latter was quite unnecessary, Julius, and frankly a bit unseemly so early in the day.'

'As I recall, I only flirted with Miss Harkstead during breakfast.' Clearly on a mission, Julius was striding across the lawn, but not so fast that Marcus didn't see his smug grin. 'You can hardly blame me—she is uncommonly pretty. And, for the record, I thoroughly intend to flirt with her some more tonight.'

The temptation to grab him and punch him on the nose was overwhelming.

'I don't think she would appreciate it.'

'Surely you mean that *you* wouldn't appreciate it, big brother?'

Marcus opened his mouth to speak and then promptly shut it until he could temper his words. Silently he fumed, only to watch his brother's smug grin being replaced by a bark of laughter.

'I knew it!' He waved his finger too close to Marcus's face. 'Your blatant jealousy has revealed the truth. You are smitten with her! Admit it.'

'I am not smitten.'

Yes, he was. And the fact that he was, so soon, was ridiculously rash, when he was never rash.

'I hardly know her.'

But he desperately wanted to. Everything. Every last fascinating minute detail.

'We have exchanged a few pleasantries over two meals. That is all. And during one of those I hardly got to say two words to her, thanks to you, our mother and that dreadful Lady Broadstairs.'

'Only twice?' His brother feigned unconvincing innocence. 'Gibson must be mistaken, then, because he said the pair of you were chatting for ages yesterday. In the library...' Those damn eyebrows rose again. 'Completely unchaperoned.'

'I really do not appreciate what you are insinuating!'

'Did you kiss her?' His brother's eyebrows wiggled suggestively. 'You know Mama's views on kissing. It only takes one kiss to recognise *the one.*'

This needed to be nipped in the bud—and then he would hunt down Gibson like a dog and give him a piece of his mind too. Butlers were supposed to be discreet and loyal, not tittle-tattle turncoats who spread gossip to the rest of the family.

'Absolutely nothing untoward occurred during that brief meeting. I will have you know I was a perfect gentleman!'

His brother rolled his eyes. 'Of course you were. Sadly, I expected nothing less.'

'Sadly?'

Julius stopped dead on the pathway to the stable yard, so abruptly Marcus almost crashed into him, and then had the gall to look annoyed.

'Heaven forbid you should act on impulse once in a while! Everything always has to be so measured and pragmatic and blasted *sensible* for you!'

To add insult to injury he grabbed Marcus by the shoulders and shook him.

'Sometimes you need to forget you are a blasted duke!'

Marcus prodded his brother firmly in the chest. 'I *am* a blasted duke! A job with such crushing responsibilities I wouldn't wish on my worst enemy. Unfortunately, it is not something I can ever forget!'

'I know, but...' Julius sighed as he let go. 'What if Mama is right? What if there is one special person for each of us? Where the connection is instant and undeniable and draws you like a magnet? Meant to be? Fate...'

'Have you been at the wassail early?' Marcus pointed to the shadowy crowd of ladies still watching them from the driveway. 'Rabid husband-hunters, the lot of them! All dragged here by their mamas to entice and then trap us both!'

'I appreciate that one of Mother's dreaded house parties isn't the ideal place to meet the woman of your dreams, big brother—largely because Mama will become unbearable on the back of it and make my life intolerable as a result—but...' He huffed out a breath. 'I've seen the way you look at Miss Harkstead and she at you...'

Miss Harkstead had been looking at him? His heart instantly swelled in his chest at the thought.

'Wouldn't it be awful if you were *so* sensible, *so* measured, *so* pragmatic and averse to the idea, purely on principle, that you missed the chance fate has thrown at you?'

'Surely you, of all people, do not believe all Mother's fairy tale nonsense about fate and history repeating itself? Love at first sight is a myth, Julius. I hardly know her.'

Although, bizarrely, he felt he did. Know all that truly mattered at least.

'Or at least I know nothing beyond the fact she seems refreshingly different.'

And lovely and clever and gloriously unimpressed with his title...

'Nor will you, unless you take a chance. You have a few hours, Marcus. Tonight, tomorrow, one ball, and then she leaves first thing the next morning with everyone else. Don't waste them. *Seize the day!* Take some time to really get to know her and at least explore the possibility before you dismiss it completely.'

And there was the rub.

'In case it has escaped your notice, this house is teeming with eager ladies all doing their level best to monopolise my every spare second. Amongst all that, do you seriously think I will have the time or the privacy to get to know any one of them better.'

'Do you think I haven't considered that?' Julius's answering grin was smug. 'I have a contingency plan all worked out. In fact, if my exceptionally cunning plan works, you will owe me such a huge debt of gratitude I fully intend to take the whole of Mother's next dratted house party off.'

'I don't follow...' But suddenly he desperately wanted to.

'Lady Trumble, deaf Lady Audley and a couple of the other old dears aren't going to go wassailing, because the walk is too far for their legs. They are going to stay behind at the house. Which means either Miss Harkstead remains with them, as Lady Trumble's companion, or she joins the circus over there and you will never have a moment's peace together.'

'So?'

'So I have come up with a brilliant idea to include the old dears in the wassailing festivities whilst also giving you some time alone with the bewitching Miss Harkstead.'

'She's not *my* Miss Harkstead—' He found himself talking to his brother's gloved hand.

'I am well aware of that fact, cretin. Just as I am well aware of the fact you would very much like her to be. Therefore, you either grab the bull by the horns, and commit yourself to riding upon it for the next few hours, or regret it for the rest of your sensible, measured, pragmatic and miserable life.'

A depressing scenario indeed.

'What's the plan?'

'I have arranged for the old dears to be driven to and from the village by carriage. Lady Trumble has agreed with me that she cannot possibly ride in that carriage without her indispensable companion by her side. But, as there are only four seats in the carriage, Miss Harkstead will have to ride alongside the coachman.'

'I still don't follow.'

'That is because I have yet to apprise you of the shocking

calamity which has necessitated my dragging you so unceremoniously away from all those hideous husband-hunters.'

Julius slapped him firmly on the back, obviously very pleased with his own ingenuity.

'In a cruel coincidence, the entire staff of the stables have been laid low, after eating something which didn't agree with them, and there is nobody fit enough to drive the elderly ladies tonight. But I know that you, being selfless, pragmatic and egalitarian, will want to offer to step in and save the day and drive them yourself.'

Which would give him a blissfully solitary fifteen minutes with Miss Harkstead beside him on the way there, and another fifteen on the way back.

'I suppose it is only right that I drive them—as the head of this household, the stables and our guests are ultimately my responsibility after all.'

'That's the spirt!' Julius grinned as he gazed towards the stables. 'I shan't accompany you. The ladies are waiting in the carriage for the hero of the hour to save the day, and they would probably unanimously much prefer *me* to do it if I present them with the option, so you'd best get cracking while I give all the other ladies the bad news. We will meet you in the village.'

'Don't hurry.'

'I won't—and I would advise you to take the long way around to give Cupid a greater chance. Oh, and before I forget, I have brought you a little something which might come in handy if you do miraculously discover she is the one.'

His brother rifled in the pockets of his greatcoat before slapping something into Marcus's gloved hand.

'Mistletoe?'

Julius shrugged before he sauntered away. 'Well, it *is* Christmas, big brother. It would be a crying shame not to make use of it. *Carpe diem* and all that.'

# Chapter Seven

Eliza did not believe in sulking. She had always thought it a childish and fruitless endeavour when actual communication was better in solving a dispute. However, being banished to ride in the carriage with the older ladies rather than walking with all the others galled and, despite her using all the communication skills God had given her, even resorting to a full-on arm-waving tantrum, Great-Aunt Violet had refused to be moved.

But now that she was stuck in the carriage with the old ladies, forced to sit on the driver's box in the cold, while they enjoyed hot bricks inside, she was sorely tempted to sulk regardless. And all because she suddenly had foolish and fanciful ideas about a certain handsome and charming gentleman who happened to be a duke.

Miserably, she arranged the thick blanket she had been issued as consolation tightly around her legs and gave herself a stiff talking-to before the off. Yes, he was a duke—which, of course, rendered her silly, pulse-flittering fascination pointless.

He enjoyed her conversation and her company, but to read anything more into his interest would be folly. To add to that, he had the pick of all the young ladies present and swathes of eligible and aristocratic beauties who weren't, so why on earth would he be interested in *her*?

She had no fortune. No connections. No real clue how to behave properly in his world. And—and this also galled—none of the ethereal prettiness most of those young ladies possessed. She was too dark, too tall, and altogether too sensible even to try and compete.

So why did she want to?

In the midst of tonight's inevitable melee, she really did not stand a chance of a minute alone with him to engage in any conversation. Today she had been lost in a sea of eager and significantly better dressed young ladies, only standing out perhaps because she'd positively refused to be eager. She might well be too dark, too tall and too common for a duke to woo, but she had her pride and she knew she was still a rare prize in her own right, exactly as her parents had always told her.

She was a long way from ugly. In fact she was intelligent, quick-witted, outspoken and fun. She had always secretly wanted a man to fall head over heels in love with her for all those qualities and flatly refused to settle for anything less. So if he wasn't interested that was entirely his loss. She would be sensible about it rather than bereft.

There would be another man whose eyes twinkled. Whose mere presence made her pulse quicken. Who were as handsome and as charming and as attractive as him. Who called to her soul as he did.

The Duke of Manningtree wasn't unique.

Surely?

'Good evening, Miss Harkstead.'

As if she had somehow conjured him up, he strode through the entrance to the stables looking sinful in a dark greatcoat. Largely because he had the shoulders for it. He was hatless, and his dark golden hair was windswept. It suited him, making him seem more approachable and more human than he sometimes did when he was obviously being the Duke.

'Good evening, Your Grace.' Then, because she couldn't think of a single other thing to say, she stated the obvious, pointing to the empty seat next to her. 'We are awaiting our driver. Apparently the usual coachman has been taken ill.'

'I am told the whole stable staff have been taken ill. Some

mysterious ailment has forced them all to their beds, I'm afraid.'

'Oh…'

That probably meant she would be staying here, now that Great-Aunt Violent had suddenly and selfishly decided she couldn't be without her. She couldn't help thinking that Aunt Penelope had got to her and insisted Eliza remain below stairs, where she belonged, on the off-chance a miracle occurred and the Duke suddenly became interested.

'So I am the cavalry.'

One big hand grabbed the footplate before he hoisted himself up and to her great surprise seated himself next to her.

'I hope you don't mind being stuck with me for the duration—but somebody has to ensure the safe delivery of the wassailing pot to the village.'

A kaleidoscope of butterflies instantly flapped in her tummy.

'Not at all, Your Grace.'

In the confined space, those big shoulders touched hers. She could feel the warmth of his body all the way down her right side. Smell the seductive spicy scent of the fresh cologne on his skin. As he snapped the reins and the carriage lunged forward over the cobbles, she bounced against him repeatedly because she couldn't keep her balance. How could she when the only thing to hold on to was him?

They rode in silence as he effortlessly manoeuvred the large conveyance out of the stable yard, taking a different route down the driveway from the one she was familiar with, which went past the house. Instead he turned to cut across the parkland until they were shrouded in trees.

The only sounds she could hear were the crunch of frosty gravel beneath the wheels and the rapid thump of her excited heart. There were no stars, just the hazy shadow of the full moon behind a dense blanket of low clouds which threatened snow. As Eliza tried to calm her slightly erratic breathing, she watched her breath and his mingle in frozen

mist in the frigid air, wondering what it was about him that
called to her so.

'Can I let you into a secret?'

His voice whispered past her ear and down her neck,
leaving a trail of goosebumps in its wake.

'I loathe wassailing. It's all so…cringingly embarrassing.'

Pride forced her to make conversation, even though she
had the overwhelming urge simply to sigh at him. 'My father
used to feel that way too—until he discovered the liberating benefits of wassail. He claims the only way to do it is
three sheets to the wind. He has a point. It's actually rather
enjoyable after the first few cups.'

He laughed. It was a soft, deep, seductive sound which
came from somewhere deep in his chest. 'Perhaps drunk,
I might enjoy it.'

'And I think I might enjoy the sight of you drunk, Your
Grace. It's not every day a girl gets to witness an illustrious
duke stumbling around and singing carols with abandon.'

'Ah…but then who would drive the old ladies home?'

'I am sure I could manage it, Your Grace.'

'You can drive a coach and four?'

'I confess I have never done it, because society has strange
rules when it comes to females and big carriages, but…' She
glanced at the loose reins in his hands and shrugged with
haughty bravado. 'It doesn't appear particularly hard. I can
drive my father's phaeton perfectly adequately, and I sincerely doubt four horses are more troublesome than two.'

'Then give it a go.' He gently waggled the leather ribbons
at her in challenge. 'You'll have to prove your mettle before
I relinquish command later and drown myself in wassail.'

Never one to shrink away from a challenge, Eliza took
them. The well-trained horses didn't blink an eye.

But if she had hoped having something to do other than
be aware of the Duke would calm her nerves, she was wrong.
As she attempted to concentrate on the dark road ahead she

could feel the weight of his stare as he watched her, which inevitably led to self-consciousness.

'Am I doing something wrong, Your Grace?'

'You are doing a splendid job. But you know that already, don't you, Miss Harkstead? You are not one to feign ignorance or weakness to make a man feel superior.'

'Do you need to feel superior? Because as an illustrious duke, Your Grace, surely you already are?'

He smiled, then shook his head. 'I thought we had an agreement whereby you don't fawn or defer to me in any way.'

'I was hardly fawning. If anything, I was being impertinent, Your Grace.'

'And there it is again…the fawning. There's at least one toadying *Your Grace* in every sentence. Call me Marcus and please try to forget I am a duke. For it is only a title and really says nothing else about me at all.'

In that moment she realised he didn't particularly enjoy being a duke—and he was right. Dismissing him as nothing but a duke did him a great disservice, because the man beneath the lofty title was actually rather…lovely.

'All right, Marcus…' How delicious that sounded on her tongue. 'You have my word I shall never *Your Grace* you again.'

'Thank you, *Eliza*.'

He lingered over the vowels as if savouring them, thankfully unaware his disarming deep voice played havoc with her nerves.

'However, you do realise this new informality between us is going to put a great many noses out of joint? My aunt Penelope's especially. She has still not forgiven me for apparently stealing Honoria's thunder.'

Mortifyingly, she realised that sounded as though she was suggesting he had taken a fancy to her—mostly because Great-Aunt Violet had repeatedly told a po-faced Aunt Penelope she was convinced of it, which in turn had given Eliza false hope that perhaps he might. That was a far-fetched prospect in the grand scheme of things, no matter how much the fanciful romantic part of her approved of it, so she quickly clarified in case he ran a mile.

'We servants are supposed to be seen and not heard, remember?'

'As if Honoria could ever steal *your* thunder, Eliza. Or anyone else for that matter.'

He gave her an odd look, then quickly looked away to stare at the road, leaving her wondering as to the exact meaning of the compliment.

Was it a back-handed compliment, on account of her customary forthrightness in comparison to all the other ladies at the house party? Of course it was. Because if it wasn't then the only other way to take it was that he considered all the other ladies paled into insignificance against her. Much as she would love that to be true, and as much as the mere thought of this intoxicating gentleman being enamoured with her thrilled her, she had to face facts.

She could call him Marcus until she was blue in the face, but he was still a duke and she was still a bookkeeper's outspoken daughter. Assuming it was a back-handed compliment was undoubtedly more sensible.

'My father despairs of my forthrightness. He is much more even-tempered and reserved than me.'

'But not so reserved that he didn't run away with his employer's daughter. Tell me that story. Your parents' *scandal* intrigues me.'

'It began just before Christmas...'

'Really?'

'Really. One week before, to be exact, when my father started a new job as bookkeeper to my grandfather. To hear my mother tell it, she took one look at him and her heart was lost.'

They both smiled at the improbability of that claim.

'And was your father similarly afflicted?'

'Apparently so, because he recklessly took advantage of a piece of mistletoe.'

'The impertinent scoundrel.'

'I believe my mother was not the least bit offended by the impertinence, for she kissed him back and has always claimed that one kiss was all it took to know they were destined to be together.'

'And they eloped off the back of it?'

She nodded. 'On Christmas Eve.'

'Astounding…' He frowned, staring off into space before shaking his head. 'That really is the most bizarre coincidence. It eerily echoes my own parents' story.'

'How so?'

'My mother met my father just days before Christmas, and also claims that just one kiss was all it took. I believe there also might have been mistletoe involved—although knowing my mother I wouldn't be at all surprised to discover it wasn't. But my father proposed on Christmas Eve and they were married by special licence.'

A bizarre coincidence, indeed. 'Then we are both the products of reckless unions.'

He stared at her oddly. 'Successful reckless unions. Perhaps there is a moral there?'

Was he suggesting they be reckless too? Her pulse quickened at the thought.

'It looks like snow.' A nicely inane thing to say to cover a potentially awkward moment. 'I should imagine Manningtree Hall looks beautiful in the— *Oh*…' Out of nowhere, the driveway had ended and there was a crossroads. 'Which way?'

'Left.'

She tugged on the ribbons but couldn't seem to get the horses to move quickly enough as they barrelled towards a bank of grass and the inevitable ditch. All at once his arm came around her and he added his strength to the task at hand while enveloping her completely with his big body.

'I am so sorry.'

...ds

...to be
...w her, or
...t's chance
...ite his name
...d then, perhaps

...ce the full spirit of a
...que ensemble, complete
...sk sprouting dyed ostrich
...ked him up and down with

...ndsome this evening. Even if
...tume. All we need is the finishing
...sh, she turned towards an extensive
...s on the table, part of the vast collec-
...ulated over the years at eye-watering ex-
...ered them.

...beg of you. No mask for me. Everyone pres-
...w who I am when I greet them anyway.' Not to
...ey would probably have to be daft not to recog-
...in a stupid mask.

...nsense, dear. It is a *masquerade*. As the host, you
...olutely *have* to wear a mask to the festivities. It is our
...hristmas tradition.'

'I didn't *have* to wear one last year, and I cannot recall you complaining then, so it's not that much of a tradition.'

'That was last year, dear. This year I positively insist. Family traditions are almost as important as family, and as

'My fault.'

His lips were next to her ear now, which made it difficult to focus on anything other than them.

'I should have warned you sooner. Four horses take a bit longer to turn than two.' With inches to spare, he managed to straighten the carriage. 'That was close.'

As was he. It felt wonderful.

'But no harm done.'

He let go of the reins and shifted slightly. Eliza made the mistake of turning towards him to agree and found herself gazing into the fathomless depths of his eyes, still partially caged by his arms and entirely happy to remain so.

'Thank goodness...' She couldn't seem to look away. Didn't have the strength to move. It felt scandalously intimate.

She watched a single snowflake land on his face a moment before another landed coldly on hers, and they both smiled in wonder as more magically followed.

'You were right about the snow...' His fingers brushed a flake from her cheek and she felt his touch everywhere. 'I hope it settles.'

'So do I.' Recklessly, she hoped there would be a blizzard—one which snowed them in and gave them more time together.

His gaze searched her face, then dropped to her mouth where it lingered. Then lingered some more.

She found herself worrying her bottom lip with her teeth, because she now tingled with awareness, silently willing him to close the distance between them and put her out of her misery. Wanting him to kiss her. Needing him to kiss her. Desperate to discover if just one kiss really was all it took to *know*...

His head dipped.

She leaned closer.

Then their foreheads crashed together, thanks to an enormous pothole in the road.

# Chapter Eight

Seize the blasted day?

He was sorely tempted to strangle Juli[us] [for putting such] ridiculous ideas into his head. The only [reason he] was because it was hardly his brother's f[ault he'd cho]sen to 'seize the day' at the single mo[st dangerous mo]ment and had nearly killed four swee[t old ladies because] of his recklessness.

For at least the fortieth time that [day, he rubbed the] throbbing bump on his head and [wished that hitting] the pothole had shaken him out [of whatever spell he'd] been cast under, thereby forcing [him to slow down be]fore they careened into the pre[vious] [one that had spun them] in the other direction.

If that wasn't bad enough, [his spur-] of-the-moment attempt to st[eal a kiss had caused an awk]wardness between them wh[ich meant that instead] they had spent the final ten [wretched minutes of the] journey making tortured small talk. [The one bright spot of Ju]lius's blasted mistletoe had been burning a [hole in] his pocket as fate and Christmas had both laughed a[t him.]

Since then it had gone from bad to worse. He had hardly seen her during the wassailing, and as he had been formalising the right words for the journey home, in order to subtly probe if she might be as interested in him as he was in her, disaster had struck.

Although it had been blatantly obvious that it wasn't a *real* disaster, it would have been downright bad manners to call the tenacious daughter of an earl a liar at the time. Hence, instead of driving the old ladies home with Eliza

*Invitation to the Duke's Ball*

his mother's guests properly—as he had faithfully prom-ised when she had been a surprisingly good sport about the radical and chaotic changes he had implemented upon her carefully orchestrated mealtimes. With another one hun-dred guests invited on top of the fifty or so who had been here for three days, she genuinely needed to have all han[ds] on deck tonight.

That, of course, wasn't his only motive. He wante[d to be] there in case Eliza slipped in early. As soon as the se[rvant] his trusty lookout Gibson did, there was not a c[hance] in hell Marcus wasn't going to immediately w[hisk her onto] on her dance card for the very first waltz. A[nd the second] rashly, the second too.

'Good evening dear.'

His mother, always one to embra[ce the spirit of the] masquerade, was dressed in a baro[que] with an ostentatious Venetian ma[sk] feathers. She smiled as she loo[ked him up and down with] approval.

'You look especially h[andsome tonight, I can see] you aren't wearing a cos[tume, only a] touch...' With a flouri[sh she gestured to her own] array of gaudy mask[s] tion she had accu[mulated at great ex]pense, and pond[ered]

'Please—I [hope the gentlemen of the eve]ent will kno[w...] mention t[hat you didn't] nise hi[m...]

abs[ent...]

him[self with calm] assurance. One [by one, all the] other aspect of his nor[mal life had] been thrown up in the air.

Realising he was wasting precious time, [he] shoved the wilting piece of tragically unused mistle[toe in] his pocket, then put on his coat. After one final look in the mirror, he dashed down the stairs early, to receive all long as there is breath in my body I shall uphold ours. Masks are so romantic, don't you think?' She sighed. 'Besides, you know they have a soft spot in my heart. It was thanks to a masquerade that I met your father...'

Right on cue, here came the guilt. A weapon his dear mama used ruthlessly.

'Don't you remember how he adored our Christmas masquerades? What would he say if he heard you refusing to wear a mask?'

'You can spare me the lecture, Mother.'

Behind him, Julius was sprinting down the stairs to join them.

'I'll take the biggest one you've got. That way I can use it as a shield if any of the ladies get out of hand.' He slapped Marcus on the back. 'I suggest you do the same, big brother. In fact, if you go for one of those painted plague mask monstrosities, you can protect yourself from the tenacious ladies who will be doing their best to accost you under all those ridiculous balls of mistletoe dear Mama has hung everywhere.'

Before their mother could select one, his brother snatched up a terrifying-looking devil's face which was framed in a halo of sharp metal flames.

'This should do the trick. If all else fails I can use it as a weapon as well. Now, where's the brandy?'

Marcus was sorely tempted to follow him. There was so much nervous energy pumping through his veins, such an uncharacteristic sense of haste and fear of time running out, a bit of Dutch courage wouldn't go amiss.

'This one is perfect for you, Marcus!'

As his brother stalked off, his mother held aloft a surprisingly small but expensive-looking mask which he had never seen before. It was painted with harlequin diamonds in varying shades of blue, each diamond no bigger than a quarter of an inch in height and edged in what looked suspiciously like gold.

'Please tell me you haven't been shopping again? I swear you must already have a mask for every day of the year.'

'Not at all, darling—well, perhaps I did buy one or two.' She grinned unrepentantly. 'But this one is old. Practically an heirloom. In fact, this was your father's favourite and it matches that lovely waistcoat perfectly. He always loved blue too.'

Before he could argue, she lovingly traced her fingers over the surface with such tragic longing that any attempt at reasonable argument evaporated, and he didn't have the heart to be unreasonable. Beaten into submission by his own noble conscience, he allowed her to tie it on.

When she stepped back to admire her work there were obvious tears in what he could see of her eyes behind her own mask.

'You remind me so much of him in both looks and character, Marcus. You are so alike that sometimes it is uncanny… and I forget he is gone…' Her bottom lip trembled slightly before she banished her tears with a brave smile. 'You are such a credit to the Dukedom. So very diligent and responsible. Sensible to your core.' She smoothed her hand down his cheek before straightening his lapels to hide the obvious catch in her voice. 'He would be so proud of you.'

'I know.' They had all adored his father. 'But I cannot take the credit. He taught me everything.'

'Not everything. You have built on his good work, just as he did on his father's, and that reminds me of him too.' She stepped back to assess her work. 'And, exactly like him in his prime, you look so handsome tonight that all the ladies will be fighting over you.'

If she was trying to buoy him up, that was the most depressing thing she could say. If he couldn't even manage a bit of peace at breakfast, thanks to their aggressive guests, things didn't bode well for tonight, when they would all be demanding his attention.

'There will be some diamonds in the room tonight,' his mother said.

Only the one diamond. As far as he was concerned, all the rest were paste.

'So make sure you dance, darling. Even if it is only just once. You never know...history might repeat itself and—'

'The first carriages are arriving, Your Grace.' Gibson interrupted before she could finish her sentence, and thankfully it distracted her from whatever hopelessly romantic pearl of wisdom she was about to share.

Instead, she ushered him towards the ballroom, retrieved his fearsome brother Beelzebub from the refreshment table and made sure all three Symingtons were in their correct places in the receiving line before she instructed the waiting footmen to throw open the doors.

# Chapter Nine

'Whoops.' Aunt Penelope feigned shock as red wine quickly soaked into the front of Eliza's coral evening gown. 'I do apologise.'

Eliza could barely breathe, staring down at the huge bleeding stain as her stomach sank to her toes. Her beloved silk dress—her one and only remotely fancy evening dress—was completely ruined.

'You did that on purpose!' Great-Aunt Violet's face contorted with rage. 'I watched you throw it!'

'I tripped on the rug.' The other woman shrugged, unrepentant. 'It was an accident.'

About as much of an accident as the uncharacteristic glass of wine her aunt had insisted on drinking to calm her nerves this evening, when she rarely drank at all. She'd planned this. For the first time in her life Eliza had been genuinely looking forward to attending a ball, and her spiteful aunt had ruined it.

Unable to form words, because she couldn't breathe, she stared at the damning stain in shock.

'Hurry and put something else on, Eliza. We don't want to be late.'

The smugness in Aunt Penelope's voice confirmed her suspicion. Slowly she lifted her eyes from the devastation to stare at her, undecided whether to launch at the witch like a banshee or cry.

'She doesn't have anything else and you know it!' Great-Aunt Violet went on the rampage for her, practically spitting in the other woman's face. 'Of all the mean-spirited, dirty, jealous, disgustingly low things to do, Penelope! How *could* you?'

'Oh, for goodness' sake, Auntie. It's not as if it matters. It wasn't much of a gown in the first place and Eliza can wear anything—nobody ever notices a companion.'

'*He* noticed her. That is what this is about, isn't it? Do you seriously think that by sabotaging Eliza the Duke might switch his allegiance to your daughter?'

'I do not like what you are implying, Aunt, but I am not going to spoil my evening by arguing with you.'

Penelope wrestled her hands into evening gloves, checked the position of the laurel crown which matched her pristine trailing silk toga costume, just to rub salt into the wound, then idly flicked one silk-clad wrist in Eliza's direction.

'It's only a bit of wine. I'm sure one of the maids will be able to get it out. If that fails, feel free to borrow something of Honoria's. You don't mind, do you, Honoria?'

'Of course not.'

Her faerie-themed cousin, complete with protruding translucent wings, smiled, her gaze quickly taking in the size of Eliza compared to her, troubled in case she was wrong in her assumption that absolutely nothing she had in her over-stuffed trunk would fit.

She looked distraught when she finally managed to work it out. 'My pink gown might do. It's a little bit long for me.'

In forlorn desperation, Eliza dabbed ineffectually at the enormous stain with her handkerchief, praying for a miracle even when she already knew nothing short of an act of God himself could save her poor dress.

'That is very kind of you, Honoria.' She would not lower herself to sniping at the poor girl in her frustration, any more than she would give her cruel aunt the satisfaction of see-ing how much her malicious actions had hurt her. None of this was Honoria's doing and the child meant well. 'I shall give it a try.'

Bravely, she forced herself to smile past the lump in her

throat. Aside from the fact that the gaudy cerise colour of her cousin's most capacious gown really would not suit her at all, even if the garment was too long for Honoria, it would be a good six inches too short for her—and probably a good ten inches too narrow. She and her petite cousin were cut from different cloth in every sense of the word.

'There—a solution has been found.' Aunt Penelope's eyes were cold as they stared back at her triumphantly. 'Eliza will change and we will see her shortly downstairs. In the meantime, we cannot leave Their Graces waiting. As honoured house guests, it would be very poor form for us all to arrive late.' She strode to the door. 'Come, Honoria!'

'I would rather wait for Eliza, Mama.' Incapable of artifice of any sort, her cousin rushed to her side. 'I am sure Their Graces will forgive us any tardiness under the circumstances...'

Pride had Eliza smiling brightly, ridiculously glad that her papier-mâché mask hid the sudden tears swimming in her eyes. 'It's all right, dearest. I shall be down as soon as I can.' The quicker they were gone, the quicker she could mourn the death of her silly dreams about tonight. 'You go. Have fun.'

'But what if my pink gown doesn't fit you?'

They all knew it wouldn't. Like reality returning with a bang, it was a foregone conclusion.

'Eliza is a resourceful girl. I am sure she can sort it out to everyone's satisfaction without us getting in the way. Are you coming, Aunt? I would hate you to miss out on one of the chairs.' She shrugged when Great-Aunt Violet violently shook her head and glared at her through narrowed eyes. 'See you downstairs.'

The decisive click of the door closing as they left sounded like a death knell. That was it, then. Eliza would never discover if the Duke had actually intended to kiss her in the carriage. She had been sure he had wanted to, she'd felt it overwhelmingly in her heart. Until she'd spoiled the magical moment by losing complete control of the carriage and the precious, poignant moment had been lost.

Stupidly, she had been too embarrassed to broach the subject last night. But, after lying awake for hours chastising herself for her cowardice, she had tried repeatedly all day to catch him alone and pluck up the courage to ask him about those strangely loaded moments last night as the snow had begun to fall. But there were too many other ladies clamouring for his attention. Not to mention Aunt Penelope, who had stuck to her like glue.

Had her snooty aunt seen her longing glances? If she had, she must have also caught him staring back at her. Their shared smiles... Was she reading too much into them too? But Great-Aunt Violet was convinced Marcus had singled her out for special attention and, whether it was vain or not to think it, something told her that her new, complicated and giddy feelings for him were reciprocated.

The masquerade was her last chance to find out, and now that was gone she would likely never know. In the circles she walked in, she would never collide with the Duke.

'I'll fetch a maid.' She felt Great-Aunt Violet's arm come about her slumped shoulders. 'Perhaps she'll be able to get the stain out. A quick rinse and an iron and it might look as good as new.'

'We both know that's hopeless. The dress is ruined.'

'Then we'll find another dress, Eliza! A better one! There are enough gals at this soiree—surely one of them must be your size?'

They both also knew those same *gals* would be as ruthless as Aunt Penelope in doing all they could to keep Eliza out of the equation tonight. As far as they were concerned she had dominated more of his time these past few days than a lowly lady's companion ought to, and they would have no sympathy for her plight. She couldn't walk past any gaggle of girls without feeling their hostility. All day it had been positively palpable.

'It doesn't matter. Really,' she said, even though it did.

Pragmatically, she reluctantly acknowledged that this was doubtless for the best. Especially when she was destined to be disappointed by it all in the long run.

'I've been waiting for a chance to finish *Don Quixote.*'

With decisive fingers, she undid her mask and tossed it on the dresser. It was hardly as if she had seriously expected Marcus to pay her special attention tonight, when he was technically the host and she was still very much just a lady's companion and a bookkeeper's daughter. If she'd gone to the ball, they might have exchanged a few pleasantries in the crush, but ultimately she would have ended up wandering back to the tiny room next to this one, feeling miserable that nothing had come of her silly daydreams after watching him dance with young lady after young lady.

And even if he had paid her special attention, then what? He would only have wanted an oasis of undeferential conversation to keep him sane for the duration of this house party. She had witnessed first-hand how difficult he found it all and could hardly blame him for seeking sanctuary from all the madness. To assume, to dream he wanted anything beyond that was as fanciful as a child's fairy tale, and Eliza was not prone to flights of fancy—not when in truth he would likely wave her off with all the others tomorrow without so much as a backward glance.

This way *was* for the best. Harder, certainly braver, but the sooner she accepted what might have been had never really been a possibility in the first place, the better and the quicker she would get over it.

'I might even ask for a bath to be drawn and make the most of the peace.' Then she could weep to her heart's content and lick her foolish wounds in private.

'Out of the question!' Great-Aunt Violet stomped to the door, then wagged her finger decisively. 'You are due an adventure! Do not get in the bath! If it is the last thing I do on this earth, I *will* find you a dress, missy, and you *shall* go to the ball!'

Alone at last, and feeling entirely deflated, Eliza slipped through the connecting door to her room. A room which screamed of her status as companion. It was small and neat, with the minimum of fuss, and close enough to her mistress to be at her beck and call. Then, still hopelessly stained and feeling wretched, she lowered herself to lie on the mattress. She stared dejectedly at the ceiling, trying not to listen wistfully to the strains of the orchestra wafting from the floor below and wondering what might have been regardless...

'Miss Harkstead?' The light tap seemed to come from behind the panelling rather than from the door. 'Can I come in?'

Before she could answer, a hitherto unnoticed secret door in said panelling swung open to reveal, of all people, the Duchess of Manningtree.

'Lady Trumble said you'd had a bit of a mishap.' She smiled kindly as she stared at Eliza's ruined dress. 'But now I see it's not so much a mishap—more an outright catastrophe.'

It had taken her almost half an hour to talk herself into a state of calm acceptance and to suppress the tears, yet apparently just one mention of her ruined gown could bring them all flooding back. As wiping them away and showing her pain to the Duchess was out of the question, she tried not blinking instead, in the hope they would not fall.

'A famine is a catastrophe, Your Grace, not missing a ball.'

'Oh, pish!' She waved that away. 'You will not miss the ball, dear. Because I have come here expressly to rescue you.' She held out her hand and pulled Eliza to stand, then eyed her dark curls thoughtfully. 'It is as I thought...we are more or less the same height. I'll concede I have a bit more padding nowadays, but back in the day I was as slim as you—

which is most fortuitous, for I am bound to have something suitable you can wear.'

'Really...you do not need to go to any trouble...'

'Oh, I do, my dear! I absolutely do! It is Christmas, and if ever a miracle is going to happen it is now. Come.' Still holding her hand tightly, she dragged Eliza through the hidden door before she could argue otherwise. 'Let us seize the day!'

Too stunned by the bizarre turn of events to know what to think, she obediently followed. The world behind the panelling was astounding. As they sped along, a warren of identical narrow passageways veered off in every direction.

'It is like a maze, Your Grace. So confusing...'

'It is—but you get used to it. After thirty years, I think I've finally memorised the route of most of them. The Third Duke of Manningtree had them built into the structure as the house was built. He hid priests during Queen Elizabeth's reign, by all account, or so my husband told me.'

They came to a sudden halt at the end of one long lit corridor and the Duchess briskly opened the door. Behind it was the most sumptuous bedchamber Eliza had ever seen.

'It comes in very handy when you need to save time, rather than traipsing along all the official hallways, or want to avoid people. It is especially good for avoiding people.' She strode straight to an enormous oak wardrobe. 'Now... Let's find you a nice dress...'

She almost disappeared as she rummaged through the shelves, then emerged with a heavy garment wrapped in a long garment bag made of calico which she lovingly laid out on the velvet comforter on an enormous carved and canopied bed.

'This one should be perfect!'

As the gown emerged from the bag, Eliza sucked in a breath. Even in the dim lamplight of the Duchess's bedchamber the pale sapphire silk shimmered. Yards and yards of fabric emerged, full skirts and sleeves exquisitely embroidered with bold peacocks, their intricately iridescent tails fanned out on glimmering shafts of golden thread.

'It's lovely, isn't it?'

'Stunning...'

Eliza had never seen anything so fine. The way the fabric moved was like water, and the lace on the fluted elbow-length sleeves was as delicate and sparkling as a spider's web kissed with dew.

'My dear papa was a merchant who specialised in importing silks from the Orient. When he discovered this fabric he bought it for me, because he knew I loved blue. My mother's modiste turned it into this magnificent gown, which I wore to my first ever masquerade. Oh... I was *so* excited—and this dress made me feel like a princess...'

She sighed at the memory for a moment, then snapped back to efficiency and business in the blink of an eye.

'It's a sack-back—or if you want to be fancy a *robe à la française*—they were the height of fashion and sophistication when I was a girl. I did feel very daring wearing it. I suppose the style is a bit dated now—but not for a masquerade. It will take the two of us to put you in it, though, as sack-backs are not the easiest things to put on...what with the panniers and stomachers and all the complicated hidden laces. But, oh, my goodness...' The Duchess reached out and cupped her cheek, beaming. 'It will look *wonderful* on you.'

## Chapter Ten

Marcus scanned the ballroom frantically from his prime spot in a raised alcove for at least the fiftieth time in as many minutes, but there was still no sight of her, despite the presence of both Lady Broadstairs and Lady Trumble.

Thanks to the majority of those present having embraced his mother's masquerade theme to the full, finding anyone in the sea of ostentatious costumes and exuberant masks was near impossible. Added to that were the plethora of giant mistletoe balls, mere feet above their heads, hanging from the vaulted ceiling on long strips of scarlet ribbon.

He couldn't think where she had got to and was starting to fear she was not going to come at all.

'Still no luck?'

Like Gibson the butler, Julius had been dispatched to assist with the search—which meant they were both being remiss in their duties as hosts by flatly ignoring all the other guests.

Marcus didn't care if he was being rude. He didn't have any interest in the simpering and fawning—especially not tonight—and had stomached about as much of that nonsense as he could take.

'No.'

Even sending Gibson up to her room had proved fruitless. That room, as well as Lady Trumble's, and the library where they had first met, had been depressingly empty.

'I have no clue where she could possibly be.'

Time was running out so fast. They had already missed the first waltz, and if she failed to appear soon they were doomed to miss the second at midnight.

'Something must have happened.'

Or else he was reading far too much into their fledgling relationship. That was a distinct possibility. Just because he was completely smitten, it did not mean she was. Worse, it was quite possible she might be entirely ambivalent to him, as she was to society gatherings in general, and had chosen *Don Quixote* over the ball.

With Eliza, his being a duke was more to his detriment than a bonus. She was not impressed by rank and there was every chance his had put her off. She preferred bookkeepers.

'I might just check the library once again.'

'Allow me,' said Julius. 'You're more likely to spot her in this crush than I am.'

No sooner had his brother left his side than Lady Broadstairs replaced him, with her daughter in tow. 'Your Grace, you have clean forgot to add your name to Honoria's dance card and I would hate for you to miss your chance. It's practically full.' She thrust the card and the pencil at him. 'But she has saved you the next waltz.'

He stared at the outstretched card with disgust. 'I'm afraid I am already engaged for the waltz.'

Until the first bars were played he would cling on to hope.

'The cotillion, then? Which is next, if I am not mistaken...'

All of a sudden the atmosphere in the heaving ballroom seemed to shift, and he sensed her even before he turned around. When he did, it was as if all the crowds and chaos disappeared, evaporating like magical puffs of smoke as his eyes locked on hers.

Not caring if he was making his intentions or his feelings obvious, he ploughed through the swirling couples on the dance floor to get to her. Later, he would liken Eliza's pull on his heart to a Siren's call. Completely impossible to ignore.

He didn't notice his mother smiling next to her. Nor his brother close behind. All he could see was her. In a magnificent gown of vivid shimmering cobalt, her dark curls piled loosely on her head and falling artfully about her shoulders, her lovely eyes sparkling behind an exotically feathered mask, she was smiling just for him. A beautiful blue beacon in an ocean of mundane brown.

As he came nearer she dipped into an exaggerated curtsy, those same eyes dancing with mischief as they held his through the sooty fan of her ridiculously long eyelashes.

*'Your Grace.'*

He took her hand to help her up and didn't let go. 'You solemnly promised never to call me that, *Eliza*.'

'And there I was, thinking I was incognito...completely disguised. I wanted to be a mystery for once.'

'I would recognise you anywhere.' Her hand felt so very good in his. Perfect, in fact. 'What kept you?'

'A small mishap. But I am here now.'

'Thank goodness.'

He wanted simply to stand exactly where he was and stare at her, revelling in this odd moment they were sharing and the odder feelings coursing through him, and would have done so had he not spied Lady Broadstairs barrelling towards them as if her life depended upon it.

'May I have this dance?' It wasn't a waltz but, under the circumstances, it would have to do.

As if she read his mind, she turned slightly, took one look at the determination on her brazen aunt's face, and nodded. 'Yes, please. As far away from her as is humanly possible.'

With the cotillion in full swing, he led her across the floor but as they took their places the music abruptly stopped. A quick glance at the musicians' gallery confirmed why.

Gibson.

His wily retainer beamed down at him from his position next to the conductor as the first strains of a waltz began. While all the other couples dispersed hastily, to find their correct partners for the dance, he and Eliza were blissfully left all alone.

All alone, that was, apart from at least one hundred pairs

of eyes, watching their every move from the sidelines. Yet, oddly, none of that mattered.

He took her hand, she placed hers on his shoulder, and as he pulled her close and began to move his gaze never once left her face.

'You look beautiful tonight.'

'Thanks entirely to your mother.'

'My mother?'

'When my gown was ruined by my spiteful aunt Penelope your mother came to my rescue and lent me one of hers. Otherwise I wouldn't be here at all.'

'Then I shall thank her later.' For once all his mother's meddling was entirely welcome. 'She has saved the day.' Or seized it, as she was prone to. Either way, he was supremely grateful.

'She has.' Her face briefly clouded. 'Although I feel bad to be wearing this particular gown when she had so many others I could have borrowed—but she insisted. She said it absolutely had to be blue. No other colour would do. I wonder why?'

'I have learned, in all dealings with my mother, it's usually best not to ask.'

'Still—I'm so glad she insisted. This gown is lovely. She wore it to her first masquerade, apparently, and thought it would be a fitting choice for mine.'

Of course she did.

He found himself smiling at his dear mama's unsubtle machinations. It had been at her very first masquerade— here at Manningtree, during a Christmas house party, no less—where she had first met his father. The irony was not lost on him. His mother's gown. His father's mask. The hope of history repeating itself and romantic Christmas miracles…

He was beginning to believe—no, to hope—that there might actually be something to it. Because this, dancing with

Eliza under these chandeliers, felt suspiciously like fate. It was astounding how perfect and right she felt in his arms.

As they danced, she gazed into his eyes as if searching for something elusive, and he found himself extremely content to stare back, enjoying the way the hundreds of candles which lit the room brought out twinkling flecks in her dark irises, and the way just being with her made him feel.

'I cannot tell you how relieved I am that you are here, because there is something I've been meaning to ask you since last night,' he said.

'Then ask away.'

'You see, the thing is…'

Out of nowhere, the formerly deserted dance floor had apparently filled while he had been oblivious. All around them now were eyes and ears. Most making no secret of the fact they were eavesdropping.

'I see we have company again,' she said.

'Not for long.'

Deftly, he twirled her to the furthest edges of the dance floor before he attempted to speak about anything personal and private. But before he could tell her all the things he still had no earthly idea how to say the music came to an end. It was only when he became aware of the other couples on the floor curtseying and bowing to one another that he remembered to release his hold.

He gave her the briefest and stiffest bow and held out his arm, his nerves returning with a vengeance. 'Will you take a turn with me?'

'If that is what you wish.'

She seemed nervous too, and perhaps she also felt the peculiar atmosphere which had engulfed him, heavy with the weight of words that desperately needed to be said and feelings neither of them fully understood.

He led her towards an alcove, in the vain hope he could find a quiet spot as well as a convenient ball of mistletoe, but then in his peripheral vision he noticed that his choice of direction had galvanised several of the duke-snaring husband-hunters to follow.

So far they were edging ever closer subtly, but that wouldn't last long. If he was ever going to say what he absolutely had to, then he now had only two choices—drag her outside through the French doors into the chilly snow-covered gardens, or scandalously sneak her through the hidden door in the panelling.

Unsure which was better, he clumsily deferred the decision to her.

'I really wish to speak with you, Eliza…but I fear I cannot do it here.'

If she turned him down flat, he would rather not be humiliated in front of an audience. He saw her eyes flick to the unsubtle clump of young ladies who had suddenly decided to loiter behind a pillar and to his utter relief she nodded.

'We do seem to be being followed. Or rather you do. As I am not a duke, they are certainly not following *me*.'

'We could take a walk around the terrace, or we could…'

'Escape through the panelling? I am assuming there is a door hidden near here too, seeing as there seem to be everywhere else.'

'There is indeed.'

She gestured towards the dance floor with a curt nod of her head, alerting him to the wholly unwelcome sight of Lady Broadstairs, who was forging through the crowd, dragging her poor daughter behind her, with a look of sheer but furious determination on her face.

'Then shall we make a dash for it? Only Aunt Penelope has already destroyed my gown and I'd hate to give her the opportunity to ruin your mother's too.'

In a rush, Marcus helped her gather up her skirts and then, with her hand wrapped wonderfully in his, spirited them towards the corner of the ballroom and salvation.

There really was no time to lose. As they came closer he abandoned all decorum and broke into a very un-duke-like run, and to his delight Eliza kicked off his mother's quaintly heeled shoes from another era to keep up.

As soon as they disappeared behind the last marble column he pulled open the secret door and only managed to close it softly behind them with scant seconds to spare.

'I am sure they came this way.'

Aunt Penelope's voice was unmistakable.

'I thought I saw them head towards the garden, Mama.'

'Without her shoes, Honoria? Don't be daft, girl! There is six inches of snow…'

Marcus pressed a finger to his lips, silently turning the key in the lock as they listened to her family wander off in search of them. Then he took Eliza's hand once more.

Stealthily, they made their way down the narrow passageways. As he seemed to have a very clear idea of their destination she was content to follow, acknowledging it made no earthly difference because she would probably follow him anywhere.

When he finally opened a door she recognised the library, lit this time only by the dim moonlight as it streamed through enormous windows.

'That was close.' He breathed a huge sigh of relief. 'For a moment, there, I thought we were done for.'

They were both a little breathless from the exertion. Both giggling at the madness of it all.

'But we are alone at last…'

All at once he appeared very serious.

'You see, the thing is, Eliza…'

He seemed to be choosing his words very carefully.

'Yesterday—in the carriage…'

Exactly as he had in the carriage, he looked suddenly awkward in his skin. He raked a hand through his hair, leaving it delightfully dishevelled as he huffed out a sigh.

'I am really not very good at all this, so please bear with

me. Since I met you I have felt the overwhelming weight of
the hand of fate...'

He had started to pace, apparently wincing at his own in-
eptitude while he struggled to get out what he wanted to say.

'And, as much as it pains me to agree with my fanciful
mother's fairy tale nonsense, I find myself curious to see
if just one kiss really is all it takes to know for sure...' He
suddenly stopped dead to stare at her, patted his waistcoat
pocket for some reason, then sighed. 'But now apparently
I've lost my mistletoe.'

'I don't need mistletoe.'

And to prove it, before she lost her nerve, she quickly
closed the distance between them and pressed her lips to his.

His mouth was soft and gentle and, as kisses went, this
one began as quite a chaste affair. Yet it still held the power
to rock her to her core.

She sighed and melted against him, utterly powerless to
do anything else. When he deepened the kiss she wound her
arms around his neck, whispered his name like a benedic-
tion and pulled him closer, needing every inch of the contact as she kissed him wantonly back.

And what a kiss it was—passionate, honest and blissfully
sublime—and it told her so much more than mere words
ever could.

Breathless, he broke the kiss for long enough to look at
her, and huffed out a giddy sigh of relief when he saw she
was as overwhelmed and undone by it as he.

'That was...enlightening.' She was still shamelessly plastered against him and she didn't have the wherewithal to
care.

He smoothed his palms along her curves possessively,
sending a wave of scandalous tingles to parts of her body
which had never tingled like that before.

'Yes, it was, wasn't it?'

She sat on the desk, her heavy skirts rucked around her
knees, so consumed by passion she had no recollection of

getting there. Their masks had somehow been discarded on the floor at his feet, alongside his cravat, which she had a vague recollection of removing while his mouth had been doing sinful things to her neck, although for the life of her she couldn't remember the exact details.

He had also thoroughly destroyed her hairstyle. A riotous cascade of unmanageable curls now tumbled about her face and down her back, and he wound his index finger in one of them before he kissed her again, smiling against her mouth as she felt the strength of his desire all the way through the heavy skirts, petticoats and panniers. An unnecessary barrier she was now impatient to feel there at all when she wanted to feel his skin against hers.

She decided to blame the gown for her complete lack of propriety. It made her feel very bold. 'Did the kiss tell you all you needed to know?'

'It did. Completely.' He tugged her hips closer and nibbled on her ear. 'For me, apparently, it is exactly as I feared. You, Eliza, are the only one. You?'

'My heart is hopelessly lost too.'

'In that case, I was wondering if...'

The wretch paused, because he had found the most sensitive piece of flesh at the nape of her neck. And as her needy body demanded more, so too did her heart.

'If...what, Marcus?'

'If you would consider seizing the day with me.'

'Just the day?'

'Well, I'm a cautious man by nature, so I thought we'd start with the day and build up to discussing for ever after breakfast.'

'For ever sounds absolutely perfect.'

'Then, seeing as we are undoubtedly the source of much fevered speculation already, and before we create a full-blown scandal which makes it into *The Times*, we should probably go and announce our engagement to the ballroom. Let's enjoy the outrage on your snooty aunt's face that her scandalously impoverished niece is about to outrank her, and suffer my mother's inevitable gloating that one of her tedious traditional Christmas husband-hunting parties has finally borne fruit.'

Those talented lips nuzzled her jawbone.

'Unless I can tempt you into seizing tonight first...'

Eliza pondered the dilemma for less than a second as somewhere in the distance she heard the clock strike twelve.

'I've secretly always wanted to be in *The Times*...'

\* \* \* \* \*

# A MIDNIGHT MISTLETOE KISS

Catherine Tinley

For my inner circle of Wise Women—
Emma, Leslie, Margaret, Niamh and Gilly.


Dear Reader,

I do hope you are enjoying these Christmas Cinderella stories. Here's mine. Poor Nell has been grieving since her father's death, and things look bleak for her this cold Yuletide. But never worry—a happy ending awaits!

Watch out for my next Regency novel, which tells the tale of a rather laid-back baronet and an outspoken governess with secrets who shakes up his hitherto quiet life.

*Catherine*

# Prologue

*London, 1818*

The Honourable Thomas Beresford, known to his brother and a select number of intimate friends simply as Tom, set down his pen. Ensuring it was aligned neatly with the papers on his inlaid mahogany desk, he addressed his man of business.

'Thank you, Merton. You may proceed with the purchase of the tavern in Winchester, but I have decided not to acquire any of the ships you have highlighted. Keep looking.'

Merton bowed. 'Yes, sir.'

'Now to the country houses. How many have you found?'

'Two, sir, with a possible third.'

Handing over three packages, each tied tidily with a leather thong, Merton stood impassively while Tom perused the contents. This took some time, but the man did not speak or move. He had been working with the Beresford brothers for long enough to know how things should be done.

'You have not included an estimated price for this one in Kent—' Tom tapped the middle sheaf '—Wyatt House, near Chiddingstone.'

The man nodded. 'Wyatt House is not yet officially available for sale. But I am assured by my various contacts that it will be very soon.'

'Tell me more.' Tom leaned back in his chair, stretching his long legs out in front of him.

'It is owned by a widow—Mrs Godwin. Her husband died almost two years ago and since then she has amassed substantial debts.'

Tom raised an eyebrow. This sounded promising. 'This purchase is to be different from my usual acquisitions, Merton. This house will be for my own use.'

Merton's eyes widened. 'Forgive me for asking, sir, but are you seeking a house that you will make your home?'

'Home? No!' Tom heard the vehemence in his own voice. With some effort, he continued in a milder tone. 'I have no need of a *home*, Merton. This house is a business acquisition that I will use when it suits me to entertain—nothing more. Dealing with business matters during a private house party is much more effective than endless London dinners and balls. My brother the Earl has use of the family properties for his own purposes, and I now believe it is time for me to acquire my own building.'

*There*. That had struck exactly the right tone. Tom had no need of a home. Boarding school had been the only home he had known for most of his life. In truth, any notion of *home* had left him once Mama had died...

Merton nodded, disapproval clearly apparent in his rigid posture. He spoke again, a little stiffly. 'You asked me to find options within reasonable reach of London, large enough for entertaining, yet not too large?'

'Correct. I do not want the encumbrance of a large estate.' Thankfully, all was businesslike again.

Merton pursed his lips thoughtfully. 'In that case, Wyatt House is the best of the three possibilities I have presented. The first, I understand, is modest in size and capacity, while the third has substantial lands which would have to be managed or disposed of separately. Wyatt House, I am told, is sizeable, yet comes only with gardens, not farms.'

'Very well. I shall consider how to approach this Mrs Godwin. Does she go out in Society?'

His aide gave a wry grimace. 'She does. Indeed, she is well-known for her lavish parties, both here in London and at her country home.'

'Ah—hence the debts.' Tom flashed a knowing smile at his man.

'Indeed, sir.' Merton paused. 'Last year, once she had come out of mourning, Mrs Godwin held a house party at Wyatt House for Christmas which lasted all the way until Twelfth Night. That is how I was able to ascertain that the house is large enough to host a sizeable party.'

'Excellent. You never fail me, Merton.'

His secretary remained impassive.

'Now, to cultivate an acquaintance with Mrs Godwin! Tell me about her.'

'She is young for a widow—not yet five and thirty. She was only married to the unfortunate Mr Godwin for a matter of months.'

Tom nodded. 'Perfect!'

Merton coughed discreetly.

'Yes?'

'I believe Mrs Godwin is in Town at present, sir. I also understand she is acquainted with Lady Jersey, who might help you secure an introduction.'

'Whatever it is I am paying you, it is not enough!' Tom declared with a grin, abandoning the frustrations of a moment ago. He stood and rang the bell for his valet. 'Now to don my best evening coat.' He flashed Merton a wicked smile. 'I have a widow to charm!'

# Chapter One

*Kent, December 23rd*

'Dash it all!'

Feeling slightly guilty about her shocking expletive, Nell glanced around furtively, but there was no-one nearby to hear her. The copse and the lane were entirely empty, save for her and a brace of pert ravens. The day was grey and miserable. In truth, her entire existence was grey and miserable. Melancholy was part of her now.

Sighing, she picked up the basket she had so carelessly dropped and began replacing all the holly and mistletoe she had been collecting. Her hands were already cold, and her old wool dress, dyed a dark winter green, was marked with mud along the hem. She brushed at it ineffectually, finding it hard to care.

It did not matter. Nothing mattered.

*Surely by now I should have adapted to my new life? One without Mama. Without Papa. Without love.*

It was not true. In truth, she might never adapt. Even now, nearly two years since Papa's death, she still expected him to come riding along this very road, to rescue her from the emptiness of her current existence.

But Papa and Mama were gone, and her chances of marrying were slim. She had never met a man she had the slightest inclination of marrying even *before* Papa's death and her loss of status. She was, it seemed, destined for a life without affection or warmth. And today, at the beginning of Christmastide, her unhappiness felt particularly acute. She was eternally downcast, spiritless, empty…

Her ears pricked up. *Hoofbeats!* A shiver went down her spine. No-one ever took this back road, for it led only to the abandoned cottages at the edge of the copse, and then on through open countryside. No-one but she and Papa, that was. They had walked and ridden this lane together through all the seasons of the year, collecting bluebells in late spring, blackberries in August, and Yuletide greenery in December. This had been their special place. Now she came here alone.

Visitors and tradesmen knew to take the main road linking Wyatt House with the village. Stopping at the edge of the copse, she glanced curiously up the lane. Her breath fogged in front of her in the crisp winter air.

A lone rider sat astride a magnificent black stallion. He had clearly seen her, for he slowed as he approached. They eyed each other, she taking in various details at a glance. Riding boots by Hoby, if she was not mistaken. Pale breeches clinging to muscular thighs. A Weston jacket hugging a well-built figure. A strong jaw, handsome features. Flashing dark eyes currently showing wicked amusement.

'Oh!'

'Quite,' he agreed, pulling up and dismounting smoothly. 'The surprise, I assure you, is entirely mutual. I did not expect to find—' his eyes swept over her, making her suddenly conscious that her dress, while demure in cut, was altogether too close-fitting, '—a Yuletide damsel in the area!'

Nell ignored this, asking directly, 'Are you lost? This lane leads only to Wyatt House, though from there you may take the road to the village.'

'You might say I am lost,' he replied obscurely, 'and yet I have found you, so today is already a success.'

She snorted. 'You would do well to abandon any attempt at flummery, sir, for it has no effect on me!'

'How refreshing!' He took her hand and bent over it, then frowned. 'Your hand is cold.' Taking both hands in his, he gently chafed them in his large warm ones.

She raised a shocked eyebrow and removed her hands. *He is very forward!*

'Now my hands are miraculously warmed,' she said dryly, 'you may be on your way.'

Stepping out into the lane, she turned left towards the house.

Gathering up the reins, he walked beside her, his horse following dutifully. 'It seems as though we are destined to follow the same path.'

'The difference,' she offered, 'is that you have a horse, sir. Might I suggest you ride it—' she pointed ahead '—in *that* direction? I have things to do.'

'What things?'

She indicated her basket. 'The house is to be greened to-morrow, for it will be Christmas Eve—as you must know.'

'What house is that?'

She tilted her head to one side. 'Why, Wyatt House, of course! It is the only house of any size nearby.'

'Ah! You work at the house, then?'

*I used to just live there. Now I work there too.*

'Yes,' she replied shortly. 'Can I offer you assistance, sir, by giving you directions to wherever it is you need to be?'

He slapped a hand to his chest. 'She wounds me! I am unused to having my attentions spurned in so heartless a manner.'

She raised a sceptical eyebrow. 'Again, I shall ask: where is your destination?'

He grinned, then replied in a more natural tone. 'Very well. I have reserved a room at the inn in Chiddingstone for tonight, but somehow I have found myself here, on this back lane. Cutting across country for a good gallop is refreshing, but it can leave one a little…lost.'

He had abandoned his attempt at charm and, strangely, had become instantly a little more attractive to Nell. His explanation also made sense.

*Oh, how I miss riding!*

Nell was much too busy these days to indulge in such luxuries. She straightened her spine. No point in dwelling on impossible things.

'If you follow this lane for a little more than a mile it will take you to the house. You can find your way to the village easily from there.'

'I believe I shall walk,' he announced, 'as I should not overtire my horse.'

His horse did not look particularly in need of a rest, but she decided not to point this out. He made no attempt to remount and leave her, and, stupidly, part of her was glad. It was a long time since she had been in the company of a good-looking young man. And now that he had decided to speak to her like a sensible being, she discovered she might quite like to share his company on this dreary day. So long as his behaviour remained gentlemanlike.

The implications of his earlier statement began to sink in. He had a room booked for *tonight*. Presumably he had broken a longer journey by stopping in Chiddingstone. He would, then, be gone on the morrow. She smiled inwardly. What harm would it do to enjoy his company for a short time? There was little pleasure in her life these days. Sparring with a high-handed but undeniably handsome man would lighten the darkness of her day a little.

*Oh, Nell!* she told herself. *Your foolish romantic leanings will bring you trouble some day!*

She tossed her head, shaking off the sensible voice in her head, and walked on.

They ambled slowly up the lane, idly debating the weather, the idyllic views, and the antics of a couple of startled rabbits who crossed their path. It took something more than half an hour.

Nell felt strangely at ease with him.

*Perhaps it is because here is where I am closest to Papa, even now.*

'We are nearly at the house—it is just around yon bend.'

'Indeed?' He had stopped.

She halted, eyeing him with puzzlement.

'Before we round the bend, then, I should like to thank you for your company today.'

He took her hand again, and this time she did not protest. *I like him!*

His dark eyes never leaving hers, he lifted her hand to his lips. His kiss sent shivers of delight racing through her and she caught her breath.

He, too, seemed somewhat stirred, for he stood unmoving, his gaze locked with hers, for a long moment. Then his horse moved, breaking the spell between them.

Confused beyond measure, Nell patted the greenery in her basket as if checking it would not fall. It gave her the chance to adopt a more usual demeanour.

They rounded the final bend in silence, and the house came into view.

'So this is Wyatt House?'

'It is.' Her voice shook a little.

*My home. My family's home for generations. Now in my stepmama's control.*

He was eyeing the building with what seemed like a keen interest.

'Is it not a fine-looking house, sir?' She could not help but ask. Here she had been happy for much of her life. Until Mama had passed away and then Papa had become ill…

'Actually, it is a handsome house indeed!' He sounded surprised. 'As someone who has lived mostly in London in recent years, I can appreciate a fine dwelling in an idyllic setting such as this.'

His hand swept wide, indicating the gentle slopes of the Downs in the distance, the woodlands to left and right, and the well-designed gardens in front of the house.

'The gardens are much prettier in summer,' she offered, leading him to a mounting block.

*Why am I seeking his approval?*

He mounted his stallion, then looked down at her. 'I thank you for your company. I assume the drive will take me to the Chiddingstone road?'

'It will. Turn left at the gate.'

He smiled, his handsome features alive with warmth. 'Might I ask your name?'

For an instant she considered announcing herself as Miss Eleanor Godwin, daughter, granddaughter and great-grand-daughter of the Wyatt family, but then, conscious of her now lowered status, decided against it. 'I am called Nell.'

'Nell.'

A thrill went through her at the sound of her name on his lips. They looked at each other for a moment, before she shook herself out of the unaccountable stillness that had settled around them. 'Good day, sir.'

As she walked towards the house she could sense he was still there, watching. It was only after she had heard him ride away that she realised he had not told her his name.

## Chapter Two

Inside, all was chaos. Nell's stepmother's guests were expected before dusk, and the servants were busy cleaning, setting fires in unused bedchambers, and preparing a mountain of food for the Christmas feast. Thankfully, they were too busy to notice anything different about her. Some of the servants had known her from babyhood and were altogether too perceptive.

Her stepmama, in an attempt to make economies, had let go two scullery maids, a housemaid and a footman this year, so everyone else—including Nell—had to work doubly hard to make up for it.

'Ah, there you are, Miss Nell!' It was Mrs Hussey, the housekeeper. 'Did you get some greenery?'

Nell nodded. 'I did!'

'Well, I hope you did not bring it inside the house! We have had quite enough bad luck already!'

'Never worry. I left it outside the kitchen door, ready for tomorrow. I see others have been gathering too, for there is quite a substantial pile ready to be used.'

The housekeeper nodded. 'All I can say is I hope Christmastide brings us all a change in fortunes.' She paused. 'Oh—the mistress has asked to speak to you, me, and Jemett when you arrive back. We are to go to her drawing room.'

Nell's heart sank, but she kept her features neutral. 'Very well.'

Beatrice, Nell's stepmother, was idly studying some fashion plates in a periodical when Nell and Mrs Hussey, along with Jemett the butler, entered the drawing room.

'Finally!' she declared, frowning. 'Where on earth have you been, Nell?'

'Gathering greenery for tomorrow.' Nell felt her heart flip a little at being with Beatrice. Sometimes her stepmama was perfectly cordial. At other times she was decidedly *un*-cordial.

Beatrice snorted. 'Avoiding work as usual, no doubt.'

Nell bit her lip against protesting at the injustice of this. Beatrice might behave rudely in front of the servants; she herself would not.

Beatrice brandished a piece of paper in front of them. 'Mrs Hussey, here is the final list of guests for the house party.' She handed it to the housekeeper, who ran an eye over it.

'I see, madam,' she offered tentatively, 'that there is a new addition to the list.'

Beatrice gave a self-satisfied smile. 'Indeed. A gentleman will join us who is a darling of the ton, brother to an earl, and one of the most sought-after persons in society.'

Mrs Hussey, Jemett and Nell exchanged worried looks. Nell, knowing it was up to her to speak up, did so.

'Beatrice,' she began. 'As you know, we have been preparing for this party for nigh on a month. Mrs Hussey has been organising bedrooms, sheets, cleaning and supplies, while Jemett has been polishing the silverware and bottling wines, and Cook has been preparing enough food to feed an army.'

Mrs Hussey sniffed, and bravely intervened. 'Never have I had so much to do with so little information!' She drew herself up, clasping her hands under her ample bosom. 'At least last year we knew who was coming in good time! *And* we had enough staff to manage it!'

Beatrice frowned. 'I am sure you will cope. You always do. Besides, these are mostly the same people who come to all my parties. It is the first time they have brought their children, it is true, but Nell tells me you have prepared the nursery on the top floor. There are plenty of beds for all the children and their nursemaids there.'

Mrs Hussey seemed unable to speak. Jemett paused, then pointed to the last name on the list. 'This extra guest, The Honourable Thomas Beresford...?'

The name meant nothing to Nell.

Beatrice smiled. 'His letter came only this morning. He will join us tomorrow—a day late, but it is quite the accomplishment for me to have attracted him!' Her brow creased. 'I do not know why I am seeing all these frowning faces. Why should one more guest matter so much?'

'Because we have nowhere to put him! Nowhere at all!' The words erupted from the housekeeper, in a tone of angry indignation.

Beatrice's brow cleared. 'Is that all? But that is easily solved.' They all looked at her, perplexity in their expressions. 'Nell will move out of her chamber during the house party and then you will have an extra bedchamber to work with. Nell, you can sleep with the servants.'

Nell could not believe what she was hearing. There was a roaring in her ears, spots before her eyes, and for a moment she worried that she might faint. The shame, the intended insult, the sheer *humiliation* was clear to all of them.

'Indeed she will *not*!' Mrs Hussey was outraged. 'As if she has not suffered enough indignities since—' She stopped abruptly.

Beatrice narrowed her eyes. 'You were saying, Mrs Hussey?'

The butler placed a calming hand on his colleague's arm. 'It would not be seemly for Miss Godwin to sleep with the servants,' he said.

The housekeeper clamped her lips together and gave a tight nod.

Seemingly satisfied that the housekeeper would not forget herself again, Jemett asked carefully, 'Is there no other solution?'

Everyone knew what he meant. Mrs Godwin occupied a large suite of rooms. She could easily have a bed set up for Nell in the corner of her own room, or in the smaller antechamber.

Beatrice, her expression carefully blank, feigned ignorance. 'Well, I am sure I have no idea what you mean. Nell, you will sleep with the servants and I shall hear no more of it.' She laughed. 'It is not as if I am telling you to sleep in the stables, after all!'

They stood in stony silence. Nell was incapable of speech.

Beatrice picked up her periodical. 'You may go,' she said absentmindedly.

They went.


Tom climbed the creaking stairway to his chamber in the Chiddingstone inn. The evening had been most enlightening. He had wondered if it would be useful to travel into Kent a day early, to explore the village and the area around Wyatt House, and his ploy had been amply rewarded. He had been free with his purse in the taproom tonight too, and had gained some useful information from the locals about the place.

They were proud of Wyatt House, and of the long connection between the Tudor village and the Wyatt family, but had no particular attachment, it seemed, for the Godwins.

Tom had pieced together what he thought was the true tale. Mr Godwin had married the last Wyatt descendant—a daughter—over twenty years ago, and then remarried after her death.

'They say,' a local farmer had confessed, his tongue loosened by the fine ale Tom had been purchasing in copious amounts, 'that he married *her*—the second Mrs Godwin, that is—because he knew he would soon cock up his toes and he wanted her to look after the lass.'

Godwin had died only months after his second wedding—as Tom already knew—but it was helpful to know that Mrs Godwin had no particular connection to the house or the area, and that the villagers had no particular connection to her.

*So much the better!*

Mrs Godwin, along with her husband's child from his first marriage, could start again elsewhere once she had sold Wyatt House to him and paid off her debts. If she had responsibility for a child then he might even use that to pressure her, if things became difficult. A life released from debt would certainly be better for anyone who had guardianship of a child.

In truth, he did not anticipate any difficulty. He had made it his business to cultivate Mrs Godwin's acquaintance, encountering her many times in London in recent weeks, and had already ascertained her type. Young and silly—although at five and thirty she was his senior by quite seven years— she had flirted desperately with him.

*She will always be young and silly,* he thought, *should she live to fourscore years and ten!*

Naturally he had easily managed to secure an invitation to her Yuletide house party. He had shown her a little charm and the merest hint of ennui at the thought of spending Christmas with his brother at the family estate and she had issued the invitation. He had written to say he would arrive on Christmas Eve, but had travelled here a day early to see what he might discover.

For a number of years after their father's death Tom and his brother Jack had, through financial necessity, done without the services of a valet—until their hard work in turning around the family fortunes had begun to bear fruit. Tom, having developed a taste for independence, still tended to dispense with the services of his man when he could.

When asked, Mrs Godwin had assured him that others among her guests would bring their personal servants, and she would ensure there would be someone to serve him at Wyatt House during the house party. So, as a consequence,

Tom had given his astonished and grateful valet a full fort-night's paid holiday and travelled to Kent by himself. His trunk would arrive tomorrow, carried by John Coachman.

So now there was no valet in his chamber to greet him. The landlord, who had accompanied him upstairs, helped him out of his boots and jacket, then bade him goodnight. The man had lit a small but cheerful fire in the grate, and the sheets seemed dry and clean.

Tom began to disrobe, reflecting on his earlier ride. He had seen Wyatt House itself, and been impressed. Well proportioned, in a good state of repair, and elegant in design and setting, it would make the perfect backdrop to his business-focused entertaining.

*I believe I shall acquire it*, he decided, quite surprising himself, since he had not yet seen the interior.

But this would not be just a paper transaction. It was something he would *use*. Live in for a substantial part of the year. He shrugged off the niggling emotions at the edge of his awareness. No, he was *not* buying it because of some absurd emotional response to the place. Of course not. He was buying it because logic told him it was the most suitable option.

Flinging his waistcoat on top of his jacket, he let his thoughts drift to his earlier encounter with the beautiful young woman in the woods nearby.

*Nell.*

Instantly a visceral response washed through him—mostly desire. Her hair autumnal auburn. Her skin pale with the fragility of winter light. Eyes hazel, flecked with green—the colours of the idyllic copse where he had first encountered her. Her figure svelte and elegant, with curves exactly where he liked them.

*My, she was beautiful!*

Her beauty was unquestionable, but he had also found himself intrigued by her character. She had not responded to his initial attempts at charm, and yet later in their walk, once he had been more straightforward with her, she had rewarded him with simple conversation unaffected by simpering flirtation or archness. She had been engaging, witty and intriguing. And he had been quite overcome when he had kissed her hand and heard her catch her breath.

Like most men of his age and status, Tom had had his fair share of liaisons. He tended to pursue women with the same single-minded dedication with which he pursued a business ambition, and then tire of them fairly quickly afterwards. He and his brother were alike in that regard. They were aware of their ability to charm, and used it ruthlessly, but both knew that succumbing to emotion was dangerous to their most important cause—that of financial security.

Having lost his mama—the person he had loved most in the world—at a tender age, he was determined to guard his heart. He was tempted by Miss Nell, but to be distracted right now might interfere with his aim of acquiring the house. He must be careful.

Who was she, though? She had indicated that she worked at the house, and yet there had been something in her demeanour that suggested she had not always been a servant. Her clothing had been of good quality, though rather faded and worn. Her voice had proclaimed her to be well-educated. And yet her simple dress and hairstyle implied she *was* a servant. A paid companion or governess, perhaps?

'That has to be it!' he said aloud, unfastening his cravat and flinging it onto the chair. She had to be governess for the Godwin child.

*She thinks she will never see me again.*

He had deliberately given her to understand that he was a random traveller, staying at the inn only briefly, knowing it would assist his chances of a kiss. His inner smile turned wolf-like as pride in his achievement suffused him. She had moved from her initial coldness to allow him to kiss her dainty hand.

*There! That is better.*

Treating it as a casual flirtation felt much more comfortable than examining the strange flutterings she had caused in him earlier.

He considered this further as he took to his bed. Oh, he was looking forward to encountering her again.

He grinned in the darkness, considering the mortification she would feel when she encountered him at Wyatt House. The beautiful Miss Nell, flirting with a stranger, only to find him a house guest for a full fortnight.

The possibilities were endless.

Yes, a light flirtation would do no harm, surely?

# Chapter Three

*Christmas Eve*

'Morning, miss.'

It was one of the housemaids.

Nell looked up from her embroidery. She had found refuge in the small parlour—a tiny room at the back of the house which no-one else wanted to use, and to which Beatrice had banished Mama's portrait. It had used to hang in pride of place in the main salon, but Beatrice had persuaded Papa to replace it with a painting of herself.

It galled Nell every time she thought about it, but she had learned to bite her tongue. And she now spent much of her time here, in this small room, when she was not busy with household tasks. Today, between final Christmas preparations and the needs of their guests, she had had very little time to herself.

'Well, Mary.' She smiled at the girl. 'Am I needed?'

Mary grimaced. 'The mistress wants you to help entertain the children again.'

'Very well.' Nell set down the handkerchief—a gift intended for one of Beatrice's guests—squared her shoulders, and made for the salon.

There she found a sizeable group of guests, chattering and flirting like a flock of exotic birds. They ranged in age from debutantes to middle-aged, but it was clear to Nell that the Marriage Mart was central to the thoughts of most of them.

There were numerous doting mamas or sets of parents with daughters to marry off, and a number of single and widowed gentlemen had been provided so they might all survey and measure one another.

None of the gentlemen, Nell had decided last night, were in any way engaging.

Some of the families had also brought their young children—three girls and a boy—who were permitted to join the adults only for brief periods, spending the rest of their time with their nannies and nursemaids. Last night Nell—who had always adored children—had taken the time to learn their names and help them feel at ease, and Beatrice had been uncharacteristically grateful.

'Nell!' she had proclaimed, as the last of her guests had departed for bed. 'I am so glad you were here to entertain the brats earlier. Why anyone would wish to spend time in the company of children, I do not know! But everyone whined so much at being separated from their children last Christmas that I found myself forced to invite the little fiends!'

Beatrice herself was currently holding court at the far side of the room, and she indicated with a nod that Nell was to busy herself with the gaggle of children currently sitting stiffly near the fireplace, seemingly intimidated by the watchful eyes of their parents.

Nell did so, and her gentle conversation soon drew them out. After just a few minutes they had started to warm to her again, and were soon vying with each other to tell her their favourite things about Christmas.

'Today,' she confessed to them in a confidential tone, 'we must green the house with sprigs of holly and mistletoe. The servants will help with the high boughs, which must be positioned with the use of ladders, while I shall make some for every room, and for the tables and mantels. But I do not know how I am to get it all done, for it is no little task!'

'We can help!' offered the girl called Alice, her eyes shining. At eight, she was the oldest of the group.

The others agreed enthusiastically, and Nell was just about to suggest they ask their parents for leave to come with her when the footman announced the arrival of the final guest.

'Mr Thomas Beresford!'

Nell, who happened to be looking in her stepmother's direction, was intrigued to see a slight flush appear on Beatrice's cheek. At the same time Beatrice's friend, the Dowager Lady Kingswood, gave her a knowing look.

*What?*

But the thought was forgotten as Mr Beresford entered. He was a handsome gentleman, slightly taller than average, and fashionably dressed. His hair was dark and coiffed *à la* Brutus, his figure was strong and lean, and his dark eyes held the wickedest delight Nell had ever seen.

Eyes that had gazed into hers just yesterday as he was kissing her hand.

Her heart lurched. *What on earth...?*

Mortification rushed through her and she bent her head lest anyone see her discomfort.

*What was I thinking? I should never have been so familiar with a stranger. Oh, if anyone were to discover the truth about my behaviour... I was shockingly intimate with him. And what must he think of me?*

She dared not contemplate all the ways in which she had compromised a lifetime of good behaviour with one lapse. Already she had been anxious about surviving Beatrice's Christmas gathering. With this added complication her anxiety had become anguish.

Tom bowed and said all that was proper as Mrs Godwin began introducing him to her other guests, many of whom he was already acquainted with. He had hoped Nell would be here, and so she was. As his gaze had swept around the room he had spotted her instantly, seated amid a cluster of young children.

*Just so. A governess, clearly.*

She was wearing the same green dress as the day before,

and her confused blush on seeing him was just as delightful as when he had seen it yesterday, after that unforgettable moment between them.

This was a sizeable party, he thought. And he had barely made it around half the people in the room when there was a flurry of agitation among the children. The young boy had taken exception to something another child—possibly his sister—had said or done and was protesting in the strongest terms.

'Mama!' he appealed to one of the ladies seated with Mrs Godwin. 'Alice says I am too little to help with the greening!'

Nell intervened. 'Of course you are not too little! Alice, I shall need everyone to help—including John. Now, I think we should begin without delay, for there is much to be done.' She stood, offering her hand to little John. He took it, smiling at her with something like adoration. 'Thank you, Miss Nell. I *knew* I was big enough!'

She smiled back at him, and Tom's breath caught in his throat. John looked to be about five—the age at which...

Had his mama, before she died, looked at him in such a way? It was too long ago. He could not remember.

*You will never marry,* he reminded himself. *Never be a father.*

'And this is Mr and Mrs Bridgeton...' Mrs Godwin, ignoring Nell and the children, was continuing with the introductions.

Tom replied automatically, conscious that the delightful Nell was even now making her escape, accompanied by the chattering children.

*You may run now,* he thought, *but you will have to face me eventually.*

He reassured himself briefly with flirtatious thoughts. But underneath them his attraction to her raged on, stronger than anything he had ever felt before. It was unsettling, and he did not like it.

He pushed thoughts of the governess away.

* * *

Nell accompanied the children to the red drawing room, where the servants had placed five large baskets of greenery—not just the mistletoe and holly that would form the core of the greening, but rosemary, laurel, and even bay leaves, which would be made into wreaths, boughs and garlands.

She gave each of the children one of the empty wreaths, their wicker twigs overlapping and intertwining to form a twisted diadem, ready to be adorned with greenery. As the children gradually fell silent, becoming absorbed in their task, she began to make up garlands, weaving boughs together and tying them with ribbon with practised efficiency.

While she worked diligently, replying appropriately to the children's occasional comments, in truth Nell's attention was elsewhere.

*He tricked me!*

She would never have flirted with The Honourable Thomas Beresford, nor allowed him to kiss her hand, had she known he was to be a house guest. Indeed, she had never done anything so daring in all her nineteen years. It was only because she had believed he was a passing stranger that she had done such a shocking thing.

*And because I wanted to.*

Honesty spoke in a small voice within her. Since Papa's death she had dwindled into a housemaid, a timid companion for Beatrice and a sometime governess. In the process somehow she had lost sight of *herself.*

Yesterday, in the company of the unknown gentleman, Nell had been fully and gloriously Nell again. Just for a short time. Today the greyness of eternal sadness had settled around her again—the invisible cloak she had worn since Papa's death.

No, she would never have done it had she known he would be a guest here. And he had probably known that. She had seen the keen intelligence in his eyes. It was one of the things that had attracted her to him. That and his handsome face, flashing dark eyes, well-formed figure...

But his quickness of mind, along with every other of his attributes, had been used against her. She bunched her hands into fists, wishing she, like the children, could voice unfairness as soon as she felt it.

In truth, unfairness had been her portion these past three years. First on her father's remarriage—what a catastrophe *that* had been! On being informed by his London doctor that the growth in his throat would prove fatal in the not too distant future, Nell's papa had courted and married Beatrice in a two-month whirl—without ever telling Nell.

'I wanted you to be looked after,' he had told her afterwards, ill and frail, and she, swallowing her hurt and concern, had thanked him. Well, what else could she have done?

Losing Papa had been the hardest thing in Nell's life, and her grief had not been eased by Beatrice's presence. The young widow, mourning a man she had barely known, had sighed with relief on putting away her black gloves and, lacking all sensitivity to Nell's suffering, declared what a relief it was that she could go out in Society again. Her lack of concern for Nell came not from any studied or deliberate coldness: rather, she was entirely unaware of Nell's feelings.

Nell's papa had left his widow with a generous portion, the exact terms of which had been agreed as part of the marriage settlement. And Beatrice seemed determined to spend every last guinea of it as rapidly as possible.

When Nell talked to her of economies, Beatrice simply looked at her blankly, before brushing away any suggestion of parsimony saying, 'Stuff!' or similar utterances. She continued to spend as much as she wanted on dresses, hats and slippers, while telling the housekeeper there were too many staff. It had been left to Nell to make the housekeeping budget stretch to cover the regular entertaining Beatrice insisted on—with the Christmas party last year causing the greatest expense.

This year, in anticipation, Nell had worked with the female staff to harvest every last morsel of food from the Wyatt House gardens. The horses had got fewer carrots and turnips, for the excess had been sold to the village store, while Cook and her remaining scullery maids—with Nell's assistance—had made as much bramble and rhubarb jam as they could manage, generating extra pennies to help buy wines and meat for Beatrice's guests.

And now Nell was expected to behave naturally with a man she had allowed to be quite outrageously familiar! For the next fortnight she would have no option other than to be in his company.

*Oh, how mortifying!*

Thankfully, the children had provided her with a means of escape today.

*I foresee myself spending a lot of time with the children in the next two weeks,* she thought wryly.

She ordered lemonade for her charges after an hour, and helped John with some of the holly twigs that were refusing to stay where he wanted them. By late morning the children's wreaths were ready, and Nell herself had created a sizeable pile of garlands and mistletoe boughs, complete with the red ribbon with which they would be suspended.

But even with all their efforts, three of the baskets remained full to the brim with uncompleted work. So it was with mixed feelings that Nell responded to an offer of help from two of the guests as the party gathered in the dining room for nuncheon.

Lady Cecily was a young lady around her own age with whom she had become friends over the past two years. Cecily was the daughter of Beatrice's close friend the Dowager Lady Kingswood, who was just as flighty and bird-witted as Beatrice. Nell had often wondered if Lady Cecily suffered the indignity of having more wit and common sense than her mama.

*Like me with Beatrice.*

To her right, she heard Beatrice laugh out loud at something Lady Cecily's mama had said. 'My dear Fanny,' Beatrice declared, 'I have never met anyone so amusing as you are!'

*Amusing?* Nell thought uncharitably. *Lady Fanny is about as amusing as a severe dose of the flux!*

She realised that Lady Cecily was still eyeing her evenly. 'Of course!' Nell said in a rush. 'I shall welcome the assistance, for there is much to be done!'

'Wonderful!' gushed the other young lady, Miss Bridgeton. 'I recall as a child there was nothing more exciting than the thrill of Christmas Eve. Don't you agree, Mr Beresford?'

Nell's heart skipped as she realised Mr Beresford had joined them in the dining room. She stole a quick glance at him. Same handsome features. Same air of confidence. Same wicked gaze. She looked away, ignoring the inconvenient increase in her pulse.

'Oh, I cannot agree, Miss Bridgeton,' he drawled, 'for I can think of many more exciting things than Christmas. What is it, anyway, save forced gaiety and wasted food?'

Miss Bridgeton looked uncertain for a moment, and then her brow cleared. 'You are roasting me!' She laid a playful slap on his arm. 'Why, *everyone* loves Christmas!'

Nell, who had decidedly fallen out with Christmas over the past few years, said nothing. She no longer allowed herself to think of her happy childhood Christmases. The thoughts only made her sadness worse. However, it did not sit well with her to be in agreement with the deceiving Mr Beresford, so she remained silent.

'After nuncheon we are to help with the greening. You should join us, Mr Beresford!' Miss Bridgeton was all charm.

'I should like nothing better!' declared Mr Beresford.

Nell's heart sank. As they moved towards the side tables,

where a cold collation had been laid out for them, she took the opportunity to go to a different part of the room than that favoured by Mr Beresford and the two young ladies. It was best to stay as far away as possible from him—and from his unwelcome effect on her.

Somehow that kiss on the hand had set off an unexpected and inconvenient response within her, like ripples in a pond. And instead of decreasing, her heart, mind and traitorous body seemed ever more focused on Mr Beresford. Flirting with him had been a mistake. A mistake her body would—she hoped—eventually forget.

She could not, however, escape him for ever, and before long nuncheon was done. Leading the way to the red drawing room, she decided that appearing bright and cheerful was probably the safest mask to wear.

'I am so grateful to all of you,' she declared generally, as they moved through the small parlour and into the drawing room. 'As you see, there is plenty of greenery to be dealt with.'

'But this is perfect!' Lady Cecily smiled. 'I much prefer to have something to *do*, you see. Idleness does not sit well with me.'

The two of them spent the afternoon idly conversing over holly prickles, laurel leaves and assorted lengths of ribbon, while Miss Bridgeton flirted with a rather distracted Mr Beresford.

Nell could not help but be amused by Miss Bridgeton's increasingly desperate attempts to secure his interest. Mr Beresford either replied in the most general of terms, or seemed not to hear some of his companion's sallies, so intent did he seem on crafting the most perfect garlands and wreaths. Nell, her eyes dancing, met a similarly amused gaze from Lady Cecily, and their friendship, already strong, was sealed.

Eventually it was too much, even for the heedless Miss Bridgeton, who began including the other two ladies in her conversation. At this point Mr Beresford seemed to spring back to the present, engaging with all of them in a charming manner.

*I must not let him work his charm on me.*

Unfortunately, Nell's heart was continuing to race in a most inconvenient manner in his company. She focused her efforts on behaving naturally. It was difficult at this moment to remember exactly how to do that...

After a time Miss Bridgeton excused herself, stating that she would return shortly. She was presumably destined for the retiring room or her chamber. With a brief glance towards Nell and Mr Beresford, Lady Cecily made her own excuses a moment later, saying she was going to fetch the small scissors she had brought with her, which would be ideal for trimming ribbons, rather than all of them having to share the kitchen set.

*No! Do not leave me with him!*

Nell's thoughts must have been apparent on her face, for Lady Cecily frowned slightly, as if surprised. Nell, belatedly re-establishing her polite mask, assured Lady Cecily that her embroidery scissors would be just the thing.

Silence fell as the door closed behind her. Nell kept her eyes downcast, focused on her work.

After a moment Mr Beresford said, 'So...'

'So what?' Nell looked up, her tone defiant.

He grinned. 'Such pertness from a member of the household towards a guest!'

She snorted. 'A guest who has already breached good manners!'

'How so?' He looked unperturbed.

'You should have told me you were to be a guest here.'

'Ah, but then I would not have had the delight of spending time with you.' His voice deepened. 'Or the opportunity to kiss your hand.'

'Precisely!' She glared at him.

'Precisely,' he echoed softly. 'That kiss will stay in my memory for a very long time.'

She quivered, uncertainty replacing her righteous anger. Did he, too, think it special? 'I do not know what to make of you, Mr Beresford.'

*Is he a heartless flirt or not?*

'The feeling is entirely mutual, Miss—' He frowned. 'I do not know your name. Much as I should wish to continue to refer to you as "Nell", it would not be appropriate.'

Ignoring the thrill tingling through her at the sound of her name on his lips, Nell lifted her chin.

*It is time to tell him who I am.*

'I am Miss Godwin.'

'Godwin?' A frown creased his brow. 'So Mrs Godwin is your…?'

'She is my stepmother.' Nell grimaced at his raised eyebrow. 'Yes, she is only sixteen years my senior.'

'I see.' The frown had returned. 'Then this—' he gestured vaguely '—is your family home?'

A painful lump formed in her throat. 'Yes.'

He was looking at her closely. 'And you assist your stepmother here?'

She nodded. 'I do. My stepmother is not particularly— that is to say…'

'Household management and economy do not come easily to everyone,' he murmured diplomatically.

She nodded, grateful for his subtlety. Hopefully he would assume her assistance was limited only to tasks befitting a lady of quality.

'Thank you for telling me,' he continued. 'This conversation has been most enlightening.'

*It has? Why?*

Aloud, she said only, 'Can you pass me another holly bough, please?'

He did so, and a moment later Miss Bridgeton returned.

Her eyes widened briefly, and she asked after the where-abouts of Lady Cecily with a hint of suspicion in her tone.

Lady Cecily entered—with her scissors—an instant later, and they all resumed their work.

# *Chapter Four*

*Christmas Day*

So far the Christmas party was going smoothly. The staff had served an excellent breakfast, the children had been delighted with their small gifts, and the adults, too, had exchanged little presents.

Beatrice had gifted each of her guests an embroidered handkerchief. The ladies had received lace-trimmed pieces embroidered with spring flowers—bluebells and daisies and primroses—while the gentlemen had each received a fine cotton square with their initials.

Nell—who, of course, had done all the work—had stayed up until almost two in the morning, embroidering Mr Beresford's initials in fine blue silk.

The guests had all expressed their delight and gratitude, and Beatrice had taken their praise with equanimity.

Nell had kept her gaze on her clenched hands. When eventually she had managed to hide her hot temper enough to raise her eyes, Mr Beresford had been looking directly at her, a puzzled frown creasing his forehead.

So it was unsurprising now, when he sought her out as they walked to church. The carriages had dropped them in the village, and he took the opportunity to fall back until he was beside her.

'Do you sew, Miss Godwin?' he asked baldly.

She shrugged. 'On occasion.'

He took a handkerchief from his sleeve. A sideways glance confirmed it was the one she had embroidered. 'Did you sew this?'

What to do? She could not lie, and yet she did not wish to expose Beatrice. By doing so she would possibly reveal the misery of her current existence; her pride would not allow it.

Glancing at Beatrice, who was gliding ahead alongside Lady Fanny, she gestured airily. 'Possibly. Beatrice and I often help each other on our sewing and embroidery projects.'

Beatrice's assistance was generally limited to instructing, criticising and taking credit, but she did not say this.

'Oh, look! They have added candles to the windows of the store!'

Candles in the window were a Yuletide tradition, barely worth commenting on, but she pretended to be interested in them long enough for Lady Cecily and Miss Bridgeton to join them. Thankfully Mr Beresford did not pursue the topic.

The day was crisp and clear, and people were generally in a jovial mood. Mr Beresford continued to walk with her and the other young ladies as far as the church—which meant, somehow, that they ended up beside one another for the service.

While singing one of the traditional carols, she sensed his head turning towards her. Unthinkingly, she turned to look at him, and their gazes collided. Ignoring her racing heart, she sang on, eyeing him steadily. He seemed to forget the words for an instant, and she flashed him a challenging grin. He smiled back, and her heart felt warmer than at any time since Papa's death.

After nuncheon they played spillikins, at the request of the children, with the young ladies and some of the younger gentlemen taking part. Nell was surprised to find that Mr Beresford, showing the same good grace he had exhibited while helping with the greening yesterday, joined in the parlour games with enthusiasm.

At one point she caught him looking at little John, and there was sadness in his gaze.

*Why?*

He was charming to all the ladies in equal measure, and was already a favourite with the matrons. The gentlemen liked him too, with many seeking him out for advice on matters of business. Their comments had given Nell to understand that Mr Beresford and his brother Jack, the Earl of Hawkenden, were both wealthy and knowledgeable on such matters. He was somehow different when he was discussing matters of business, Nell observed. Sterner. Colder, even.

The children flocked around him like bees to nectar—which gave Nell the greatest trouble. Being herself drawn to him, and knowing she was as yet unsure whether to trust him, she was still to be convinced that there was true sincerity beneath his charming mask. But children, she had always found, were often more insightful than adults in the detection of falsity, and it confused her to see how much the little ones had warmed to Mr Beresford.

*He will be gone soon,* she reminded herself. *It will not matter then who he is or what his reasons for being here are.*

The thought was decidedly poignant.

Once the children had been taken away by their nursemaids to rest before dinner, Mr Beresford suggested a brief walk outside for those hardy enough to enjoy it. Most of the guests declined, but Lady Cecily, Miss Bridgeton and Mr Emerson all agreed with alacrity.

Lady Cecily pressed Nell into going along. Glad of the invitation—for she hated being cooped up indoors for long periods—Nell joined the others in donning cloaks, boots and hats, before they all stepped out into the quietness of a cold Christmas Day.

The day was midwinter-dark, the clouds steel-grey, heavy and portentous. Nell shuddered. Some whisper of fear had sent a cold shiver up her spine.

Ignoring it, she walked on with the others.

On reaching the copse they began to wander apart a little, collecting fresh holly boughs to brighten the older ones in the house. Unexpectedly Nell, with her arms full of greenery, came upon Mr Beresford, who was reaching up to snap off a leafy branch festooned with red berries and glossy green leaves.

'Oh!' She could not help but exclaim. He was in her thoughts at all times, so to see him suddenly alone was like a wish come true.

He turned and stilled when he saw who was there. His eyes pinned hers, and she was lost in her own longing—and his. Her heart was racing, her palms moist, and she could feel herself quiver. Who *was* he to have such an effect on her?

Unaccountably, they were now standing face to face. Had she stepped towards him or he towards her? It mattered not.

He lifted a hand to caress her cheek. She remained still, knowing what would happen next.

*I want this!* she thought fiercely. *Good things never happen to me, so I shall kiss him, and never see him again after the party, and always remember this moment.*

A moment later his lips touched hers, soft and warm, and she responded instantly, taking every ounce of pleasure she could.

Minutes later they drew apart, both breathing hard.

*What a kiss!*

Her heart was racing, desire was pooling in her stomach and her hands were trembling.

He had noticed, and was sliding his hands down her arms to claim both hands. Oh, how wonderful it was to feel the warmth of his hands on hers, his breath on her cheek, the heat of his body where it aligned with hers.

During their kiss snow had begun to fall softly, caressing them gently with whispering coolness. It was perfect.

His lips curved into a radiant smile, and she returned it with one of her own.

*What on earth am I doing?*

Some strange madness had taken hold of her, filling her with daring, exhilaration and, somewhere deep down, defiance.

*Inside I am still me. I am alive yet.*

Voices alerted them to the impending arrival of Lady Cecily and the rest of their party. Swiftly he turned, reaching again for a high holly bough.

Nell bent to pick up her own twigs and stems, which had been abandoned to the undergrowth during their kiss.

Praying her breathlessness and flushed cheeks would settle quickly, Nell hoped the others would think it due to the weather and her exertions. Thankfully, they seemed to notice nothing amiss, and amid excited chatter about the snow they all made their way back along the lane.

Tom's head was awhirl, his body ached with need, and his heart—he simply could not work out *what* was happening with his heart.

When she had looked at him in church he had been overcome with a longing so intense it had closed his throat. Kissing her just now had been wonderful, inevitable—*necessary.* Never had another person, man or woman, disturbed him as much as Miss Nell Godwin was disturbing him. And he hated the discomfort of it even as his heart soared.

He walked on with the others through the gentle snowfall, but in all the world to him there was only one other person. *Nell.*

## Christmas Evening

Nell glanced around the salon. The Yule Log stretched right across the large hearth, barely touched by flames, so imposing was it. Around it smaller branches and blocks blazed merrily, ensuring the large room remained warm and bright. Branches of candles had been placed on most of the side tables, and the shutters had been closed to block out the darkness of the winter night.

Beatrice's guests were grouped in twos and threes in different corners, chattering, laughing and sharing the fine selection of expensive wines that Jemett had prepared for this Christmas Day. The children were gone to bed, dinner had been a clear success, and the gentlemen had recently joined the ladies after their port in the dining room.

Christmas Day as a whole had gone well, Nell reflected with some satisfaction. The staff had outdone themselves in ensuring the comfort of all their guests, from the early breakfast before church, to the extravagant dinner tonight, when a fine fat goose had been the centrepiece, flanked by a range of well-prepared dishes including suet puddings, dumplings, vegetables in sauce and white soup, along with blancmanges, cakes and ices.

Throughout all the feasting, praying, singing and games Nell had remained intensely aware of Mr Beresford—and of the momentous kiss they had shared earlier.

Right now he was engaged in conversing with Beatrice, who was flirting outrageously with him using fan and eyes and—presumably—words. As she observed them it occurred to Nell that, while his attention seemed entirely devoted to her stepmama, in truth he was rather distracted.

Nell was old enough to understand that a widow was free to do things denied to an unmarried maid like she, but the thought that Beatrice wished to share Mr Beresford's bed disturbed her more than it should. Much more.

There was no reason to believe he was returning Beatrice's flirtatious intent. In truth, he might simply be interested in what Beatrice had to say. But that was unlikely, and therefore puzzling. Her stepmother's conversation was rarely raised above a discussion of fashion and gossip—hardly the most interesting of topics. Yet no other explanation presented itself.

'Thank you for a wonderful Christmas Day.'

It was Lady Cecily, a hint of embarrassed kindness in her eyes. Had Lady Cecily drawn the same conclusions about the conversation between Beatrice and her handsome guest?

'Oh, but I did nothing!' Nell replied airily, grateful to tear her eyes away from them.

Lady Cecily gave her a sceptical look. 'My mama— whom I love dearly—has no more common sense than a kitten. I have been looking after her affairs for a number of years now.'

Nell understood perfectly. 'My stepmama and Lady Fanny are great friends,' she offered carefully.

'They are so alike!' declared Lady Cecily, with a grin.

Nell gave her an answering smile. 'As young ladies, we must always be careful not to criticise our elders...'

'But we may look after them when needed!'

In perfect charity with each other, they took a turn about the room, their shawls draped over their elbows in matching pose.

Nell was wearing an evening gown of pale gauze, worn over a daring cherry-coloured underdress, with Vandyke points edging both the neckline and hem. She had not worn it since last Christmas, having refashioned it from an old dress. New clothes were no longer a regular part of her life. Beatrice had taken away her allowance, deeming it unnecessary because, she had said, Nell's requirements were all met without the need for coin. Since then Nell's talents with a sewing needle had regularly been put to good use...

Lady Cecily's gown was of blue silk, which emphasised her angelic beauty.

While it was good to walk, after nigh on two hours seated at dinner, it was also gratifying when they received a number of compliments from men and women alike as they sauntered around the large salon, chatting lightly. As they passed the corner where Beatrice and Mr Beresford were still conversing Nell was careful not to look in their direction. She *felt* as though his eyes were upon her, but of course that might be simply her imagination...

They regained their seats, and Nell began to inform Lady Cecily of their habits for the morrow—St Stephen's Day.

'We shall give the servants their gifts, and they will have the day off to visit their own families. Our guests' personal servants will remain, of course—no doubt they will be given time off after they leave here—but apart from that we shall fend for ourselves.' She grinned. 'I shall take to the kitchen and serve the food, but it will be cold collations all day, I'm afraid.'

Lady Cecily shrugged. 'We have the same tradition at home. I confess I enjoy invading the kitchen on that one day in the year.'

All the time Nell's attention was partly on the far left corner—where *he* was. That feeling was still there...

Unable to resist, Nell stole a glance in Mr Beresford's direction. His dark gaze met hers, sending a shocking thrill through her.

*I was right—he is watching me!*

She felt herself flush as she and Mr Beresford locked gazes. There was hunger in his expression—a hunger that matched her own.

With some difficulty, she tore her gaze away. Her insides were melting and her heart was pounding so loudly she feared others might notice.

She glanced at Beatrice. Oh, dear! Her stepmama looked most put out—presumably because Mr Beresford was no longer paying her any attention.

*Did she see how he looked at me?*

An entirely feminine wave of triumph rippled through Nell—followed by guilt at her own uncharitable thoughts. Still, to have disrupted Mr Beresford's concentration in such a manner *was* rather gratifying.

'Then let us take over the kitchen together!' she suggested brightly.

'An excellent notion!' agreed Lady Cecily.

*I like her so much!*

Nell's friendship with Lady Cecily was an excellent distraction from other, less clear connections that might possibly be made.

Mr Beresford was taking up too much of her attention. If something serious were to happen between them she would welcome it, but she did not wish to have her heart bruised by a gentleman set on a simple interlude.

*Stop looking at her!* Tom admonished himself silently, as his gaze drifted yet again to the place where Nell was.

Lord, she was beautiful! And bewitching. And intriguing. Memories of the intimate kiss they had shared had not faded, and his desire for her seemed to be increasing by the hour—fuelled not just by her beauty, but by her charm, and her kindness, and her lively mind.

This fixation was entirely outside his control, and it was not a feeling he welcomed.

Add to that the fact that old memories from his childhood were reawakening, and it seemed as though there were moments when his heart was being torn in two. It was to do with Nell, he knew, but also with his own family, and the little ones here at Wyatt House. He did not often find himself in the company of families.

Thankfully the children had now gone to bed. It was difficult to forget that little John was the exact age Tom had been when his own mama had died. Just before Christmas.

Yes, being with loving families at Christmastide was bringing back memories of long, long ago and leaving him feeling exposed, heartsore…almost *frightened*.

That lump was back in his throat.

Between inconvenient memories and raging desire, he knew he had, until tonight, somewhat stalled in his task of persuading the widow to sell him this beautiful house.

Business. Calmness. Certainty.

*That is exactly what I need right now.*

With some effort, he pasted a smile on his face and turned back to Mrs Godwin.

* * *

Nell eyed the mistletoe bough with disfavour. Seeing it suspended from the crystal and bronze chandelier in the small parlour that had become her own particular haven was bad enough. Noticing that not one but *two* of the pearly seeds had disappeared was bothering her enormously. She had sought refuge in the parlour before bedtime, believing she could have a half-hour's peace before ascending to the tiny chamber she shared with some of the serving maids. Now, her peace was disturbed.

Tradition held it that each time a couple kissed under a mistletoe bough they had to remove one of the seeds. Earlier today there had been three; now there was but one. That meant people had been kissing each other right here, in her sanctuary, under the watchful eye of Mama's portrait, and Nell was not at all happy about it.

She stood beneath the offending greenery, regarding it with a baleful eye. Who were the offenders? Some of the servants, perhaps? Or the guests?

She recalled the attention Mr Beresford had given Beatrice earlier tonight. Had he kissed Beatrice—or some other woman—in this very spot?

*Of course he had not!*

Yet it seemed unfair that others were sharing kisses while she was yearning for another kiss from a particular person. It would probably not happen, she knew. Mr Beresford, sadly, would be gone soon, and with him any chance of another romantic moment to lighten the dreariness of her existence.

She frowned.

*No, it was more than that.*

In truth, she admitted, she believed the kiss she had shared with Mr Beresford was different. Special. *Magical.* Yet he had made no attempt to seek her out today.

Oh, he *looked* at her. Constantly. She felt his eyes follow her any time they were in the same room, and the gossamer threads of an unseen connection grew between them each time they met. But he had made no obvious effort to fix her interest. Indeed, he had probably spoken with her *less* than he had the other ladies. This evening he had shared his attention equally among them all—save for Beatrice, who got more, and Nell, who got less. It almost seemed as though he were avoiding her.

Yet still she understood in her heart that the way Mr Beresford looked at her was *different*, somehow, from the way in which he engaged with the other ladies. There was fire in it. And it had lit an answering flame in her—one that had disturbed both her sleep and her waking thoughts since they had met.

At times it felt as though she burned for him—for a man she had only recently met. And the Christmas magic in the air seemed to be leading her to impossible thoughts, unachievable dreams. That kiss, the snow…all pointed towards something wonderful—something just out of reach.

Fleetingly she wondered if she, just like Mama, could *know* this early on that she had met the man who was her destiny.

*Oh, how absurd!*

Mama had been exceedingly romantical, and Nell had long since dismissed her mama's description of her courtship with Papa as memories based on wishes rather than reality. And yet…

For heaven's sake—what woman could deny the attraction of Mr Beresford's handsome features, wicked smile and well-formed figure? For Nell, though, the attraction was much more complex than an earthy appeal—although that pulsed through her constantly. What she felt was more than a simple physical urge. It fired her heart and her mind as much as it did her body. And while he watched her, she also watched him…

Having succumbed in less than three days to this unanticipated obsession with Mr Beresford, she had become conscious of the certain sadness that crept into his expression from time to time—particularly when he was unaware of being observed. It was particularly apparent when he looked at the children.

Nell had no idea what was behind it, but her heart melted each time she noticed it. And, whatever his frailty was, it was not apparent to the others in their circle, who laughed and played and conversed with seeming ease. No, there was more to Mr Beresford than met the eye. He was, she understood now, a puzzle she needed to solve.

Despite the attraction and the obsession and the need he had created within her, she continued to remain wary of his effect on her and her lack of certainty about his motives. So when he suddenly entered her sanctuary via the red drawing room, real and immediate, her instinctive reaction was to take a step back.

He was no fool, and his eyes narrowed at her response. 'Good evening, Miss Godwin,' he declared formally.

'Good—good evening, Mr Beresford.' Her heart was pounding and her mouth suddenly dry with a disconcerting mix of excitement and nervousness.

*The last time we were alone together we kissed.*

'I came to offer my services for tomorrow. As there are to be no servants, I thought you might need assistance in carrying trays to the dining room.'

His dark eyes fixed on hers, making her stomach tighten and her knees feel strangely soft.

'That is kind of you. Thank you.' Her voice sounded remarkably normal. 'We shall dine at the usual time tomorrow, so I would appreciate your help—perhaps half an hour beforehand?'

'Perfect!' He grinned. 'Like you, I enjoy peace and quiet at times.'

She smiled wryly. 'I do hope you do not think me rude for disappearing now and again?'

'Not at all! I believe we are similar in that regard.'

There was silence. A silence in which the air took on the

heaviness and anticipation Nell associated with thunder-
storms and lightning strikes. Their eyes locked. Nell's heart
was pounding so loudly she could almost hear it in the room,
and the air prickled with suspense. In the background, the
clock began to chime. It was midnight.

Nell gazed at him hungrily, drinking in the sight of him,
unable in that moment to hide what she wanted.

'Dash it all!' The words exploded from him as he took
three steps forward, taking her into his arms. 'Kiss me,
Nell!'

She did so, glorying in the passion between them.

Propriety, reason and common sense were abandoned
as she devoured him and he her. Crushed against him, she
pressed ever closer, seeking contact from chest to hip, his
heat fanning the conflagration within her. Her hands were
in his thick dark hair, while his were busy on her back, her
bottom, her hips.

'Nell!' he groaned against her mouth, and she claimed
him again, her desire for him the only reality.

Eventually they paused, forehead to forehead, both
breathing noisily.

'What are you doing to me?' he murmured. 'I have never
felt anything like this!'

*He feels it too!* Her heart sang at his words. *It is real!*

Abruptly, he stepped back, his breathing still ragged. 'I
apologise. I should not have—' His face had hardened. 'I
cannot offer you anything, Miss Godwin.'

She watched, agape, as he turned on his heel and left, the
door closing behind him with an audible click.

*What on earth...?*

Nell put a hand to her head, trying to understand what
was occurring. He wanted her—that much was clear. And
there was no obvious barrier to a marriage between them.
So why had he left her? Why was he trying to deny what
was between them?

Mama's portrait looked down upon her. Nell closed her

eyes and tried to steady her breathing, to calm her racing thoughts.

*Mama would have approved of that kiss, I think.*

She well remembered how affectionate Mama and Papa had been, and had no doubt that they had known passion in their marriage. And Mama had *chosen* Papa the first time they had ever met.

'I want *that* one,' she had apparently said to her friend, on first seeing the young Mr Godwin. 'I knew, you see,' she had told Nell. 'I knew he was the man I should marry.'

*Marriage.* Never before had Nell seriously considered marriage with anyone. But if her instincts were right, and he was a man of good character, then it seemed her heart was well on the way to choosing Mr Beresford as her ideal husband. She had known him for only a few days, but already her gut was telling her he could be the right man for her. That midnight mistletoe kiss—and his response to it— confirmed it in her mind. This was more than lust. It went deeper than anything she had ever known.

Exhilaration rushed through her at the realisation, but she bit her lip. Judging by his hasty—one might say *panicked*— departure, Mr Beresford was not yet of the same view. That would have to be managed.

Reaching up, she plucked the last lustrous white seed from the mistletoe above her head and slipped it into her reticule with a secret smile. She had much to think about.

Tom made it to the safety of his chamber, his mind, heart and his body all in disorder.

*What the hell is happening to me?*

Never had he experienced anything like the attraction he felt for Nell Godwin. It consumed him.

He paced around the chamber, unable to think clearly, his mind overwhelmed by the instinct to return downstairs and kiss her again.

*Damn it! I have known her only three days.*

It felt much longer.

He disliked this feeling of not being in control of himself. Even the warmest of his *affaires* had never disturbed his equilibrium.

*I must master this!*

After quite half an hour of anguished pacing, he gradually began to feel more rational again, yet still he was not ready to sleep. Pulling open the drawer in the mahogany desk in the corner of the room, he removed his folio of papers. Focusing on matters of business for a while should further calm his spirit.

He sharpened a pen and began making notes, including his observations on Wyatt House as the location where he would entertain his contacts in future. The problem was that each time he tried to imagine how he might use the various spaces he saw Nell. Nell in the dining room. Nell in the salon. Nell in this bedchamber, he on top of her.

He groaned, then exclaimed with frustration as his pen snapped in two.

'Hell, damn and blast it!'

He began flinging drawers open at random, sure there must be another pen somewhere. And in the bottom left drawer of the desk, at the back, he saw something which gave him pause. A book. And written in a neat hand on the cover were the words *Miss Eleanor Godwin—a journal*.

Knowing he should not, he lifted it out, his hand caressing the cover, lingering on her name. Opening it with what felt like reverence, he saw it was filled with multiple entries, dated between 1815 and 1817.

*Nell's journal.*

Her handwriting called to him, being both mysterious and beautiful. The temptation to know her better was too strong to resist.

*I must not read it,* he told himself, opening it at random.

A moment later he shut the book with a snap. Here was just punishment for the sin of invading her privacy. He had happened upon the entry in which she wrote of her papa breaking to her the news that he was ill. Dangerously ill.

*May 25th, 1816: Papa is returned from London, where he saw the doctor about the lump in his neck. It is, the doctor informs him, a malign growth, and it will before long obscure Papa's windpipe.*

There was no emotion expressed afterwards. The rest of the page remained empty.

Tom knew just how distressing the news would have been to Nell. He closed his eyes briefly as grief washed through him. But why should he feel grief for the loss of a man he had never met? Then he knew. It was grief for Nell's sake.

And there were other shades in it too. For the first time in many years he felt again the bewilderment of a small boy whose mother had suddenly vanished, called to live in heaven, far away from home.

*Mama.*

# Chapter Five

Tom glanced around the chamber, slightly dazed by his abrupt return to the present. Placing the journal back where he had found it, he began mechanically to undress.

A thousand thoughts were swirling around his disordered brain, like leaves in autumn. One drifted into focus.

*Why is her book here, in this chamber?*

The journal was so intimate, so personal—surely Nell would have kept it in her own chamber?

He stopped, stunned by a sudden moment of clarity. Abruptly he began opening closets and drawers, searching for confirmation. Here a comb. There a length of ribbon.

*This is Nell's chamber!*

So why on earth was she not sleeping in it?

He slapped a hand on the bedpost as the answer came to him.

*Because the house is full of guests, of course.*

Guilt washed though him as he realised she had been displaced from her own chamber in order to accommodate him. She should not have been so discommoded! Presumably she was sharing a bedchamber with one of the young ladies—or possibly her stepmother.

Grimly, he considered his options. There was no way he could see by which to remedy the situation. Under no circumstances could he admit to having found her journal. He would therefore have to pretend he did not know.

He glanced at the bed. Nell's bed. There she slept, night after night. And tonight he would sleep there again. The thought was disturbing, exciting and comforting all at once. Nell Godwin was altogether too interesting.

*I am my own master, and I choose my own path.*

As he climbed into bed, it did not occur to him to notice how completely she was occupying his thoughts.

## December 26th

Nell felt as though she were in a beautiful dream. As she worked in the kitchen, serving bread, meat, pies, cheeses and precious fruit onto platters and into serving bowls, she sang softly to herself. Not since losing Papa had she felt so happy, so light of spirit.

Mr Beresford had come into her life and brought light and wellness and happiness. Yes, he had left her rather abruptly last night, and there had been as yet no opportunity for private speech with him today, but he would surely be warm again when next she saw him. She did not know exactly how events would unfurl in future, but at this moment the future was not her concern.

Lady Cecily had helped earlier, but was now gone to dress for dinner. Finding a large pot of soup in the second larder, Nell decided to reheat it so the guests would have something warm on this cold winter's day. Stoking up the kitchen fire, she accidentally got some soot from the cinders on her hands in the process, but soon had the fire burning merrily and the soup pot suspended from the iron chimney crane.

She washed her hands, then stirred the soup gently, enjoying the sense of purpose in so simple a task. Absentmindedly she hummed another tune, enjoying the feeling that for the first time in a long time, her burdens felt lighter, the darkness around her less dense.

She did not hear him enter, but some sense told her he was there. She turned, unable to prevent a welcoming smile lighting her face.

He blinked, as if walking into strong sunlight, and then, as if nothing at all had passed between them last night, remarked cordially, 'You have been hard at work.'

'I have.' She dimpled at him. 'It is surprisingly satisfying.'

'You told me that you worked here...'

There was a question in his tone and Nell felt suddenly nervous. She should not reveal Beatrice's true character to a near-stranger. For that, she reminded herself, was what he was, despite this connection between them.

She felt herself flush. 'It is *partly* true,' she offered carefully. 'Since Papa died I have sometimes felt more like a servant here than a member of the family.' Frowning, she reflected on her own words. 'That is unfair. Beatrice—my stepmother—has never sought to treat me badly...'

*Is that true?*

Remembering Beatrice's insouciant demand that she vacate her chamber, and the way in which she had been gradually expected to help more and more with the physical work around the house, she felt a blinding realisation come to her. She *had* been treated badly! Many times. And she herself had allowed it.

'And yet,' she added frankly, 'I do seem to have been badly done by.'

He was frowning. 'So would it be true to say that you work here, or not?'

'No...' That sounded weak. 'No,' she said again, with more certainty than she felt. 'And so I must apologise to you for giving you the impression at our first meeting that I was a servant.'

His expression softened a little. 'That small deception was harmless in its intent.' He grinned. 'Like my decision not to tell you I would be a guest here.'

She laughed. 'You have me there! Very well—you are forgiven for kissing my hand under false pretences.'

'You accepted the attention under equally false pretences,' he shot back, his eyes dancing with mischief.

'So we both got what we wanted,' she said softly.

There was a pause as they eyed each other.

He swallowed. 'You have soot on your cheek.'

He pulled out his handkerchief—the one *she* had embroidered. The cinders! She stood immobile as he gently cleaned them away, enjoying his nearness…the delicious scent of him. His warm fingers were on her chin, tilting her face up a little. Had his breathing become a little louder?

'I, too, suffered a change in circumstances when my parents died.' His voice was low, and the air between them seemed charged with the enormity of the secrets they were sharing. 'My mama died when I was five—at Christmastide.'

Nell felt her face crumple with compassion. *Poor little boy!*

'My papa,' he continued, 'sent me away afterwards. First to distant relatives, then to boarding school. In truth, I became an orphan when Mama died.'

She nodded, felt her throat close painfully, making words impossible. They looked into each other's eyes for a long moment—until they heard, in the distance, the chiming of the clock announcing that it was dinner time.

Dropping his hand from her face, he strode to the scrubbed table and picked up the first tray. 'Do you want this anywhere in particular?' His tone was clipped, his expression shuttered.

*He is upset because of what he has just told me.*

She needed to assist him to retain control of himself.

'Let us just bring everything to the dining room first, then we can display it properly.' Her voice shook a little. She pointed to the plates of meat. 'Please take those first, then come back for the bread.'

'Yes, milady!'

The mischief was back, despite the emotion still swirling around them both.

She took a breath. *Oh, but he is wonderful!*

'Well, go on, then! And do not tarry!' she retorted sharply, joining in the game.

With an ironic bow, and a decided glint in his eye, he obeyed.

*December 28th*

Two days had passed—days which, for Nell, had been both dreamlike and agonisingly frustrating all at once.

Having discovered the truth in her own heart, she gloried in the exhilaration of finding the person her soul had craved. Everything about him was fascinating to her. The way he spoke, and how it revealed or concealed his thoughts and opinions. The way he moved, with a fluid, long-legged grace that confused her senses and made her heart skip. The habit he had of pulling his right ear when he was irritated by someone—often Fanny or Beatrice.

She wanted more. She wished to know everything about his life so far. More of his childhood. How it had been for him to lose his home and his mama at five and be sent away. His hopes and dreams. His favourite foods. What books he enjoyed. Whether he was a proficient dancer or had any talent for music.

So much to discover about him and so little opportunity!

She had observed the proprieties, of course. Not for her an obvious flirtation, such as the one tried by Miss Bridgeton. Nell, determined to learn from the transparent behaviour of some of the other young ladies, was subtle and restrained in her interactions with Mr Beresford while they were in company. Or at least she hoped she was.

She made sure to spend time with everyone in the party, sharing her attention and her conversation fairly among them. Yet when everyone walked each day she and Mr Beresford automatically and naturally fell in together. It was their opportunity to talk, and they took it with enthusiasm.

She found herself telling him much of her own history— her happy existence before Papa's illness, the trials she had endured under Beatrice's guardianship, the black moods that sometimes threatened to overwhelm her.

In turn, he entrusted her with memories of his beloved

mama, although he was reticent about his lonely years in boarding school.

'My brother Jack suffered more than I did,' he offered, with seeming reluctance. 'He, being two years older, appointed himself my protector. There was no-one at all to protect *him*.'

Nell had shivered at the words. *Poor boys!*

Nell knew that Cecily understood she had a partiality for Mr Beresford, but was much too well-bred to comment on it. Together, in the house, they entertained the children, laughed together, and chose to seek each other out during the long winter evenings, when the party was gathered in the large salon.

Mr Beresford sometimes opted to sit with them, but Nell could honestly not point to anything that might signal they favoured each other.

Except for the fact that she *knew* they did. Knew it with a conviction that was implacable, unalterable, unquestionable.

Tonight there was an added air of excitement, for members of the local gentry had been invited to boost their numbers and lift their mood. Beatrice had even hired musicians to play for them. Naturally it had been Nell who organised it—but, as hostess, Beatrice would get the credit.

Jemett, Mrs Hussey, Cook, and the entire staff had been busy all day—cleaning, polishing silver, cooking, and moving furniture. The salon now contained numerous additional chairs, arranged against the walls, while the sofas had been moved back to create a space for dancing. The musicians had arrived a few hours ago, and the strains of instruments being tuned and their practising all afternoon had increased Nell's excitement.

Nell was not normally encouraged to attend Beatrice's parties, but tonight she was deaf to Beatrice's hints and determined to be part of it. Earlier, when Beatrice had idly wondered if Nell might prefer to stay in her bedchamber this evening, Nell had pointedly reminded her that since the arrival of Beatrice's guests she'd *had* no bedchamber, and was not enamoured of the idea of spending all evening in the tiny attic.

'Well, I suppose you might make yourself useful with the younger ones,' Beatrice had conceded. 'But once they are taken away to the nursery you should go too.'

Nell had answered noncommittally, knowing that, for once, she was planning to defy her stepmother.

'And make sure you do not disgrace me!' Beatrice had added. 'What will you wear?'

Nell had shrugged. 'One of my remade evening gowns.'

Beatrice made no reply. Well, she knew quite well Nell had no other option.

'There you go, Miss Nell!' Sally, the housemaid who had used to look after Nell, had finished working on her hair.

'Thank you, Sally,' said Nell with a smile. 'We have no mirror here, but I am sure you have done an excellent work on my coiffure. Now for the dress!'

Nell's favourite evening gown was hanging from the curtain rail in the cramped attic room she was currently sharing with Sally and two other maids. It warmed her heart even to see it hanging there. The dress was of white net, over a white satin slip. Tiny pearls ornamented the bodice, the short, slashed sleeves and the hem trimming. Embroidery in the pattern of holly leaves had been added, the red berries and dark green leaves giving a subtle splash of colour to the gown.

Nell had reworked the skirt to match the modern, fuller style, and it moved against her legs with a satisfying swish. Tonight was her first time wearing it since that last happy Christmas before Papa's illness and his death.

Sally helped her with the buttons, then Nell added Mama's pearls and picked up her ivory and jade fan. 'I am ready—and in good time, too! Thank you again, Sally. Now, let us go to our duties, for the guests will soon begin to arrive.'

Tom fixed a diamond pin to his cravat, not even bothering to check how he looked in the mirror. Mr Bridgeton's valet had assisted him into his Weston evening jacket and a snowy cravat, and the waistcoat, knee breeches and dancing slippers that were required evening wear were all perfectly adequate. He dropped his watch into his pocket, ensured he had a clean handkerchief, then dismissed the valet.

He glanced at the clock. Hmm… There were two options. He could descend now, and risk a solo conversation with Nell—who, he had no doubt, would have been left to lead the arrangements for tonight's event. Or he could linger here for another ten minutes, ensuring that others would be there to prevent any intimacy between them. The intimacy he craved, yet must not seek.

He knew himself to be in great danger. Never before had his heart been so moved by a young lady. He was convinced he must never try to become a husband or father. He would, he feared, fail spectacularly, and condemn some poor woman and her as yet unborn children to the agony of disappointment, abandonment, or bereavement.

The orphan in him cried out for love, yet he knew he could not take on the responsibility for the happiness and safety of any other person. He had been determined to engage only in a light-hearted flirtation with Nell. That was proving impossible, leaving him with the feeling of being ripped apart inside.

He and Jack managed well in their fraternal connection. And Jack, as head of the family, would have to marry eventually. Tom, as younger brother, was under no such compulsion. Therefore, despite every part of him wishing for nothing more than to be with Nell every hour, every *minute* of the day, he knew he must resist.

Refusing to listen to the inner voice denouncing him as a coward, he crossed to the desk and withdrew her journal. Although he had successfully kept a reasonable distance from her in company, in truth he remained preoccupied with Nell Godwin to quite an astonishing degree. He lived for their walks, and for the conversations they shared.

From those conversations he now knew that Nell had been mistress of Wyatt House since her sixteenth birthday, with the housekeeper Mrs Hussey supporting her as she became increasingly confident in the role. She had told him many tales of everyday household mishaps and challenges, and was unafraid to be self-critical and self-deprecating, even while pride in her successes came clearly through.

Her wit had had him laughing out loud at times, as well as reinforcing for him her keen intelligence. He also saw how her stepmother had been using her most selfishly. It angered him, yet he had no power to change it.

Quite why he found Nell so fascinating he could not say. She was beautiful, it was true, and yet he had encountered many beauties in his time. Perhaps it was her wit, her intelligent conversation and her lively mind? But no, for other ladies he knew were equally sharp-witted—including Lady Cecily, who was also present at this very house party.

He shook his head. There was neither rhyme nor reason to it. It was an unanticipated quirk of fate, temporary in nature, no doubt.

His gaze dropped to the book in his hands. As before, he had been unconsciously caressing her name on the cover. *Eleanor Godwin.* Once again he reminded himself that he could not read her private journal. Last night the temptation had been strong, yet he had resisted, and had retired without so much as a peek into the seductive world of Nell's mind.

It had done him absolutely no good whatsoever, for his dreams had been haunted by her just as much as they had been since he had first encountered her. Alone in this chamber—her chamber—he was surrounded by her spirit.

'It will not do!' he declared aloud. 'I am a rational man, not given to emotion or sentiment. I choose not to indulge this flirtation any further.'

His own words stabbed at him, and he dared not look inside himself for the reason. Deeply uncomfortable, he squared his shoulders, put away the journal and left the chamber.

## Chapter Six

Beatrice was in fine fettle. Nell watched her greet each guest as they arrived, all smiles. Her stepmother was sparkling with good humour, a spangled gown and her own wit. Nell hovered nearby, in case she might be needed.

While Beatrice detested work of any kind, she simply adored hosting events. Having Nell there to organise and plan, to lead the staff and ensure that all went smoothly, meant the Widow Godwin's reputation as an excellent hostess was building. Wyatt House was held to be both elegant and convenient to London, and Mrs Godwin's house parties guaranteed good food and wine, pleasant company and excellent entertainment.

That was why, Beatrice had informed Nell, people like Mr Beresford—younger brother to an earl—had deigned to choose Wyatt House for his Christmas sojourn.

If that was true, then Nell was entirely grateful for her stepmother's reputation, for it had enabled her to meet the one man above all others who had managed to hold her attention, pervade her dreams, and make her think of impossible things. A wedding. A wedding night. Becoming a mother.

*Stop!* she told herself. *None of these things are real.*

Yet she could dream, could she not?

But something in her remained wary. Mr Beresford occasionally acted with great reserve towards her, and she knew instinctively that he was not yet sure of what was happening between them.

She sighed. Men could be stubborn and lacking in insight at times. Even Mama, who had loved Papa dearly, had occasionally lifted her eyes to heaven at some of his less discerning pronouncements, before correcting him in a gentle but effective manner.

Mama had died of a lung infection the winter following Nell's fourteenth birthday. At fourteen, Nell had still had much to learn from her mama.

*Oh, I wish she were here to advise me about Mr Beresford. What should I do?*

Mama had always behaved with perfect propriety, and yet had managed to ensure Papa married her—despite his initial slowness to understand that that was what was to happen.

Mama had also had an added complication, in the form of Grandfather Wyatt, who had died when Nell was a baby. That formidable gentleman had insisted on a marriage settlement which ensured the bulk of his wealth and possessions remained in trust for his daughter and her children. Papa, who had had no need of the Wyatt wealth, being himself a gentleman of means, had agreed with alacrity, but apparently the two men had nearly fallen out over it.

'It was their pride you, see,' Mama had told Nell. 'Your grandfather was determined to see my future protected, while your Papa took umbrage at any suggestion he was a fortune-hunter.' She had laughed, before saying, 'Nell, understand this: men are wonderful creatures, but they are much more emotional than they admit. Nonsensical notions of pride and how others see them can drive even the most sensible of men to foolish actions. They have been reared to deny they even have sensibilities, which means we women must use all our ingenuity at times to ensure they do the reasonable thing.'

Nell needed every ounce of Mama's wisdom to guide her now. Mr Beresford was due to leave when the house party broke up after Twelfth Night, and Nell sensed her campaign to win his heart was faltering.

*Perhaps he does not feel as I do?*

Nell considered the notion. He had been just as affected

as she by their kisses, and yet she knew she could not read too much into just two kisses.

*Tonight I must see progress.*

She nodded to herself, as if deciding so would make it happen.

*There he is!*

Finally Mr Beresford had appeared in the line of guests. Relief and excitement warred within her. Evening wear suited him. If such a thing were possible, he grew more handsome each time she saw him.

He was unexpectedly late. She knew Mr Bridgeton's valet had seen to him before returning to his own master, and Mr Bridgeton had been downstairs for more than half an hour already. What could have delayed Mr Beresford, she had no idea. Still, at least he was here now.

She kept a close eye on the footmen as they moved in and out of the salon, bringing fresh trays of drinks—wine, ratafia, and even lemonade, in order to cater to all tastes. The housemaids, including Sally, were assisting guests to don their dancing slippers in the front parlour, and Jemett was standing stiffly at the entrance to the salon, ready to announce each guest as they entered the room.

Nell's gaze returned to Mr Beresford as he reached the front of the line. He made some polite remark to Beatrice, and kissed her hand, but even from a distance Nell could tell he was somewhat distracted. Timing her walk carefully, she approached Jemett just as Mr Beresford left Beatrice.

'All is well so far, Jemett,' she declared calmly.

'Indeed, miss. I am content,' was Jemett's reply. 'Are you going inside?'

She could sense Mr Beresford was behind her, and slightly to the right. 'I am.' She turned. 'Good evening, Mr Beresford.'

He bowed, but did not kiss her hand. 'Good evening.'

Her heart sank.

*He looks...closed, somehow. Why?*

'I shall announce you both,' said Jemett.

Nell, in something of a daze, walked in step with Mr Beresford.

*What ails him? And what does it mean?*

They paused briefly, once inside. A number of the local guests had turned at the announcement of an unfamiliar name, and Nell could see interested gazes—and even a few quizzing glasses being utilised in Mr Beresford's direction.

'Nell! My dear!' Mrs Hoskins was the first to reach them. 'You look ravishing, dear girl!' She paused, eyeing Mr Beresford expectantly.

Nell introduced them, and Mrs Hoskins promptly claimed him, inviting him across to meet her three unmarried daughters.

That set the tenor for the evening. Mr Beresford was fêted, flattered and courted by all the local families. Hardly surprising since he was, as Beatrice kept reminding everyone, brother to an earl, and possessed of a creditable fortune. He was also pleasing in face, figure and manner.

None of the guests, Nell would swear, had discerned the lines of tension about his face tonight, his slight air of distractedness, the subtle stiffness of his tall frame.

*He is deeply troubled about something and is masking it.*

Quite how she knew this, Nell had no idea. But she was convinced that something had occurred to disturb him. She had no idea what it might be. Remembering their conversations about his history, the truth he had shared with her, she felt her heart ache for him. She hated to see anyone in distress, but Mr Beresford had become so dear to her, so quickly, that she could not help but feel distressed at his pain.

She had no way to reach him—no way to discover what might have disquieted him today. All she could do was watch from a distance and hope his worries would ease in this pleasant company.

And pleasant it was. The evening, from many perspectives, could be described as a great success. The house guests mingled easily with the county families, conversing, playing cards, eating and drinking, and finally dancing.

Nell's hand was claimed for every dance, and she noticed that Mr Beresford did not sit out any of the dances either. He danced with Lady Cecily, with Beatrice, and with every one of Mrs Hoskins's smiling daughters. Then, just when Nell was beginning to give way to doubt, he finally approached her.

'Miss Godwin.'

His expression was grave. Stern, even. As if he had not wished to approach her but had been compelled to do so.

*Perhaps he is fighting against this connection between us?*

The realisation came to her as she glanced up at him.

She curtseyed. 'Mr Beresford.'

'Might I have the pleasure of this next dance?'

She nodded, and preceded him towards the centre of the room. His visage remained unyielding as she turned to face him. But his male beauty, she noted, was undiminished by his unsmiling harshness. Indeed, the air of danger about him served only to heighten Nell's inner response. He was a fox. A wolf. An unbroken stallion.

They moved together through the first figure, silently executing the steps with grace, fluidity and perfect harmony. It was *easy*, somehow—so much so that it seemed to Nell as though they had danced together a hundred times before. And yet at the same time all was new. For the only time in her life to date she was dancing with a man who called to her heart as no-one ever had. Happiness rose within her, and she gave herself over to the moment.

Gradually, as they moved through the second figure, then the third, she sensed a subtle change in him. The stiffness was leaving his shoulders. His expression was now more open. His eyes clearly showed hunger. The same hunger that had overcome them each time they had kissed.

*Yes!* she thought, relief flooding through her. *Yes! And yes!*

Before long the dance came to an end, and with it her time with him. He bowed, offered to fetch her refreshment, then excused himself when she declined.

Nell turned away with equanimity, understanding that he needed to leave her in this moment. She had once more pierced his mask and scored another hit in her assault on whatever fortress it was guarding his heart.

For the remainder of the evening she carefully stayed away from him, concentrating on all her old friends who were there and giving Mr Beresford the chance to retreat for a time. Inside she felt satisfaction, and confidence, and the renewal of hope. Her heart was singing.

# *Chapter Seven*

*December 31st*

Tom urged his stallion into a gallop, desperately trying to escape the demons that pursued him night and day. It was late afternoon, the sky already darkening with the coming dusk, and occasional snowflakes drifted in the air.

On this New Year's Eve, the feeling of endings and new beginnings was raging within him. Like Janus, the ancient two-faced god of doorways, Tom could see two worlds at the same time, and he knew not which to choose.

On the one hand was his usual life—familiar, solitary and safe. A life in which he and his brother focused on financial security, consistent with the vow they had made to each other at their father's funeral. Unlike him, they had resolved to be clever with money—they would rebuild the family wealth, not waste it on fripperies, women and gambling. And they had achieved it. It had been Tom's dedicated path for years now—a path that focused on success, and comfort, and an understanding that he needed no-one else. He could trust in his own wits to gain him all he needed. He had no notion of marriage—of course not.

Emotion flooded through him, and he recognised it. *Fear.* He could never marry. Marriage meant children, and he could not bear the thought of creating a future orphan. Or of hurting a wife through his inability to ensure her happiness. No amount of sleepless nights could change that fact.

At present, his aim was the purchase of Wyatt House. He would do well to remember that. He had no doubt the widow would sell to him, and owning Wyatt House would be another marker on his journey of success. His brother had the family home. Wyatt House would be a suitable residence for a man of Tom's gifts and stature.

But the thought disturbed him, somehow. Confidence in his own talents, along with financial security, had been Tom's purpose for most of his adult life, and yet today he felt strangely distant from it all.

Another life, as yet vague and unrealised, was calling to him. A life with Nell. He could no longer deny the compulsion within him. Never had he been so drawn to any woman. She haunted both his nights and his waking thoughts. His days were a constant battle of wanting to be near her, yet resisting the urge. The hours of darkness were torture, as he fought with himself about his future direction.

It made little difference anyway, he acknowledged, for he watched Nell constantly, hung on her every word even while pretending to converse with others.

She was exceptional in every way. Her beauty was driving him to madness—the thought of her skin, her luxuriant hair, that divine form, those haunting eyes... And he was also drawn to her character. She lit up a room just by being in it. He noticed her accomplishments, her quiet assurance, her generous heart. The children loved her. Sensible people like Lady Cecily were drawn to her.

She was discerning in her own friendships, choosing Lady Cecily over the more vacuous young ladies present at the house party. She conversed in a well-informed way on a range of topics, being firm in her opinions without seeking dissent with others.

To spend his life with her would be bliss—yet how could he, when the notion of becoming a father filled him with fear? They were both orphans, he and Nell. Although she had enjoyed her father's company until recently, and even her mama had lived until she was well in her childhood. Yet still he saw how lost she was—adrift among strangers, friends and servants, with no-one she could truly rely on.

Gritting his teeth, he had endured Nell's tale of her father's unexpected marriage, and the efforts she had made to welcome the bride who had arrived so unexpectedly during one of the most difficult episodes of Nell's young life.

What a fool her father must have been! Why had he not seen that Nell needed *him*, not a bird-witted bride who disturbed everyone's comfort?

His anger on Nell's behalf was heightened each time she spoke of her papa—or reported, with determined good humour, the latest incident with Beatrice. It had become clear to him that the new Mrs Godwin was incapable of household management, and preferred Nell to carry that burden.

She had also spoken to him of her father's death. It gave Tom real pain to think of what she had endured these past years, and it had reawakened in him old, unfinished feelings of loss and grief from his own childhood.

Each time he thought of Nell he faced an inner assault of grief, regret, desire and pain. He could not sleep, and had spent the past few nights in frustration and an agony of mind. During the day he was struggling to concentrate, and he felt sleepy and distracted much of the time.

It was too much.

*I cannot live like this. I must turn away from this madness.*

The wildness within him had to be tamed.

*I must take back control over my life. She is simply a girl I met at a house party. I have known her for little more than a week.*

His thoughts returned to his purpose in coming here—the purchase of Wyatt House. If Mrs Godwin agreed to sell it to him, then perhaps Nell could have a fresh start somewhere, with a stepmother who no longer had to worry about money.

*Once I am gone from here the purchase can proceed. I will return once the house is secured and the Godwins are gone. I need never see her again.*

Summoning all his inner strength, he resolved to end this fascination with Nell.

*No more.*

The door was closed, the decision made.

The snow was now falling thickly. Noiseless and remorseless, it covered everything, living and dead, in a blanket of silent, frozen white.

Wheeling around, he turned the horse back in the direction of home. Wyatt House.

The party were all gathered before the fire, as New Year's Eve tradition demanded. It lacked only half an hour until midnight, and the enormous Yule Log that had been burning since Christmas Eve had diminished to a small remnant, now covered with new wood. Nell was seated alongside Lady Cecily who, like her, had lapsed into silence, gazing at the orange sparks as they disappeared up the chimney.

All around was the hum of contented conversation. Beatrice and her guests were enjoying another pleasant evening, and on the surface all looked well.

Nell, however, was concealing inner turmoil. Something had changed with Mr Beresford. He had disappeared this afternoon—riding out on that magnificent stallion—and had been gone nigh on two hours. Much longer than she had anticipated. When he had returned it had been almost fully dark, and she had been relieved to find he had not suffered any injury.

But he had come back changed.

Nell could not say exactly what was different. She simply knew that the connection they had shared was somehow sundered. She was as aware of him as ever, but this evening he had not so much as looked at her.

Shaken, she had subtly put herself in his way as they had moved towards the dining room earlier. He had been perfectly polite, but there had been nothing in his eyes. No emotion, no struggle, no passion. Instead she had felt a cold emptiness, as if the snow outside had taken hold of his heart and left him hollow and cold.

This was entirely different from his previous attempts to avoid her, which had been part of the passion for her that had sprung up in him as surely as it had blossomed in her. No, this was an absolute absence. It was as though she were of no more import to him than a piece of furniture or an item of clothing. He could no longer be reached.

*He is lost to me!* her heart cried.

But how? And why? What had happened to make him put her aside before they had properly begun? All evening—throughout dinner, chatting with the ladies, and playing card games when the gentlemen had joined them, Nell had been racking her brain—to no avail. As far as she knew, she had not done or said anything to make him withdraw so completely.

Inwardly, she felt a terror she had never before experienced. To have met him was a miracle. To lose him would be the worst hell imaginable.

Forcing her hands to remain still in her lap, she pretended to yawn in order to cover up her silence, which was bordering on rudeness. There he was, not five feet away, yet he might as well be as far away as London. He had been conversing easily with two other gentlemen, but as she watched he rose and went to sit with Beatrice.

Something about him—an air of purpose—alerted Nell's senses. What was he up to?

Whatever it was, he seemed to be taking his time. Straining her ears for snatches of their conversation, Nell could hear only banal comments about dinner and the weather. It had been snowing heavily all evening, causing the guests to exclaim in wonder. Safe within the warm, cosy house, and with no need to travel on the morrow, they could enjoy the spectacle in comfort.

Laying her hand on his arm, Beatrice now seemed to

be asking Mr Beresford something. After a moment's surprise, he nodded.

*What has he just agreed to?*

She soon had an answer.

'It is time, everyone!' Beatrice stood, pointing at the clock. It lacked only a couple of minutes until midnight. 'And Mr Beresford has kindly agreed to open the door to the New Year.'

*She still favours him*, thought Nell helplessly. *Cannot she see he has no real interest in her—in anyone?*

There was a murmur of excitement and, with the others, Nell walked to the front door. They all gathered round, and the men compared the time on their various pocket watches.

'In Wyatt House,' she announced firmly, 'we always welcome the New Year to the chimes of the clock in the front parlour.'

She opened the parlour door and they waited.

*This is Papa's task. It was always Papa's task*, she thought, digging her fingernails into her palms so she would not disgrace herself.

Last year she had defied tradition and gone to bed before midnight, pleading a headache. This year, with her heart and mind distracted by Mr Beresford, she could not leave even a moment early.

Finally, the clock began to chime, and Mr Beresford opened the door, ushering out the old year. There was a glad cry from the assembly, and much embracing. Nell was hugged by all the ladies, and managed to smile and behave appropriately. The gentlemen hugged their wives and daughters, shook each other's hands, and saluted the other ladies appropriately.

Nell got a bow from Mr Beresford, given with that same empty-eyed gaze. The shiver that went through her was more to do with his coldness than the frozen scene outside.

As the clock chimed on they formed a semi-circle around the open front door. Outside, the warm light spilled onto a

picture of perfect winter beauty. The snow had stopped falling, lying pure and crisp and absolutely level. There was an
air of stillness that contrasted with the crackling fire and
the conversation indoors. It was serenely beautiful, with
the starry sky gently illuminating the snow-covered scene.

For a fleeting moment Nell imagined being alone with
him in the perfect whiteness, kissing him under the stars.
The thought sent pain arcing through her, as the loss of him
once more reverberated through her. She stared unseeingly
at the perfect lethal beauty outside.

*There is peace out there. Dangerous peace.*

'Will there be more snow, do you think?' Miss Bridgeton, ever hopeful, had directed her question at Mr Beresford.

'Perhaps towards morning. But the skies are clear at present, and it is too cold for more.' He softened his words with
a slight smile—more than Nell had received from him all
evening.

The clock chimed for the final time and Mr Beresford
closed the door.

Nell felt the finality of it in her bones.

They drank, then—tea and wine and brandy—and they
danced. Nell, who was in no mood for dancing, offered to
play for the others. That way she was better able to avoid
seeing Mr Beresford dancing with various young ladies.

Lady Cecily twice offered to replace her at the pianoforte, but Nell was adamant. 'I have no desire to dance tonight,' she averred, adding a brittle smile which she hoped
would fool her friend.

Lady Cecily's frown suggested otherwise.

Somehow she survived it all without losing her fragile
control.

It was near morning before the party finally broke up. In
the salon, they clustered around the pianoforte while Nell
played 'Auld Lang Syne' and they all sang along. Afterwards, as the guests began filing out, Nell stayed behind to

tidy the music sheets back into their box. Some had been written in Mama's neat hand.

*Oh, Mama! What have I done wrong? I have lost him!*

She lifted her head, suddenly conscious of hearing voices through the open door.

'Wyatt House,' Beatrice was saying, 'is such a divine little establishment. I declare it would pain me to part with it.'

'I am sure,' Mr Beresford replied, his voice slicing through Nell's heart like a knife. 'And we must come to some agreement about the price that reflects its true value to you. But, in principle, you are open to the notion?'

Nell stood stock-still, unable to believe what she was hearing.

*She will sell Wyatt House? My home?*

Beatrice tittered. 'You must know I have lived here only a couple of years, Mr Beresford. However, that does not mean you can bargain me down. I will drive a hard bargain, I assure you!'

He chuckled. 'I do not doubt it. Let us discuss the detail on the morrow. A new year and a fresh beginning for everyone. Er…' He paused. 'I assume there are no mortgages or other restrictions on any sale?'

'Nothing you need be concerned about, Mr Beresford. I am Miss Godwin's guardian and trustee, and therefore I have the final say on these matters.'

'Miss Godwin?' His tone was suddenly sharp. 'What is it to do with Miss Godwin?'

Nell's fingernails were digging into her palms. The physical pain was a useful distraction from the shock and agony knifing through her.

'Oh, here she is—you may ask her yourself!'

They had stepped into the room. Beatrice was beckoning her, while Mr Beresford stood entirely still, as if he had sustained a shock.

'I am tired, so I am gone to bed!' Beatrice declared,

clearly unconcerned about her duties as chaperone. 'Nell, you will ensure the front door is locked?'

She swept out, leaving Nell and Mr Beresford standing facing each other, alone.

Mr Beresford found his voice. 'Wait—why should I speak to Miss Godwin about this? Are you not—?'

But Beatrice was gone.

'Can I assist you with something?' Nell, still shocked, could only hope she had somehow misunderstood.

She watched as a range of expressions crossed his face. Puzzlement gave way to resignation.

'Who owns Wyatt House, Miss Godwin?'

'It is held in trust for me until I reach my majority.' She was still frowning. 'Why?'

'Because...' he attempted a smile, which did not reach his eyes '... I should like to buy it.'

So it was true. 'But *why*?'

He shrugged. 'As a business investment. I need a house in which to entertain my business acquaintances. Wyatt House was recommended for my consideration, so I came here to estimate its suitability for my purposes.'

'Then—then you did not visit for friendship, or company, or the warmth of Christmas?' She had to ask. This new, cold Mr Beresford was entirely foreign to her.

*Where is the warm man I knew?*

He hesitated. 'I have enjoyed my time here. But sentimentality has no place in my reckoning.' His tone made her shiver. 'I have long learned to deny emotion in making business decisions.'

'To what purpose? What do you seek, Mr Beresford?'

She waited, feeling as though his answer would be the most important utterance she ever heard.

'I wish only to continue to build my fortune through business.' He glanced at her horrified expression. 'I am sorry if that shocks you.'

She found her voice. 'But you are not in the least bit sorry!'

He shrugged. 'I am sorry I have miscalculated. I believed your stepmother owned the house, so...'

'So you have been trying to befriend her in order to persuade her to sell.' It was an accusation, not a question. 'You might have done better had you focused on me.'

'I should have focused on you, it is true.' His gaze softened, yet the emptiness in his eyes remained. 'I believe selling the house to me will be good for all concerned, including you.' He hesitated. 'N— Miss Godwin, I can honestly say I have enjoyed making your acquaintance. You are a remarkable woman.'

His tone spoke of finality, of endings. Of goodbyes.

*He tried to seduce me with false flattery. His only aim was to secure the house.*

Nell stood, dumb with shock and pain, as her hopes and dreams melted around her.

His gaze became more intense. 'We have shared some fine conversations this week.' A flicker of uncertainty crossed his features.

*He's using those talks against me... Oh, who is this person?*

As if acting under some compulsion, he lifted a hand to gently touch her cheek, his expression shuttered. An hour ago it would have ignited passion, and love, and relief. Now it fired in her the strongest rage she had ever known.

'Take your hand from me!' she spat.

He recoiled, his jaw dropping.

'Do you think me so foolish, so lost to common sense, that you can seduce me with false kindness on a whim?'

'I—I simply wished to remember the friendship that has built between us.' He looked genuinely confused. 'You seemed to welcome it before.'

'Aye—because *then* I did not know who you truly are!'

His eyes narrowed. Was his face a little pale? 'And who, then, am I, Miss Godwin?'

'You are a charlatan. A fake. You think yourself so clever in business, yet you know nothing of the human heart! Tell me, have your business dealings been mostly with men?'

He could not deny it and remained silent.

'I thought as much. What made you think I would sell you my *home*—' her voice cracked '—simply because you asked to buy it?'

His eyes darted sideways. 'Your stepmother is...er... known for her generous hospitality and the joy she takes in fine things—'

Her lip curled. 'You mean to suggest, I believe, that my stepmother is in debt. Well, let me tell you that—unlike my stepmother—I would no more dream of selling my home than I would sell my person! My stepmother may try to compel me, and she holds legal rights over my affairs until I reach my majority, but I say this to you. If you and she do this thing, then I shall never, *ever* forgive either of you! And,' she finished with vehemence, 'if I *were* in debt, and needing to sell, then let me assure you that you would be the last person on this earth I would ever wish to do business with!'

'You have said enough!'

Finally, she had broken through the calculation, the manipulation. There was genuine anger in his eyes. 'I shall depart in the morning!'

'Good!' she declared.

Inside, her heart was breaking. All confusion, and overwhelmed by anger, and loss, and grief, she spun on her heel and left the room.

## Chapter Eight

Tom's hands were shaking. As the door to the salon closed behind Nell, he stood where she had left him, feeling utterly lost.

*What have I done?*

Yet the habits of half a lifetime could not easily be denied.

*Your first consideration is business*, he told himself. *You tried, and she will not sell. It is no great loss.*

The familiar words seemed empty, meaningless.

*No great loss.*

Crossing to a side table, he poured himself a brandy and stood gazing into its amber depths. His mind was in turmoil and he seemed unable to regain control. His heart was aching—indeed, his body felt racked with pain from head to toe.

He paced for a while, knowing there was no point in climbing the stairs to his bedchamber. Sleep would not come while his mind and heart were in such disorder.

*No great loss.*

Finally, he sank into an armchair beside the fire, glass in one hand, carafe in the other. Three brandies later, he was no closer to numbness. He closed his eyes, immediately seeing a vision of her hurt and confused expression. Guilt washed through him.

His mind would not let go. He kept telling himself he had done nothing wrong, that he had simply pursued a business transaction, like the countless others he had engaged in over the years. Indeed, he noted, in this case Miss Godwin had won and he had lost, for he could not, of course, pursue the purchase now.

*There is no need for guilt,* he told himself.

His conscience would not listen. It was screaming for attention, so finally he allowed himself to consider the situation from her perspective. 'Charlatan', she had dubbed him. 'Fake'.

Unwarranted, surely? Business was business, and charm was part of the game. From the start, they had each deceived the other—he by failing to declare he would be a guest at Wyatt House. She, by leading him to believe she was a servant. They had flirted, each of them practising small deceptions in order to gain the brief intimacy they had both wanted.

The kiss that had followed on Christmas Day in the snow had flowed inevitably from that first meeting in the same copse. And what a kiss it had been!

Now assailed by feelings all too physical, Tom felt his heart thunder at the memory. Closing his eyes, he gave himself over to the remembrance of their intoxicating embrace. Inevitably his thoughts moved on to that other kiss—under the mistletoe, at midnight. The experience had been overwhelming. Never had he felt passion like it.

He frowned, opening his eyes. That had been the first time she had frightened him.

*Frightened?*

He let out a brief bark of laughter at the thought. No, not frightened in the usual sense. He had not been in any physical danger. Rather, she had caused unaccustomed feelings within him…intense feelings that had threatened to overpower him.

He recalled the clarity he'd felt earlier, while out riding. He nodded as a moment of insight came to him. It was her *power* over him that was so terrifying. Where had it come from? How could she, a slip of a young lady, cause him to feel so helpless, so overcome?

His eyes became unfocused as the fire before him burned on. He added more wood, watching as the yellow flames licked along the dark wood and sparks arced and swerved towards the chimney, pinpoints of orange light. The crackling sound soothed his senses, and as his body calmed so his mind became a little clearer.

It was not power in the typical sense, he reflected. Not in the *manly* sense of the word. In business, games of power were common. In warfare, too. Those with more power generally triumphed, and weakness was to be abhorred. This was different. Her power over him came from her ability to make him feel things. Warmth. Affection. All-consuming desire.

His mind drifted to their conversations together. He had come to *know* her in a way that was unique. He knew how her mind worked, knew what she held to be important, knew how kind-hearted she was.

Daringly, he considered the people he had held in affection during his life. Memories of his mama were far away, though her loss was always with him—these past days in particular. And his brother was important to him.

*Yes*, he thought, *I care about him.*

A sudden lump in his throat had him swallowing hard.

*Papa? No. He was never close to either of us. It meant little when he died.*

The clock on the mantel began to strike the hour. Seven in the morning. Vaguely, some part of his brain noted that he had been ruminating for almost two hours.

Finally, he allowed himself to look into his heart with respect to Nell.

Instantly a wave of emotion shuddered through him. Nell the beautiful. Nell the gracious. Nell the kind. Nell who had experienced the worst of grief these past years—the loss of her father, compounded by the gaining of an unsuitable stepmother. Yet she had handled all of it with strength, and compassion, and courage. His chest ached with pride in her.

*What a woman!*

He began to pace the floor again as the shameful way he

had behaved towards her tonight returned to his mind with full force. Charlatan? *Yes.* Fake? *Unquestionably.* Even in her distress, she had pierced him deeply with the accuracy of her barbs.

The door to the salon opened. He wheeled round, somehow expecting Nell to be standing there.

It was a housemaid.

*Of course—it is morning.*

For a moment they eyed each other, and then her eyes darted about the room.

Tom's pulse increased a little, some unknown sense suddenly alert. 'Are you seeking someone?'

She curtseyed. 'Sorry, sir. Yes. Er...are you alone?'

He indicated the otherwise empty room. 'As you see.'

'Yes.' She looked uncertain. A frown now creased her forehead.

Searching his memory, he found her name. 'You are called Sally, is that correct?'

'I am.'

'Well, Sally, I strongly recommend you tell me what is bothering you.' A slow dread was building within him.

A flurry of rushed words erupted from the housemaid. 'It's Miss Nell, sir! Miss Godwin, that is.'

'What of her? Is she unwell?'

*Lord, how much have I distressed her?*

'I do not know, sir. I don't know where she is!'

Swallowing down the panic rising within him, he managed to sound calm. 'Surely she is still abed? The party did not break up until just a few hours ago.'

'She has not been to bed, sir!' Sally lifted a corner of her apron and began dabbing her eyes. 'She has been sleeping in the attic room, with me and two of the other housemaids, but she never came to bed last night. I only just found out when I woke up.'

*She sleeps in the servants' quarters? Not with one of the other ladies?*

Briefly, he allowed himself to be outraged by this, then focused on the matter at hand. 'She and Lady Cecily are particularly close. Perhaps she stayed in Lady Cecily's chamber last night, so as not to disturb you.'

Nell's kind heart made this a real possibility. Her distressed state when she had left him made it even more likely.

Sally's face brightened. 'I never thought of that, sir! I have to see to Lady Cecily's fire anyway, so I shall go there directly.'

She bobbed a brief curtsey and was gone, leaving Tom alone with his foreboding.

The next ten minutes felt like ten years. When the door finally reopened his worst fears were realised. Sally had returned, along with Lady Cecily, who was tying the belt of her robe and looking extremely anxious.

'What on earth has happened?' she demanded, in an accusatory tone.

'What do you mean?' he asked.

Her brow creased as she advanced upon him, fury personified. 'You distressed her. I know you did!' She stabbed at his chest with her finger.

Sally was watching, open-mouthed.

Tom held his ground, though he felt the full force of Lady Cecily's just accusation. 'So she did not stay with you last night?'

Lady Cecily shook her head. 'When I went up to bed there was only you and Nell and Mrs Godwin still downstairs. Nell was already troubled—I had sensed it earlier.' She lifted her chin. 'Troubled about something to do with *you*.'

He gave a rueful grimace. 'You are right. There is a—a misunderstanding between us…something I mean to put right just as soon as I can speak to her.'

Lady Cecily's eyes narrowed, assessing him. Tom held his breath.

'Very well,' she conceded, after a moment. 'Now, where on earth is she?'

They spent a few moments discussing the possibilities. It ended with Lady Cecily departing to check Mrs Godwin's chamber—though the possibility of her being there was unlikely—and Tom asking Sally to fetch his boots and cloak.

'Oh, sir!' Sally put a hand to her mouth. 'Never say you think she went outside in the snow!'

'I think it unlikely, Sally, but I must consider the possibility.'

By the time he had donned his boots, cloak and warm beaver hat, Lady Cecily had returned. 'She is not there. Mrs Godwin says we should depend upon it that she will have slept with the other housemaids, or fallen asleep on a chair in the parlour.'

Sally intervened. 'But I've looked everywhere downstairs. She is nowhere to be found. Her—her boots are gone, though. And her cloak...'

The anguish that arced through Tom at these words was almost overpowering.

*Nell!*

He could deny his heart no longer. It cried out to her with need and fear and absolute surrender.

*Nell! My Nell!*

He closed his eyes. The battle was done; he was hers.

Strangely, in giving up the fight he understood that he had *won*, not lost. She would make him a better person. He would care for her till the end of his days. He would gladly be father to her children, and love them as he loved her, for however long he was on this earth.

If she would allow him.

Opening his eyes again, he asked Lady Cecily, 'Mrs Godwin is staying in bed?' Tom knew what the answer would be, but he had to ask.

'She is.' Lady Cecily's mouth became a thin line of disapproval.

'I shall find her.' He eyed Lady Cecily intently. 'She is likely to be cold when I bring her back.'

Lady Cecily nodded. 'Sally and I will prepare blankets and a hot drink for her. Perhaps a bath as well. Mrs Hussey the housekeeper is a sensible woman. She will know what to do.'

'See that the bath is brought to Miss Godwin's own chamber.'

Sally's eyes widened. 'But, sir—'

'I shall sleep with the footmen from now on, rather than deny her the comfort of her own room.'

*It is the least I can do.*

'Besides, all this worry may be for naught. She may well have gone for a short walk only recently.'

Even he knew his words were meaningless.

*In the dark? Alone?*

By now they all knew something was terribly wrong.

Sally had brought a lantern, and Tom lit the candle inside it before closing the small brass-framed panel. Opening the front door of Wyatt House for the second time in less than eight hours, he stepped outside.

# Chapter Nine

Nell had never experienced such agony of spirit. Until tonight, Mr Thomas Beresford had seemed to her the ideal man. Handsome, well-formed, with a lively, knowledgeable mind and an easy charm. His taking smile and enticing kisses had blinded her to the emptiness at the heart of him.

*It is my own fault.*

She had allowed herself to be so taken up with Mama and Papa's tale of inevitable love that she had quite lost her mind!

*But, oh! How it hurts!*

She had sunk to the floor in the small parlour, crying bitterly. She had naturally run to the place where she had so often felt wisps of her mama's presence, but there had been no comfort in Mama's portrait. Nell's foolishness had been exposed under the same clear light that had revealed Mr Beresford to be a scarecrow, not a true, upright man. From a distance he looked whole, and complete, and—and *normal*. Yet up close he was a creature of straw, of dust, of clay.

She had wept on, for the loss of a man who did not exist, a love that could never be, and the parlour had grown colder as the clock had ticked towards morning. Yet she had not been able to think of going upstairs to Sally and the others. Disturbing their sleep and arousing their curiosity would achieve nothing.

Her grief for Papa had never left her. She had lived with the unrelenting darkness of it for two years. But since meeting Mr Beresford she had seen a glimmer of hope—the chance to feel joy again, to love and be loved.

It had been nothing but an illusion. And now the dark-

ness in her spirit had returned with renewed strength, overwhelming her with emptiness and hopelessness.

*I am no better than Miss Bridgeton.*

Indeed, she was infinitely worse, for at least Miss Bridgeton had the sense to contain her heart. It had been clear to
everyone that Miss Bridgeton's fancy had been engaged, but
she would suffer no lasting ill from Mr Beresford's lack of
interest. Nell, on the other hand, had given him her heart—
on the strength of nothing more than two kisses and her
own foolish reveries.

Nell had glanced at the ashes in the grate, avoiding Mama's eye. She had realised that before long the household
would begin to stir—the kitchen servants to wash last night's
dishes and begin the never-ending process of preparing yet
more food, the housemaids to clean out and reset the downstairs fires, before beginning their rounds of the guest bedrooms.

Suddenly anxious to avoid even Sally's well-meaning
concern, Nell had slipped silently from the small front parlour. Donning her kid half-boots and cloak, she had tiptoed
to the front hallway, opened the door, and stepped out into
the darkness.

The snow had crunched under her feet with alarming
volume, so she'd walked more slowly, placing each foot deliberately in front of the other. It had begun to snow again,
and large flakes had filled in her footprints as she'd walked
on. In a very short time, there would be no trail to show her
direction, she had thought as she'd glanced back.

The house had been in darkness, save for a warm yellow
light glowing from the chinks in the salon shutters.

*That'll be the Yule Log, still burning in the salon grate,*
she had thought. The very room where Mr Beresford had
revealed his true nature. The cold-hearted, cruel, unfeel-
ing fiend.

Dimly, she had been aware that her anger was particularly

acute and that her judgement of Mr Beresford was coloured by her own sense of betrayal.

In truth, he had not promised her anything. It had been she, building delirious wishes in her own imagination, who had created an illusion. She was to blame, not he.

Now, as her eyes became accustomed to the starlight, she trudged on. Her steps automatically took her to the lane leading to the copse—the place where she and Papa had walked together in all seasons and weathers…the place where she had met Tom, and where they had kissed for the first time.

The falling snow had brought with it a silence so absolute it seemed to her as though the world held its breath. Nothing stirred—not a leaf, nor a bird. In all the world there was only Nell, and Nell was alone.

Mama, gone. Papa, gone. No-one in the world who loved her.

*I could go into one of these fields right now,* she thought, *and lie down beneath a tree. The winter will claim me, and no-one will find me until it is too late.* She dashed hot tears away from her face, vaguely aware that she had begun to shiver. The snow had soaked through her dress, which was now damp all the way down the front, and from the hem up to her knee.

She had not bothered to wrap her cloak around her—why should she? It mattered not.

*Who will miss me? No-one. Not the servants, nor Beatrice, nor any of the guests.*

A vague image of Lady Cecily came to her mind, but she brushed it away.

*She will forget me. As will he.*

Such thoughts were sinful, she knew, and yet sin held no meaning for her. The only reality was her need to keep walking.

She passed the copse, now shrouded in pale dawn light.

*Here I met him, that first day.*

Past the old cottages. On and on towards nowhere.

Her face, ears, nose…all ached in the chilly air, and her fingers and toes had begun to tingle with pins and needles.

Blessedly, now there was no more thought. No more anger. No more pain.

The morning sunshine glistening on white, white snow meant nothing.

She trudged on…

# Chapter Ten

Tom was much more concerned than he had allowed the two women to see. He knew exactly how distressed Nell had been, how deep her wounds were. He knew because her pain was his pain. This distance between them, this coldness, division, was simply intolerable. He truly feared for her welfare.

The door closed behind him. Pausing for a moment, he lifted his lantern to search for any footprints that might give him some indication of her direction. Nothing. The snow was still falling thickly. He could see no trace of her.

Closing his eyes, as if his internal vision of her would somehow help him divine which way she had gone, he wilfully calmed his mind. Almost instantly the thought came to him. The copse lane! The place where they had first met and kissed. The place where she and her papa had loved to walk.

*If you are wrong,* an inner voice cautioned, *you might miss the opportunity to find her.*

What else could he do? His reasoning was no better nor worse than the alternatives. So he set off, trudging heavily down the frozen lane.

After ten minutes he realised he had set himself an impossible task. She could be anywhere! At each gate he passed he had to wonder if she had gone into that field. Although dawn would surely come soon, this darkness that surrounded him now was his enemy.

'Hell, damn and blast it!' He turned back, acknowledging what he should have admitted in the first place—he needed his horse.

He wasted quite ten minutes returning to the stables, and another five searching thoroughly in case Nell was there.

She was not.

Finally, he saddled his stallion, which was clearly confused by this unexpectedly early start. Dousing the lantern, Tom set it on the floor. Dawn was finally breaking—another reason why he had been better to turn back, even against the instinct that urged him to find her as quickly as he could. His pocket watch told him it was eight o'clock.

Thankfully, the snow began to ease as he rode down the lane, and it had stopped altogether by the time he reached the copse. There were still no footprints in the lane, but there had been no side roads since he had left Wyatt House.

Dismounting, he searched the copse, calling for her as he did so.

*Nothing.*

On he went, his heart sore with concern. The sun slowly crept above the horizon, illuminating an endless blue-white carpet with diamond-sharp clarity. On another day Tom might have stopped to savour the beauty of the landscape around him. Today, knowing that his Nell was out here somewhere, under threat from the freezing temperature and holding the belief that he felt nothing for her, he barely noticed the charming winter scene.

Finally he saw what he had been hoping for. He slowed, then leaned down to be sure. *Yes!* There was the merest trace of dainty footprints in the snow.

*This, then, is where she was when the snow ceased.*

His heart pounding with hope, he urged his stallion on, following the footprints.

It took another twenty minutes, but as he rounded a bend he saw up ahead a crumpled heap in the centre of the road.

*No!*

His heart pounding with fear, he urged the stallion to a breakneck gallop, snow or no snow.

'Whoa!' Barely had the horse slowed to a trot than Tom

was sliding off, running the final few yards towards her. 'Nell? Nell?'

She was on her back, her face relaxed as if she was asleep. Her skin was deathly white and her lips slightly blue. She did not move.

'Nell!'

He reached for her, hauling her unresponsive body into his arms.

'Nell!'

His voice cracked as the enormity of losing her began to sink in. Finally he had found a woman who had brought meaning to his life, and he might have killed her with his selfish cruelty.

*Enough!*

The need to save Nell was more important than succumbing to his own distress. He forced himself to look at her properly and, leaning right down to her, he was relieved to sense a slight breath coming from her nose.

*She is alive, then. For now.*

Of course he had no way of knowing if she could yet be saved. The same snow that had created the beautiful scene all around them had cruelly taken her life's warmth. Her clothes were drenched and sodden, the skin of her hands and beautiful face icy cold.

He had no time to waste. In this empty landscape, the nearest dwelling was Wyatt House. He must return with her as soon as possible.

Only a couple of minutes later, with the aid of a nearby tree-stump, he remounted the stallion. He had already placed Nell's recumbent form across the horse's withers, and now he was seated behind her. Gently, he shifted her into a vaguely upright position, with her back to him. He took the reins into his left hand while his right arm encircled Nell, holding her close. The cold from her damp clothes began to seep into him almost immediately.

*Good,* he told himself, trying to find reassurance somehow. *That means some of my heat is being given to her.*

The journey back was the longest of his life. Riding as quickly as he could, given his precious burden, he had not had the luxury of being able to check on her properly. He had, though, succeeded in warming up the parts of her that were pressed against him.

He himself was shivering a little now, and his arms and shoulders were aching, but there was definitely some warmth along his chest and torso and her back. He glanced at her again. Her head lay back against the hollow of his shoulder. Her eyes remained shut. Was that a hint of colour in her cheeks? He could not be sure.

They were almost at Wyatt House when he heard her moan slightly. He had never heard a more beautiful sound in his life. She moved a little, and he tightened the grip of his right arm around her.

'Please live, Nell,' he told her. 'Please.' His throat tightened and he could say no more.

The end of the lane was in sight. He risked going a little faster. Every moment mattered.

Someone was watching for him, for as he pulled up the front door opened. One of the footmen came running out, swiftly followed by Lady Cecily.

'Oh, thank goodness you have found her!' She looked decidedly pale. 'I have been sick with worry! Bring her inside, quickly! She must be taken to her own chamber.'

She directed the footman, who took Nell as Tom carefully lowered her from the horse. Nell moaned again, and put a hand to her head. A groom had appeared from around the side of the building, so Tom simply abandoned his horse, his attention centred entirely on the woman he loved.

Reclaiming her from the footman, he carried her so that her head was once again resting in the hollow of his right shoulder.

Mrs Hussey, the housekeeper, was waiting inside, along with the butler. Both looked distressed.

'I shall carry her upstairs,' Tom said firmly, shifting his grip to ensure he would not drop her.

As he mounted the stairs she stirred and moaned again. Her eyes flickered open briefly.

'All is well,' he told her. 'You are safe.'

Her eyelids closed again.

*Nell!*

The footman jumped in front of him to open the door to his chamber. *Nell's* chamber. Tom laid her on the bed, then stood helplessly by as Sally, Lady Cecily and Mrs Hussey bustled into the room. They began rubbing Nell gently with warm towels and covering her in soft blankets. A bath had been placed before the fireplace, and a fire was burning brightly in the grate. Tom felt the warmth in the air and was glad of it.

'Now, you men—out!' Mrs Hussey flapped at Tom and the footman like a giant bird. 'James, go and start bringing up the bath water. Not too hot, mind! We need her to warm slowly, otherwise it will be chilblains, frostnip, or worse! Go!'

The footman went.

'And you too, sir!' This was directed at Tom. 'We need to get her out of these wet clothes.'

'Of course!' Talk of chilblains was reassuring. 'You think she will—? I mean…'

Mrs Hussey's face softened. 'Time will tell. She's bad, but at least we have her home. Now, you go downstairs and wait.'

# Chapter Eleven

Tom was in an agony of mind. It had been nearly ten o'clock when they had sent him downstairs. It was now almost noon. How was she? Why had no-one come to reassure him?

He had made for the salon, where the servants had once again built up the fire. Divesting himself of his wet cloak, hat and boots, Tom had sat by the fire until his shivering had eased and his clothes had dried, knowing that all his other clothing was upstairs in Nell's room.

James the footman had come to take away his boots for cleaning, and had provided him with suitable indoor footwear, but he'd had nothing to report on Nell's condition.

'We carried the bathwater upstairs, sir,' he had confirmed. 'Tepid, not hot, as Mrs Hussey wanted. But I do not know how she is for they are all still with her.' He had paused. 'I do know the groom has been sent to fetch Dr Pagenham.'

'Thank you, James.' Tom's heart had sunk.

*Of course they will send for the doctor. Why would they not? It does not mean she must be at death's door.*

Now, his ears straining for any sound from the hallway, Tom realised that the other guests were beginning to rise, emerging from their chambers to drift downstairs. Thankfully, they went directly to the morning-room, where breakfast was laid out, and they did not bother him. He himself could not stomach the thought of breakfast—although he had had nothing since supper the night before.

*How can I eat and pretend all is well when Nell almost froze to death this day?*

He swallowed, acknowledging the truth of it. She would have died. *She would have died.* Thankfully, he had found her—and hopefully in time—but he could take no satisfaction from it as he had been the cause of her flight in the first place. He with his thoughtless, selfish cruelty.

Unable to resist any longer, he rang for a servant. Within a few moments, a housemaid arrived.

'Yes, sir?'

'How is Miss Godwin?'

'I do not know for sure, sir—though Sally might.'

'Is Sally below stairs?'

The maid nodded. 'She is having breakfast, sir.'

*Breakfast.* 'Then do not disturb her.'

Sensing the dismissal in his tone, the maid left. Tom put his head in his hands. At least when he had come downstairs Nell had been in good hands. The women had been warming her up, and Nell herself had been beginning to come round. The fact that Sally had been released to have breakfast was encouraging.

Without any further thought he rose, left the salon, and swiftly mounted the stairs. Reaching the door of the bed chamber, he hesitated. From inside, he heard a wail of pain.

*Nell!*

He leaned his forehead against the door. Whatever was happening inside, his Nell was in great distress.

*All my fault.*

Eventually the sounds decreased, then ended altogether. Tom, who was now sitting on the landing, felt dead inside. Luckily no-one had seen him in this wretched state. Not that it mattered anyway.

Summoning strength from deep within himself, he stood, straightened his shoulders, and knocked on the door.

In response to a query from Mrs Hussey, he gave his name. A moment later, the door opened.

'Mr Beresford.' It was Lady Cecily, twitching like a cat hiding its kittens. 'Is there something you need?'

'Er...yes. I should like to change my clothes. And I would like to know how Miss Godwin is doing.'

Her eyes narrowed. 'I shall send for a footman to bring you some clothes. Mrs Hussey will discuss your sleeping arrangements with her mistress later and will have your belongings moved.'

'Of course.'

They eyed each other. Lady Cecily's hostility towards him was both clear and completely warranted. Their earlier truce had lasted only until he had successfully rescued Nell. Lady Cecily was now free to make her true feelings known.

'And Miss Godwin?' His eyes flicked over Lady Cecily's shoulder, but all he could see was the foot of the bed and the window beyond.

'The doctor has prescribed rest. She is to have no visitors.'

She would say no more.

He nodded and turned away.

*I have no right to insist.*

'Wait!'

He heard it…the faintest of sounds.

'Let him in.' Nell's voice was frail, but her message was unmistakeable.

'But, Nell—'

'I insist on this.'

'Very well,' Lady Cecily conceded. 'But not yet.' She turned back to Tom. 'I will send for you when she is ready.'

He did not argue.

Nell was in agony. As her body slowly warmed the numbness gradually disappeared—to be replaced by searing pain throughout her body. Mrs Hussey and Cecily had made her bathe three times in a lukewarm bath, and treated her fingers and toes with salve.

Her stepmother had visited briefly, and seemed determined to criticise Nell for what she termed her 'stupidity'. Thankfully the doctor, taking in the situation at a glance, had asked Mrs Godwin to leave, stating that he could see she was greatly distressed. He had asked the housekeeper to prepare a tisane for Mrs Godwin and she had gladly accepted this suggestion, declaring that he was the first person to have a care for the perturbation and anxiety *she* was going through.

Lady Cecily had stayed with her during the doctor's examination. Nell had cried a little when he'd said her lungs were clear and he was hopeful she would recover fully. He'd prescribed laudanum, and continued baths, and confined her to bed. He had, as Lady Cecily had said, recommended no visitors, but Nell knew she would not rest until she had seen Tom again.

'The doctor thinks I will get better, doesn't he?' she offered tentatively now, as Cecily settled her back into bed after her latest bath. She had dressed her in a pretty white nightgown, leaving her hair down.

Mrs Hussey had left them, anxious to check that the housemaids were maintaining their duties.

'He does, thank goodness.' Lady Cecily's relief was clear. 'He says the damage has not gone too deep. It is only the skin that is affected—not the muscles or bones.'

Repeating the doctor's words was important. Reassurance for both of them.

Nell's gaze met Cecily's. Nell swallowed hard.

*I might have died. I wanted to die.*

She closed her eyes.

*And yet some part of me wanted to live, too. That is why I stayed on the road.*

She kept her eyes closed. 'It was Mr Beresford who found me, was it not?'

'Yes.' Cecily's tone was clipped, her disapproval obvious.

*She wants to protect me from him. Because she cares about me.*

'Thank you, Cecily.' Tears rolled out from beneath her closed eyelids and down her cheeks to her ears. She sniffed, and Cecily passed her a handkerchief. 'You have been a good friend to me. Better than I deserve.'

Cecily denied it, then was quiet, and Nell was left to think. She thought and remembered and questioned inside her own head, until she felt ready.

'I will see him now.'

Cecily nodded, then disappeared without a word.

Ten minutes later there was a knock on the door.

'Come in!'

The door opened.

*It is him!*

Everything depended on the next half-hour. Had she imagined it? His concern for her, the emotion she had felt in his voice, seen in his eyes, when he had rescued her? Her memories were hazy, but her heart believed *something* had happened.

It was time to discover the truth.

# Chapter Twelve

Tom stood in the doorway, suddenly uncertain. For the past few hours he had been tortured, listening to talk of Nell from Mrs Godwin—how pale she was, how ill she looked, how shocking it was that she had suffered such ill-effects after turning her ankle during a short walk.

The guests had no reason to question this version of the story, stating only that she should have taken a maid to accompany her.

Tom had endured praise for his part in finding her and returning her to Wyatt House. He had brushed this away, feeling like the lowest sinner who had ever lived.

He desperately wanted to see her, to apologise, to try somehow to convey his sense of shame. Now—this moment—would be his best chance.

There she was, in the bed that was also his, looking up at him with those beautiful autumn eyes. Her magnificent hair was unbound, and she was clad in nothing but a fine nightgown. He groaned inwardly, then pushed away his body's reaction. His task was to reach her soul. In this moment the needs of his body could only be a distraction.

She looked terribly pale, it was true, and yet to him she was the essence of beauty. He was lost for words, momentarily overwhelmed with relief that she was truly still alive.

'Mr Beresford!'

Her tone was polite, easy, restrained—just as if she was not in a bed *en deshabillé*.

'So nice of you to visit me.' From her tone, they might have been in a drawing-room.

He stepped forward, his eyes sweeping over her, noting

the bandaged hands. A pained expression flitted across his face as he felt the force of her injuries.

'Well?' she asked, tilting her head to one side. 'You wish to speak to me?'

*This is the moment. Do not fail.*

He stepped inside, closing the door behind him. 'Yes. I would like the opportunity to explain some things to you. If you are well enough for such a conversation?'

'I am listening.'

Her expression was closed, with nothing of warmth in it. Well, why would there be, when he had behaved so badly towards her?

There was an upright chair beside the bed. *His* bed. He sat, then hesitated.

'It begins,' he offered—then stopped, frowning. 'It truly begins when I was five and my mother died.'

Her eyes widened briefly. 'Go on.'

'I have told you some of it. My brother and I were sent to boarding school, where we basically lived for the next ten or twelve years. We saw our papa once or twice a year, but there was no warmth from him.' He remembered Nell's mama's portrait. 'You had a loving mama for a long time.'

Her expression remained guarded. 'I did.'

'My father had gambled away most of the family fortune by the time my brother reached his majority, and when the old man died of fever we discovered he had also run up significant debts.'

Nell was frowning now. 'I see. That must have been very difficult for you both.'

'We made a vow.' He gazed sightlessly at the window, recalling that moment. 'We declared we would not rest until we had paid off every one of those debts and rebuilt the family's wealth.' He looked at her again. 'And we have done it.'

Her lip curled slightly. 'Your business ventures?'

'Yes. We sold a small estate that was to have been mine, though we kept the hunting box. The family estate is entailed. We had to sell some of the remaining stock in the funds, but instead of using it to pay off the most pressing debts we bought a ship.'

'A ship?'

Now she looked intrigued. He hoped she *was* intrigued.

'We sent it to Brazil, with a cargo of manufactured goods, and it returned with raw materials. Thankfully it did not sink, and we made enough from that one expedition alone to pay my father's creditors. And we kept going. Ships, goods, property... My brother and I are now two of the wealthiest men in England.'

She looked decidedly unimpressed. 'Mr Beresford, is there a point to any of this?'

'Yes. Yes, there is.' His heart had begun to thump rather loudly. 'When I came here, it was with the intention of per-suading your stepmother to sell Wyatt House to me.'

'As a place of entertainment, to sweeten your business deals.' Her tone was flat.

'Yes. And there is nothing wrong with that. I have never cheated anyone or stolen anything. But my work includes a need to be persuasive at times.'

Nell tilted her head to one side, considering this. He could see her lively mind turning it over, could see that, despite his cruelty towards her, she was honouring him by giving him a fair hearing.

He took a breath. 'But something unexpected happened here.' Now he had her full attention. 'You.'

'Me?'

'I was drawn to you from the first—and in a way I had never experienced before. I believe you understand me?'

She remained impassive.

'We kissed in the copse, and then again downstairs. At midnight, under the mistletoe.'

Nothing. Not a flicker of emotion pierced her mask of impassivity.

'Afterwards I went to my chamber—to this very room—feeling as though I had been charged by an unbroken horse.'

*There!* Something flashed in her eyes, just for a moment.

'And we talked. Each time we walked together you honoured me by revealing more of yourself.'

He talked on—of how he had pieced together her journey from a happy life with her papa, through to Beatrice's arrival and her father's death.

'I felt every day of it in my own heart,' he finished. 'I learned to know and love everything about you—your indomitable spirit, your kind heart, even your wit.'

Her eyes softened a little at this, but still she sat unmoving, a vision of remote beauty. 'Pray continue.'

'Then came yesterday—New Year's Eve. I rode out across the fields in turmoil. I did not understand what was happening inside me.' He stabbed at his own chest. 'Never had I been so lost, so frightened.'

'Yes, you had,' she countered.

He felt puzzlement crease his brow.

'That is how you felt when your mama died,' she said softly.

He closed his eyes tightly, screwing up his face against the pain of it. 'Yes,' he managed.

Once he had regained a little self-control, he continued.

'I resolved to buy the house and run away. Never to see you again. Never to feel these feelings inside me. To regain control of my heart, and my mind, and my spirit.'

'So you spoke to Beatrice?'

He nodded. 'I was shocked to discover the house was yours. All my supposed business talent has been entirely absent since I met you. I had not even properly established the basic facts! This is how you have changed me.'

'Not for ever, I hope.'

*What does that mean?*

'Now to my second confession. You called me a fake and a charlatan. You were correct. Because last night, when I talked of the house and blocked out my heart, I was wearing a mask. I was lying to you, and to myself. After you left I realised I was fighting an unnecessary war and I admitted the truth.'

'Which is?'

'That I love you. I cannot live without you. When I was looking for you in the snow—' His voice cracked. 'Nell, I was in an agony of spirit. If you had died, I would not have lived without you.'

He searched her face. Slowly she lowered that curtain in her mind—the one that had prevented him from seeing her thoughts. Her eyes were shining, and a slow smile grew on her face.

His heart leapt, and he dared to gently take her hand. 'Nell! You feel it too?'

She nodded, turning her face up for his kiss.

This kiss was different from the ones they had shared before. The passion was there, but this time it was carefully banked. This kiss sealed their future together. Acknowledged their love. Marriage, soon. Children, hopefully. Never being alone again. Ever.

'Nell...' he murmured again. 'Nell.'

# *Epilogue*

Mr Beresford and Miss Godwin were married in the church of St Mary in Chiddingstone after a short courtship. The wedding was a small one, with only the bride's stepmother, some servants, and a gathering of local people present to witness it.

The banns had been called in the required manner, and the villagers were delighted to see their Miss Godwin glowing with such happiness. She wore a jonquil silk gown with Vandyke points and delicate embroidery along the bodice and hem, while her new husband—a fine-looking gentleman reputed to be brother to an earl—looked resplendent in a coat of blue superfine.

Mrs Godwin—Mrs Beresford's stepmother—had announced her intention of hiring a townhouse in London, as Wyatt House had reverted fully to Eleanor Beresford, née Godwin, upon her marriage. It was rumoured that Mr Beresford had made a generous settlement on the widow, to enable her to set up her own establishment, and that she had been only too happy to accept.

The young couple remained closeted at Wyatt House for nigh on a month after their wedding, before planning a trip to the capital.

On the night before their journey to London, Tom and Nell lay close together in their rumpled bed. Nell was idly stroking her husband's hair, her injuries now long healed. She and Tom—her darling, darling Tom—had spent most of the month since their wedding day here, in this bedchamber.

Nell, reluctant to move to her parents' suite of rooms just yet, had suggested Tom simply move back into the chamber he had slept in during the early part of his stay—the chamber where they had first and finally declared their love—and he had done so on the day they were married.

Now their cosy idyll was to end, with a visit to the capital and Nell's introduction to Tom's brother.

'You seem a little anxious about your brother's reaction,' she offered. 'Do you believe he will disapprove?'

He opened his eyes. 'I truly have no notion how he will react. His trip to France had been planned for months, but I could not wait for his return before marrying you. I wrote to him just yesterday about our marriage—though he may have heard about it already, of course.'

He shrugged.

'He *must* marry, to ensure the line. I was under no such obligation, so it may surprise him that I have married—and so quickly.' He frowned. 'I think what concerns me is that *this*—our love for each other—may seem alien to him.'

She nodded thoughtfully. 'It took something like a bolt of lightning to shake *you* out of your old ideas. I can understand how people may think us foolish.'

His right arm snaked around her, his fingers trailing up and down her spine. 'Ah, but we know it is they who are the fools, not us.'

She arched closer, kissing him softly. 'I think I knew after only a couple of days that we should be married.'

He smiled ruefully. 'We both know it took me a little longer. Yet once I knew it, I felt it with every inch of my heart, my body and my soul.'

'I do believe we are fated to be together,' she murmured, kissing him again.

'Yes,' he agreed, rolling up onto his elbow and looking down at her. 'Fated.'

And as they came together yet again it could not truly have been said which among the pair was the happier.

* * * * *

*If you enjoyed these stories, you won't want to miss these other Historical collections*

**Convenient Christmas Brides**
*by Carla Kelly, Louise Allen and Laurie Benson*

**Invitation to a Cornish Christmas**
*by Marguerite Kaye and Bronwyn Scott*

**Snowbound Surrender**
*by Christine Merrill, Louise Allen and Laura Martin*

**Tudor Christmas Tidings**
*by Blythe Gifford, Jenni Fletcher and Amanda McCabe*